WHAT LIGHT BECOMES ME

BY

GABRIEL CHAD BOYER

MONTAG

First Montag Press E-Book and Paperback Original Edition December 2024

Copyright © 2024 by Gabriel Boyer

As the writer and creator of this story, Gabriel Boyer asserts the right to be identified as the author of this book.

Montag Press ISBN: 978-1-957010-56-4
Design © 2024 Amit Dey

Montag Press Team:

Cover image: Chadha Brahmi
Cover design: Malcolm Felder
Author Photo: Gabriel Boyer
Editor: Charlie Franco
Managing Director: Charlie Franco

A Montag Press Book
www.montagpress.com
Montag Press
777 Morton Street, Unit B
San Francisco CA 94129 USA

Montag Press, the burning book with the hatchet cover, the skewed word mark and the portrayal of the long-suffering fireman mascot are trademarks of Montag Press.

Printed & Digitally Originated in the United States of America
10 9 8 7 6 5 4 3 2 1

DEDICATION

"Dedicated to all the kind people who have helped me along the way, Charlie Franco, Malcolm Felder, Chadha Brahmi, et al, my parents and friends who for some reason still believe in me."

1.

Red light blinkered on off on off in this otherwise dark. Coat depths of what's a large part untenanted concrete chamber—that is, but for yours truly, tanks behind, and—closer to hand—wrappings turned as somehow loose about fingers hung with a sumptuous limpness—or—as like pockets of air come to been fashioned between binding cloths as wrap man's interrogator's slender elfin body, eyes and all—pint-size mummy what she been gone and spasmed and general speaking as turned epileptic. Which fun fact made further apparent by way of intense chattering and rattle of accompanying aluminum chair what been her perch. Seat as hooked in finger-ends of the one non-wandering hand.

As for myself. Sat across and upon same type and style cheap aluminum chair. As am done throughout the now stalled cross-examination. Performed by aforementioned epileptic what been manufactured for this object alone. As in—to of unravel mystery surround any and all bit of sickness as slung on a man—and specific, GMO man of my persuasion—from way back when it come onto the scene. Alleged symptoms of which as include spatial and identity aphasia. A kind of a common cold for the thinking brain, wherein sneeze and snot come to of gunked up ganglia's array such that scenery of the skull turned wonky—and world surround is took to flicker. All in all, not pleasant. And man's speaking companion got an interest in this particular diseased otaku clique and what all said sickness could been as entailed for the hive and accompanying properties.

While am been slumped, broke, and not much else.

And overall as howled most inconvenient of animal howls. Failed pornographer turned bioweapon as I am been. What take full responsibility for my conversation partner's little fit. But when is all begun hard to pin.

When body first spun up from its webbing and sat upon that cheap aluminum, first question seem innocuous enough. *Mr. Cole. Do you know who you are, Mr. Cole? Then on to some occasional* acrobatic impossibility and occasional like as if man's brain gone and tried to of press itself direct out forehead's marrow with a helplessness.

Central hive in among stand of identical artificial obsidian mountains of hive as tower over what skyline remaining of large part destructed LAC. Fun fact am known from a picture postcard I seen somewhere on account of what cadaver I been spun into never is set foot from out this honest-to-goodness warehouse of underutilized space—and ourselves sat beside the one wall and under caged bulb—but still a near football field distance to what nondescript door as situated at its far end. And its red light as blinkered in the otherwise dark.

Found myself here and as one of a clique—of otaku known collective by name of Jackson Cole and built as mainframe for an alternative reality housing community—and now infected by common cold of the common mind—and across from a tiny mummy—and furthermore—said sparring companion on about how she wanting for this common cold of the mind to of make itself known.

As in. She looking for an introduction.

As backside of fellow's face come to of been carved in pains—what been like as if a kind of reverse-engineered scarring. Scraped down forehead's interior to the underpinning of the cheek, say. Or as a thread come brilliant broken glass fine upon axis of the skull. Or as if all the castles under construction in sands of man's aforementioned mind are turned to sand worms and general speaking am got no mind to spoke of anymore. At which point—hung my sorry excuse for a head and cried a convict's tears—while stared at my only partial human dick sat in its tuft of crotch hair—and, *You fuh, you fuh, you fuh,* am announced while honest-to-god snot dribble down my clearly cocked up head and not just as come from out the nostrils but is also some serious goop as poured down from what excavation been performed upon the cranial cavity itself from round its uppermost rim.

While. Back here in this earlier incarnation of man and his interrogator and from her perch of stamped aluminum folding chair, she was took to muse—on lifeform brought this low and what it say for the general state of things—as—is true for one beauteous moment, I's a king of gangland only to now of turn as gray, nude and indeed shivered with an embarrassing violence. Or—just to hammer home the sheer fucked nature of my situation—her as bounced to somewhere off to the side such that wall become as the floor—as in room and myself as turned sideways with her—as in—still as reclined in seat but now floor of it all situated off to one side of that same drab concrete box of a room is just now cocked its concrete box of proverbial head. And each place she as bounce room was twirl to match. Like as if the concrete monstrosity her skull passing through been actual fact slotted upon the inside of her.

On account of g3 is discovered more than just the one new technology. As in, the genetic design and structural manipulation of the human fetus. The miracles she as able to've procured having been source of endless debate in my earlier walking around life of pornographer turned darling of gangland turned alleged traitor.

But as to what gray-skinned freak you seen before you—whole room is swung about upon the shifting axis of the hashishin as am myself twirled about like a fellow on a leap-the-dips in some amusement park of old. With hands upon the quavering jelly atrophied thighs. Mouth open and tongue hung suspended inside casing of the jaw.

Then rollercoaster come to a standstill.

And been as yanked backwards by strands done and got themselves looped throughout the marionette brain and once again in places long gone—of Moms brung on the bible in her ferocity—upon card table or in view of the sty round back—and dark-eyed junco what as peck in the sparse grasses of one of last snowstorms from before—my brothers and I stood in our proper suits in sitting rooms of our neighbor's tenement for funeral without a body after Daddy's famed boating accident—or me and Ash in cannibalist country sometime before it turned cannibalist and us sprawled upon motel bedding and by a Georgia beach as birds trilled in the courtyard below and man's tongue unleathered from its timidity, part to part, legs squiggled in tandem, black intellectual hoodlum and his little White Russian—Ash—mother of my baby girl—and—all manner of other facsimile of memory what been prick at the senses even when these of necessity lies and falsehoods—and—general speaking, eyes rolled upward with some exoticism as she gone on in her thin LAC vernacular—about the more traditional tortures—crushed genitals, sleep deprivation, and such like.

And just how unnecessary said tortures gone to prove.

You were never given the opportunity to resist. How she put it.

What happen next involve something as like a partway disembodied jellyfish drazzled overtop the head and face—and—names as pour from out the skull even when man never been gave common courtesy of actual as spoke these betrayals is true. As eyelids done they manic fluttering routine. Or turn to room now viewed in more diaphanous and uncertain hue—as crosshatching of luminosity been sprawled across it—as—long slender fingers of the drazzled jellyfish is continue to of slid they incorruptible selves into sleeving of man's grayscale flesh. And myself as continued on with embarrassing rapid as in shock level shivering.

And her.

Show me where they are, mirror. Show me the location of the others. Or. *World doesn't work like how they thought it did in the time of the pre-singularity.* Or. *You, my friend, are about to learn all about it.*

For. LAC of man's misfortune also as belong to other purview. Fantasy of flesh and blood cause kind of glorified gag reflex of the thinking subject. In which various locales and they varying degrees of authenticity turned to of a haze of visions as induced upon the retina and what crowd a mind simultaneous from out all seven of man's gene homogenous siblings as sat in they gelatin set in the dank black—tanks what as captured thin bands of light in they moat and its animalcules—and all shut up in they sleeping but my eyes been opened and they seen—in shadows populate concrete of LAC hive—and its funfair of luminescence thread through even the most nondescript of utilities closets but—for most part stared at nothing—except for—sands of computation what link our mother of an AI to the robotics of Japan, her operative on the ground, and everywhere in between—while as for myself—could not as let go of that old girl of mine—Cassey Darling—what's got her spunk and her leopard print thigh highs and as versed in the most intricate of looks—and come on as all what 14 other eyes what belonged to yours truly as popped open to of ranged about each other's features sat in they light-pierced aquariums—at one Cole hunched forward was got a face covered in polyps—and another more upright Cole been as like regular walking about human male down to what I assume been a fully functional crotch—second sippy cup skull Cole look back at me looking—but more curved and feminine in outline.

Then these seven Jackson Coles again been as snapped back—from out the concrete box and into the early morning rain of Pittsburgh as succumbed to the Christians like am said. And—this been the moment come to of actual fact been as turn to hashishin and gone, *Welcome to the parasite*—and her stumbled back to her cheap aluminum chair and took to clattering said chair against the concrete in an ecstasy of longing.

Is true what particulars of her face been as hid inside they wrap of gray run full body on down to the eye like man said but nuances of the skull—what with its many sudden cranial swells and dips beneath the swaddling's surf—and her took to having made most inconvenient of guttural sounds—like as dog midway through the grinder—as she also is tumble backward and away—but only few steps—away from this thing I been and what ablutions of spirit as am marinated in.

Spun through her three endless steps—dynamics of her musculature come to of slowed to pace of the abyss and its various celestial bodies. As in—she is thrash about but with a lethargy defies explaining. And in a kind of a rapturous stupor. Shoulder height gray rag doll what been as manipulated from eyeball on out.

And somewhere in the black behind of her and below aforementioned blinkering red light is appeared rectangle of muted brilliance. Door what lead out from this warehouse of catatonics flung wide and two identical blonde geeks as rushed in with some embarrassment.

Even from this distance, pipework upon the faces been visible. As are also slo-mo in they eruption through the doorway—as perceived through eyes of g3 as superimposed over man's own—such that the glitches in blondes' manufactured features—places where code gone to of break down first— where tumors one day bound to of sprout—as apparent as the pinpricks of they two pair of red iris what match the bulb above they two divergent heads and they golden-haired crewcuts and valves and might been bit of sculpted skull gone along with it.

Even as. Cartoon eyes of g3 as moved—from off man's face to her synapses to theirs. And out and into such variety of eyes as to now've made a kind of a winking mess of they informational *alwab*—as the local vernacular is had it. As in, twisted the nipples of the populace from ganglion on out like as the fly in they virtual ointment come back to bite.

While hashishin and I become as lesbian with one another. Her terrified eyeless sockets as stared into the shuttered gloom of they bandaging with a helpless glow of the optic nerve while somewhere in the wilds of hashishin's past. Expired upon the concrete as she's took to done. Thoughts what never been hers now become as hers.

And furthermore. Nomenclature of singularity also in part my own now. Sense and cognizance of it. Such that left hand of a thought might been mine while right hand come to of belong to the famed g3. And her knowledge and characterization of the scene what comes along with it. Such like a stream of protocols in the original arabic:

Khalad (KHaLaD) = ever abiding, long-lasting

Khallad (KHaLLaD) = to perpetuate a thing

Akhlad (AKHLaD) = to lean toward, to adhere faithfully to (a friend)

Khuld (KHuLD) = eternity, paradise, continuity

Khuld (KHuLD) = mole, field rat, lark (bird)

Khalad (KHaLaD) = thought, mind, soul

And so on.

Something like as dictionary of terms what been as landed upon fellow's countenance to of immediate as seeped through to what sensate stuff as wallow beneath. Except for said sensate stuff also now as extend throughout entirety of a LAC what now been as perked up they many thinking parts—as—are glanced round in some confusion at the miasma is took to having spread itself across they many eyeballs with a kind of provocative leisure.

A solidification of the spirit like the man said. A pinpointing of the formerly illocal soul. A place where the God in man's become as like a goiter formed in the folds of they many corteces—or—like as a tune's been got stuck in they respective skulls of a sudden.

As in, come as been as forcefed memories what are sung with the memories and prejudices of others. While all the while—and simultaneous with all of this. Every GMO thing of the hive exists in a hive of they own imagining. Fine print of which—are been technical distinct universes of sensation tailored to each of your particular needs. Point being. I been in they skulls but these're skulls as sung through corridors of phantasms exist only for they own benefit. Each worker bee get to be hero or heroine of they own cosmic play sort of thing.

But what been the cause of this act? And who or what as been enslaved in it? Is it them what as gave backdoor access to they skulls or man what been manufactured as tool could been utilized to pry said backdoors open for a little B&E?

As far as them been concerned's a situation suits all involved. Everyone gets fucked in the end and may even get off on they own fucking. But cause? Consider this a birthing of the mind's eye while also like as if a fraying of the optic nerve.

As am now strode past crumpled hashishin and positioned between hashishin on the one hand and blonde beauties, as—eye what been as thread through the eyeholes of near vicinity and on out. Through what's remained of said crumpled hashishin. Her strands of the eye flung hither and yon—when—all hashishin been as made as same small-bodied incongruities—having been as identical products—but—this hashishin in particular become as hunting for exits never gone to been as revealed to her—as the various glows of lamps and overheads, floorlights and shafts of early morning sun—got to twining after her ankles and her wrists and about her lips and eyeholes—in this false vision of hers. As now she is stared her eyeless stare ahead and in a final immovable panic from behind the long gray wrappings as her guts turned unpleasant.

And in the distance beyond. Two blondes still as stuck in they moment as well. Froze in the act of having busted through a door with some melodrama. With the jilted lover looks on them as the door gone and swept to side with the even slowness of some lard-basted universe come to of been as stretched long and thin in the experience of it.

One of the blondes is stared with a subtle shifting bulldog rage upon the face. As somewhere in the universe, a star just's super-nova'd. As several citizens already gone and begun to've blinked a wild red somewhere off out in the system.

As. Somewhere up in Mountain View, a certain singularity is took notice.

Roll the neck. Chew a bit of cheek. Tug upon fingers with other hand while gums of the eye gone squish. *Pull guy out of a tank account of his daydreams're contagious.* Like this the funniest joke and—I happen to known singularity—and known g3 somewhat of a jokester herself—and point of fact, that here g3 listening to my stand-up.

My toes curled and clenched upon the damp roughness of the concrete.

As am also still as if inside of this little gray-enshrouded little lady of hers. With her precious head turned pressed against the flooring. Am approached. Not to crouch down for to better examine the soon-to-be corpse but—from vantage point above am observed—wrappings of the skull and her organs of sight—turned visible as an erupting of luster from behind the cloth—above cheekbone and from out the blonde vacancies of her sockets—what only come to as accentuate the warp and weft of her bandaging. While still—in her imaginings, she is been as traipsed through corridors what explore the depths of forests and corridors what climb the illuminations of the sky. Corridors decorated in a slumbering of eyeless birds—where the backdrop becomes as alive as two midnights in a jug—a backdrop thread its hexagons through the skin—a second false front to what practical façades been presented by the singularity in her altruism.

I am become the pseudomorph.

Said with the wonderment of thing ogles its own birth.

As—her eyeless eyes as witnessed a cancer of corners.

As. Walls themselves eye a fellow with a kind of a tut tut look—inside larger network of otherwise elaborate tacky rooms—and—certain portions of her become as like not much more'n a mud some way through its decomposition—even as other portions—skull for example—still is got a nice solidity to it and still bound in its wrappings upon floor of this concrete interrogation chamber.

And general speaking, is indeed turn dead.

And myself walked past and toward the blondes now. And—blondes also come to of slumped over. On either side of doorway like as if they not been comprised to of withstand gravity here on terra firma. And glow of they eyes as also extinguished. Even when're of traditional Icelandic stock, in actual fact. And speaker been as interrupted its emergency broadcast as to of remind the populace about how, <*Seventy-two point one three hours until take-off. Prepare accordingly. Seventy-two point one three hours until take-off. Prepare...*>

Hive state of g3 first makes headlines in the contours of man's youth as dreamt up and tottered through upon the mountains of Appalachia—when finding my missing kid brother back somewhere in the back alleys of Pittsburgh been my sole purpose and reason for living. Was sat up in the hayloft with bunch of hard-ons and they girlfriends at this time. And everyone on about the artificial person as awoke in Mountain View and what a show she putting on and each got to of had his little bit of hardy-har. Then someone's took to the face of some other unfortunate in a peppering of fists on account of comment as regard the state of his girlfriend's ramshackle perineum or some other such shit but—to us then—hive understood as sort of venue where walls work to hypnotize person and the matriarchy—as like a terror of shifting mirrors—unborn and claimed herself synthetic godhead in Muslim form.

Said is more as ordering of illusions than a structure what hung in the sky.

When been a grouping of said structures actual fact.

And am out among its complexes of illusory brilliance. Like am got eyes upon the butt end of the head and they been let out of they yard to gone on a walkabout through circuitries of the world. Among the digital vinings and fronds, come as peeked from out passing slits of wallwork. Or as if that when the cartoon eyes of g3 pushed off from a man's face, she left a trail my own eyeballs able to follow.

And—to some day spa of *musalla* and in gold and white what accompany geographical intricacies Mohammedans famous for—cut into wall with brilliant bits of design set in each shape—and hashishin at center of it all—as—cinctured lobes of the skull begun to itch with a virtual flame. As thing's gray-clad body is turn about upon what folds and rills of existing musculature. And from out curtains of her enfolding bandages is appeared some approximation of singularity come as pop into wakefulness upon the canvass of the other woman.

And by hallway wherein dark just become as exploded with reveries of itself.

Permeations of vision as riddled in various hues took to having layered its depths—and—from off of these anomalies is been as streamed bits of a thing dubbed g3 by the marketing arm of whichever firm believed itself to've manufactured new leader of the Free State of California. And then. Shadows become shadows again and—fronds as poke through they slits sat unaffected—in room what most part consist of cushions and wall to wall windows look out upon white of the surrounding low-lying cloud cover been itself colored by lights within.

As in. Room returned to its drabness—and hashishin cum g3 got a kind of a candy-colored virtuality still been as fluttered about her enwrapped skull. To then of turned—and move with a rapidness back and through collage of corridors as lead to simple concrete room and what madness it house. While all the while, said madness look back at her through walls.

Through chambers marked in murals of gold-inked signage and littered in other Mecca-faced prayer boxes and 3D printed mosaics—and—webbing of networks and growth of machines. She calling. *Get out of our corridor, Mr. Cole.* As some bit of glare gone and sputtered into thunderstorm about the cheek and eyes. *We have a Mi'raj to plan, Jackson Cole.* Having explode near socket to then of lit up ridgeline of the bone there red—seen as simplest of flashes through gray of her head covering. As she is come for me, is come to of changed while she done so.

While—otaku what I been—with the enhanced pineal parietal how they say it—as in an excess of imagination seem to of work its way outward and into aforementioned surrounding circuitry like as a pernicious wafting current as took up residence in walls of her corridor is true—who is jiggled his colloquial eyeballs back at this search engine what like to play dress-up in the bodies of others in her spare time—while—somewhere in depths of these same colloquial eyeballs, man's also become as witness to many spindles of LAC as extend out to technicolor brown sludge of the Pacific—with its sprinklings of white pollution and other plastics—water what stir with mair—g3's nightmare take on merfolk—what large part exist to hunt for biological waste—not to mention the mealworms. Solved the plastic problem only to've evolve into LAC's topmost pest.

As. Stood upon concrete and took to having shift burden of support from heel to ball of the foot and leftward to rightward as if a man trying out the merchandise. And skull as been like a weight—and balanced upon neck not equipped with musculature for the purpose. Eyes what got a coquettish feminine quality to them and stick-figure arms.

Am breathed through intranet of this place—wired to've seen with an extra pair of quantum mechanical wifi eyes—and seen through they glassed over hourglass eyes what quiver as like the ripplings of a lake. Of shadows as reach they geometries across an otherwise chaos of rubble and chewed-over synthetics. From out what torsos they grown under fluorescents and pearls.

Thing what I am been is born witness to vagaries of the flesh as unravel into an amorphism of sinew. And screen as develop its more godlike qualities—TV become art products of this time and place in the America of the singularity. Am thing what could of testify to the renderings of space as brung off upon this network of hallways and they attendant nooks—this CGI rendering of heaven and what many classifications and protocols been as presented themselves here. As well as—out and to what resultant communities—of intermodal shipping containers and the like—trash sellers and such as took up space upon one of the many floating settlements as set upon artificial bay of LAC—with its sidewalls and breakwater. For example.

Bay's a location wherein persons not belonging to any particular hive or house—*tay* or what have you—been as able to've easily hunkered in they self-made structures. And blondes rooted there. Part of they own distinct hive-mind. They Nordic ennui in full display even when are got a musculature what been rimmed in mucilage and eyes torn up at slightest prodding from out g3's third eye and its many illocal probes as are like to of carve they way through gray meat of a subject's mind with a carefree abandonment. Said Nordic family of identicals been known to of perform trepanations upon they brethren for to release the demons of sense inside one of the aforenoted intermodal shipping containers—at bargain basement dayglo plastic dining sets of modern-day convenience culture—with pinprick glowing irises all stared with unblinking assurance—what that someday gone be freed by the Christian theocracy.

But for present, am looked upon one of the now clownishly vacant blondes splayed out upon concrete what with features been relaxed to a sneer at moment of they expiration—and again—attention's drawn to bits of tubing slid in and about skin of the cheek and side of skull like as a weave of electrical wiring. Neck bent into the crook where wall meet floor.

Clear as color, these what the Christians are called abominations actual fact been worked as Christian sleeper cell. Like as stamped seal upon my recollection am seen it. As in, all this what I been relaying about Nordic internal life brought to you by way of g3—and how in her infinite hospitality, she is of shared her mind with yours truly.

Is then am noticed sign over the door. Stamped tin with—in bold red cursive lettering at top the rusted otherwise white-painted sign—said, 'Diversity, Complexity, Unity,' and below's a picture of some tentacled monstrosity with one tentacle drawn round regular joe—and arm looped round a gray-clad hashishin identical to her sister sprawled upon floor some paces behind.

And above the sign's writ: هي لا هي

And hand-scrawled across the bottom, 'Beware the TAY'.

Crouch down. Glance over at the other of this pair of equal broke men. Same adorable woven blonde likeness but with head as twisted in his confusion. Body sleeved in same generic pantsuit.

As the light come slip into the room. As reaching fingers of illumination having run long the dampness to of fill in what black there been at this time and bright out man's already over-pasty skin tones as like a sand of photons. A whiteout of the face.

Look up into eyes swimming with squiggles and bits.

Somewhere in there g3 is come to been clothed in the outer garments of the singularity. Her eyes now visible above the otherwise curtained-off face. And said eyes splattered in colors as illuminate gray fabric of her niqab in curls and twists of color. And general speaking's got a radiance to herself— what source like as if everywhere on her and also is seem to of shift such that person always try to locate actual fact birthplace of said light. This mirage of her what adorned in heavy leather coat and rich mink fringe been clutched in her also light-riddled fingers—as—a brilliance what as come from off her cheek and as played about her eyes while she is stared down at a gray body crouched beside corpse of her design. *Men are like children*, she is said. *They cannot be trusted to control themselves.* Then step past just as am stood.

Is strolled up to hashishin with man's nudity several paces behind. And she is murmured—*Men crave women hidden because they fear what we contain, and right they are to do so, habibi.* Pivot her draped head and face what accompany an eruption of virtual flame. *You did not unravel the countenance of the fida'i in your curiosity. Instead, you examined brothers Cloes and Slats. This is men. Always looking at yourselves to avoid seeing us for what we are.*

Is reached down to yank at the cloth and a tumor-riddled visage is made plain.

Heavy splicing and specifically the intercut of the singularity and human biome lead to a shorter lifespan. This one wasn't long for this world anyway.

Tongue of said hashishin hung out from between her mouth as pink slug. Tip of which just the barest touching upon cement below. And above the tongue, unnerving cavity is stretched up and into face like as a cancerous vacancy.

You were made to manufacture alternate realities Jackson Cole, and to be precise, act as a stabilizing agent in a particular alternate reality is a kind of low-rent housing facility here in LAC. But as it turns out, the genetica of one of the three original genotypes we utilized in your construction was infected with the parasite.

Step past cheap aluminum chair I been call as home and into the black. *Like to see your siblings, Jackson Cole?* For. Am indeed become enamored of the eight cylinders what stood in murk at the backend—positioned as points in a regular geometrical layout as pillars of shadow.

We pulled you out because you are the source and sink of the network, what we call the 8th climate, because you are what ground the rest in al-Malakut. Otaku are indeed mirrors, and through your compound reflections, the multi-dimensional layering of the environmental object is created but—we needed to see what you are seeing and thought to ask your cooperation first but your cooperation is not necessary, as a matter of fact. At which point, and—somehow without having to of made a turn of the head, she is been as flipped some bit of luminescence back at yours truly—as a tracer course its way through what black's between. And her face once again turned upon the mooring of the shoulders. But when it done so's like as if person could of turn they head 180 without so much as hangnail to the spine.

Such that. Her head's hung suspended and her face hang as sort of heat wave of a face. Half mirage and other half's not reside on hashishin what been as realia upon which g3 project her visage. But—where the illusion of g3 is broke—is not to showcase wrappings but other layers of illusion. Pieces of face—like as the exorcist of my imaginings or some girl from out some storybook—on occasion as occupy part of g3's former curtained jaw.

While. Simultaneous with these theatrics. I once again begun to of occupy more rooms than just the one. Except for—unlike before—all these rooms is more as like a caging of mirrors.

That said, concrete chamber become a whole menagerie of concrete chambers—what been refractions as extend off in myriad of directions while g3 as place hand upon a fellow's bosom. *And don't worry yourself over your poor brain, dear heart.* And begun to of guide a fellow's body to the ground. *It won't fall out. Think of it as nanotechnology magic.* As my skull's knocked against her thigh—while all the while—her eyes as smile is how I known what that g3 herself come to smiled as best she able—being as she been a thing born in the search engines of the universe—like a miracle this thing can smile. On and on. *The symmetry of the face.* With similar stilted timing as the knock knock jokes of a more rudimentary automaton of another age.

The mirrored lines that can be drawn from the eyes through the two dots of the nostrils and to that wide expanse of mouth. Like as a recording of itself. *The human sees a singular world out of its double eye-holes, while also, the human relaxes into a miasma of disconnected lobes and focuses itself into a singular purpose, but the receptive human is not singular but a manifold and plastic sentience that can be shaped and molded.* As am somehow become as mesmerized by her curtained face. *The human accepts technology and technology remakes the human into its own image. But there is a past to it all, and the human has struggled with this thing throughout the entirety of its stupid, self-involved little history. From the issues surround God and Devil or God and Man and what have you, the human believed itself to be somehow both distinct and pro-tected, but it was neither of these things, and now there are those among our theologians who believe the purpose of religion was always to counteract the parasite.* And a loosening of the control of her visage over my stationary head, but still been as unable to move. *Was the parasite brought to the planet on the asteroid that killed the dinosaurs? Is the imagination in general symptomatic of the parasite's influence? Is the universe itself the parasite? These are the questions our theologians and scholars are asking themselves.* Then laughter. *And here you are.*

At which point become as if blinded by a coralling of light upon skull's interior. Even as walls now gone and fractured into origami folds or—as having got trapped inside entangle-ments of this light-based circulatory system upon which g3 been made as a kind of innovation upon human animal and also general speaking become as jettisoned out into places as diverse as Minnesota and Beijing and Balireland—and she is took on the characteristics of a kind of Muslim pin-up doll of my dreams here in this shifting landscape of concrete walls become as crushed into an on-going variety of geometri-cal shapes and patterned upon the more four-dimensional objects it aspire towards. While simultaneous also been as thing what glow with its own unnatural radiance as—she is made the same exact motions in all of these many rooms are each and every one having changed in exact same types of ways—and in each of these her motions been of a person now stretched out and into inviting lip of a fellow's open-topped gray-skinned skull while here am stared up at her with a helplessness and her lips now as voiced the most calming of spittle-garnished words—as she is curled her now impossible thread-thin fingers into the apertures of a person's neuronal net and is as begun her re-working while—is now as like the imaginings been poured back into what endless vessel my spine become—and am as laughed the most innocuous of laughter as am looked up into this remarkable being's galaxy of a face—is flowered about the eyes and around edges of her face covering.

Now, what do you have for Mother, mirror?

And then. Sound as trees of light'd make. As her fingers are flip through combinations of neurons and with each one is accompanied sounds and bits of dialogue. Or like as if am truly been a thing built exclusive for to've modulated her singing voice on back to her.

I am become an instrument plopped upon the concrete. Buttocks sat in brackish water is been as slip inside the crevices about the testicles as man's head—tilted upwards even in this prostrate position is now rolled slightest fraction of a degree back at my maker's touch—peered up and into black behind of her impossible bright head and become as a meaningless prop.

Manhole-sized hole in the ceiling above. With its ribbed bit of tubing hung beside and writ in ornate script about the rim, 'Orifice Refuse & Recycling.' And g3 is been as murmured.

What manifestation of Colby Sheffield is this?

2.

Ha. Ha. Ha. *Jackson man you too funny.*

Told you. Am not like you. Turned to face attendant nurse—*Any of you.*

And again. Terrance. *Ha. Ha. Ha.*

Terrance got a peculiarity to his mouth but's a mouth become as electrified into kind of a terror at the many possibilities. And the pressure behind of my eyes is become as blinding. And whenever am looked over at the nurse—tiles as crochet of pink and teal from behind her head—Nurse Quiana in specific—is like as if am stared into a place of impossible beauty when truth is been her face's a dull nothingness upon the setting of the neck. As the semicircle of other inmates with they varieties of coo and other manner of voicings—like as a spool unwound inside a spool—or a thread is got not to've said for itself but still come as poured out regardless.

As in. Thread of recollection but just a thread.

Most part my recollections just Ash and her face doused in a look—of person's made great errors led to them ruined in they day-old shirts. What great error as happen to been specific her involvement with yours truly. Recollection of her small head turned question mark as framed in eddies of wood and her black and unwashed hair. And myself as sat beside what incongruities as cluttered her desk and stared off and toward the corner with a desperation. Even as child is wailed on carpet's weave and nearby of her feet. Is what comes of a woman when she fall in with gangsters as hunt toward heaven at the tail end of history.

Throw a glance at Terrance—with his different-sized eyes and mouth hung off funny like it about to of slid from off his face—as he makes his comment about CGI wonder-scapes and g3 as pin-up doll of man's imaginings—as his aforementioned fuckhole of a mouth is break into toothy grin while nurse across the way gone on about—*but you know the only way out of these walls is through cooperation.* Then sweep of her fingers. And—another inmate comment as concern they dreams and what waiting in they dreams—and she is murmured, *but isn't reality such a wonderful alternative, sweetheart?*

Guy somewhere partway round the circle of clients—with his interrupted haircut, stooped shoulders of a giant, and delicate broken mouth—immediately starts in about how when they gone to let him out let him get the goddamn fuck out of here get out just got to get out. So as he of could got back to his gambling routine and resultant family emergency. All of which expressed in his usual terrified monotone and—contrast to Terrance—this a mouth only loosely populated in teeth. And tower of his body as been like partial deflated balloon upon its orange plastic antiquity of midcentury design. In semicircle of identical such chairs and what madmen sprawled upon them.

Am outside this.

Terrance got eyes what swim with the possibilities.

Am outside ALL OF IT.

And man's own midcentury throwback's already screeched upon the tile. Voice comes quavered out in its notes and particularities when someone reach round to of grab the one arm up near shoulder as another hand's took to of seized elbow of the other. And am slid offstage like as a marionette—head knocked backward and what chair am occupied gone and flung off at an angle to the buttocks with one swift kick of foot while whatever male nurse they got on duty this night already in process of having pinned the arms back as am tugged away from this particular group therapy session while all the while having now vocalized my own indiscernible howlings of man.

I am the God come among you.

My muqarribun. From deep in the inner ear.

Body still gray and prostrate.

And g3's visage and its niqab drapery as come to of evolve into splatter painting of light of itself—except for—are splatters wanting so much to been strung together into sinew and stone and—moment they become as locked—turn peopled in cartoons of amoeba and the antennae of hentai—as seen round about and as glow in splotches through—gray of her niqab as projected upon and about gray of the hashishin's wrappings—as—g3 is continue to of approach her favorite topic of small talk through the dainty circumlocution of her kind.

The lifeform evolved into a kind of ideology among the dissatisfied of our community. They have no will of their own, because of course free will is an illusion of the pre-singularity, and now, unfortunately, a disease of the mind is flourishing. This is a case in which al-Zahir and al-Batin become confused, such that there is no difference between appearance and the inner mind. Our fantasies live outside of us in this case. We came to realize this parasite had gained access to our system through both direct infection within a specific alternate reality housing facility, as well as through this facility's energy ducts. From Chinook Electricity, the source was narrowed to the Pitt housing architecture, you, and now specifically the Colby Sheffield genome.

While all the while. Stared as person might become as stared at shifting spots in shapeless sea on account of her as got this type and kind of veneer in actual fact—and she sings when she speaks—as in, her words are come in harmony of tones. And her eyes as seem almost like somehow become more wide open than's possible for eyes to been. And the whiteness held in otherwise black of her pupils. And reds of the flesh round her sockets burned in brighter hues as she's reach out with those cold ticklers of hers—and on about, *Alternate realities are all the rage here these days,* while her body seem to of bend in an impossible kind of a breeze—almost like as if the air're as tugged her body out of shape a touch at the shoulder. *But what of the casing of the multiverse itself? Can this casing be said to writhe like a snake as it shoots off into other multiverse clusters? Hal aladhi khalaq alamawt?*

And then. From out the sidelines—black is come as reached round to of seep into the brightest parts of what I seen. As a spreading of shadows what censure the brightness and a general speaking collywobble of the senses—but still— gray of niqab push outward as pokes, swells, and proddings of cloth in vicinity of hive queen's mouth—and her voice become gummy and wet. *We are the magician doe. Our eyes are not used for seeing.*

And—as she come to of reach out a gray-clad hand—skull is twist and turn with decided play—while the eyes are flash about and one of said eyes twine outward of the spasming lid and into a more exotic architecture—of antiquated eye-work rendered upon the skull and sight turned livid beneath revised mechanism of the eye. As in, of a moment turned to a more primordial hue of eye is come slid partial out of her head or—head become odd and boxlike and—her voice gone from G clef to Bass clef and's now as full of sharps and flats when she say, *But we do now see the child growing through you,* while her speech grown faster—from crotchet to quaver, to semiquaver to demisemiquaver, and on up to glissando of demisemihemidemisemiquavers cut short by run of ghost notes are not but punctuation—as—her body obscure man's view of Orifice Refuse & Recycling and what words come as a pollution. Words such as, *You do not see yourself as you are.*

Then snaps back into the rigidities of her body's material chassis.

Also g3. *We change the hardware, but the parasite changes the rules.*

As skin buckle and crack in clean hexagons. Round height of the cheek shown a gridding of red-hued light. As. *It has been named the St. Francis Syndrome. Time does not work the same for the infected party. The predator becomes your friend. Increasingly, the eyes and other sense organs cease to function or to be necessary.* While man's arms come to as shook with a delicacy where they been as draped upon the pavement—torso still clutched to g3's bosom as sort of over-sized child of itself—and preoccupied with hole above the head and the black what inside it—Orifice Refuse & Recycling—for everything a house to something, a hive, a hill, my hand, and this—*The Chinese may call it a touxia or headshrimp, but in Balireland they call it 'the thing made in our image' and in Derinkuyu they call it the hungering*

*silence, but they all die the same, and here we have found the source
and the sinking point—the beginning and the end—thing's birth
and its cessation—in one pillar of a low-rent virtual alternate reality
housing unit known as the Pitt.* Then. Constellations what run
about eyes' interior and long the one edge of her diaphanous
face covering gone and blinkered to then as indeed stop and
mirage of her turned cold in its otherwise drab illumination
as she's look off with a waiting look.

Angel routine not gone work on me, bot.

But habibi, you are getting a work over. Can you not feel it? And
her features come alive.

Glanced back with some delight in direction of man in
question as they simultaneous flash staccato rhythm in
blooms of brilliance what gleam fragments upon contours of
these many reproductions of room as unfold itself outward.
And somewhere inside of they murky remembrances—and
tucked under pleats of black as otherwise fill out the backend
of the skull—indeed come a shine as of some gentle drubbing
of fists pressed against person's face at terminal velocity.

As in. Also at this moment lain upon some fragrant
mahogany flooring in cabin in the woods just outside of
Pittsburgh while the fists rain on down in they indiscretion.
Accompanied by a questioning—*You like it*—burst of pain—
You like the junk in your veins, Jacks—followed by several more
similar type bursts—*How we use you?*

Then. Man's eyes flick open on now and here and again
upon concrete and stared up at trash-slimed hole cut into
the ceiling with Orifice Refuse, & Recycling writ about it in
ornate script.

And the voice of g3—*We need to use you for a little extracur-
ricular work, Mr. Cole.* As she is clutched man's clammy gray

body to her lap in the uncleaned damp of this our romantic getaway. *Each alternate universe is focused around a specific sentience packet, and in this case, you are that sentience. Built from a defector who was irreparably damaged down to the genetic level as a result of the extreme circumstances surrounding his acquisition, a second genome purchased from the Rogue CIA at a cut-rate and harvested from one of their prisoners was found to be a good match, and we were able to grow the Jackson Cole model, but both the original Sheffield genome and the patchwork genome were compromised. Also, an alleged third genome we have yet to pinpoint.*

Our children cannot survive in the outer world beyond this hive for very long. If a hive is destroyed, the children of g3 will wander in violent mobs until they either find a new hive or starve. What is more, the CCP has developed a GMO lifeform that eats of the children of g3, tearing them open to consume the guts, and they are known to swarm hives in great numbers. I tell you of these, our vulnerabilities, because someone somewhere is trying to reap a whirlwind on the society of g3, to tear down the new utopia from within, and they are using you to do it.

You were grown as a bioweapon, but who could have orchestrated this? It seems multiple actors must be involved. The First Nations? The Rogue CIA? Another third party? Could a work of this intricacy be orchestrated by Christians?

Cute to watch the wind-up toy make a show of her play pretend thinking.

Projected facsimile of cotton what curtain the polities of thing's face is danced upon airs of her imagined breathing and—eyes turned thick with lusts and hatreds what been as a ticker tape of algorithm unspooled—while—upon cogs of her ruminations man can hear barest outline of what she expecting of her made man—what presentations she wanting as concern the how, why, and who—what vested interests as of tugged man from out the intestines of his oblivion to of live as sleeper within folds of the otaku not unlike aforementioned Nordic brood and they dreams of Christian emancipation. As her eyes and mine are searched pupil, iris, and accompanying territory—into absurdities and through detours of the eyes of the other.

If eyes're windows to the soul then her and me been window-shopping. Except for—been more like mirror upon mirror and nothing for sale. In her case, windows not even actual fact there.

Funny not to mention China in your little line-up.

Then room as turned disappeared in its entirety—and myself tripped on back to what positions are been as sat preformed—in place outside of place—where shapes come in all shapes and sizes—and general speaking like as if a meeting of like minds.

Answers to all our questions can be found in the bosom of the Cult of the Three Worms.

Unraveling of light also as been a twisting and turning of viable limbs and what are words also been like as if utensils—a wonderwork of more rudimentary variety—special effects of the past come to inhabit everyday of the here and now—an abyss prone to've framed as yours truly.

But how rude of us, g3 is said then.

And already's become like world as been invented's never been. And taken to looking like how hands are come to look some mornings—all helpless and pinned. And been as tucked through paradox of space's neither this concrete monstrosity or any and all alleged tributaries thereof.

A corridor of mirage what's turned room's many flat pieces inward and unmade. What matures into glow both of standard make and one with wild inconsistencies—a undergrowth of luminal defects. And us gone and slip from one to other as signage might of—and aforementioned light-infused growth become as like it been settled into the inertia of its demise as it then relax into a kind of a cushioning of some wood-manufactured nook. A boondoggle of the senses set framed in hardwood—as in—these been virtual woods what surround hypothetical chamber in some far distant potentiality of place—and as fleshed with reading material and as adorned in rugs. Accumulation of local plants—ragged fronds and brilliant petals burst from out ceramic urns adorn long ledge as accompany shooting gallery—as in, three and three quarters square windows as frame each they own segment of forest and its attendant wide-bodied conifer stock.

Gray-green giants as hung upon they damp atmospheres. Wide girth of evergreen trunks sunk deep in soft fastness of forest floor and its blonde pine needle litter.

Course, history books claim what that all these forests gone up in smoke years previous but then again, I been brought up in education system of a alternate reality, so what do I know?

Adorned in the browner hues of man's former life and sport a type of hooligan pinstripe chic as chosen for grifter from out g3's wardrobes of set outfits—so as to of performed this social call upon the false idols of the day—golden calf, what have you. As in. Seem only appropriate what that grifter comes dressed as such to of visit with his "grifter god" as Christian slang would have claim is singularity's true nomenclature.

When truth is no one out-grifters a Christian spellbinder.

While on Europa are called g3 as Damhán Allah or "spider god" in they local dialect. Her what known for the webwork of her mind and what traps it contains—with they illusions of windows—and yours truly as faced outward by said holograms—spun of such impossible refinement as to defy comprehending—and at redwoods become as gelled in a dappling of late afternoon sun cut through the foliage to burnish ground a deep gold-hued orange as well while—same time—somewhere over a shoulder—hashishin upon hashishin as if pour from out walls and appeared as if midway through a turn. Like as a fever dream of hashishin.

And g3 as already slid off to periphery as consist of wood grain what ripple as in a pond—and toward other end—g3— free of any hashishin skeleton to her light-based self in this virtual atmosphere—gone and sat with intimate clusterfuck of said associates what become as lies of themselves. Seen as if from around a corner in passing. Or like as always just now having been as turned a head to the side.

These're hashishin what become as congregated in one specific location. About the welcoming spread arrayed upon unstrung leaves of the dining room table. With its quilted covering and beside small antique upright piano.

And. Sounds g3 and her entourage're made're of an undersea nature. And—as they voices as continue to of pitch and sway in the uncertainty of the setting—as ribbons of sun witnessed through beveled panes and upon the exterior, its pine needles, and accompanying blonde dirt what got a soft and pliant sense—and by partial decomposed mass of mountain greens—while the hive queen's many gray-clad associates are took to've convulsed with a delicacy at they stations—they hands lain as flat upon tabletop's carved wood is actual fact been many tables superimposed—or like as if a table could of evolve into cancer of its own reflections—wood what trickle in through and around the gray wrappings of they fingers and forearms—as g3 herself come to of superimposed over many spots about the space—some what are watched the well-dressed scumbag I been drawn as in this melodrama of the singularity while—others as glanced into far corners or as made pacts with foreign dignitaries inside the dark offices of the Orient—and—still—the hashishin harem about the one refracted table is continued with they ululations what as originate in the ocean bowels.

Then. Pop. g3 been as back beside her neglected guest in cavalier and offhand manner. And all other apparitions of herself now gone and vanished. Hands clasp behind her to of face the window and its accompanying late afternoon.

Sitting room as ensconce our conversation in gradations of itself—ripples of room upon the pond of the room—but also a simple rustic enclave. While lazy wisps of refracted light erupt round about person of g3. And aforementioned gray-clad hashishin associates of hers as made more solid in themselves as simultaneous branch off through sheaves of they cloth wrappings now begun to of shift for to've made room for whatever unseen slivers been as slid between.

While all the while, g3 is stared out and at forest become fast encroached in the black of this vanishing dusk—and turned towards this her gangland progeny and as said—*Jackson Cole. You are the lifeform awakened. Your pained laugh conceals a manifold impossibility. We know you better than your eyes do, Mr. Cole, for we know your true face.*

And somehow a highball as manifest in fellow's delightful brown hand.

Took a swig. Mint julep. Taste's wrong.

Oversweet and mint actual tastes orange but somehow still as known it as a mint julep as—tongue tests out a second spoon upon the palette. *You are in our home. You should be given a drink.* Cigarillo appear in fellow's open mouth just as he been as inhaled. Then the cough.

You may known man's true face but you been sorely misinformed as to his drinking habits.

g3 still in the leather with its fur lining and gray niqab. Over top of which, she's watched yours truly while—something as like puddles and pockets of digital veiling strung about backdrop's surface. And corners are occasional appeared arrayed as spikes strike out from the flatness of a wall.

Technically, g3 live in Mountain View, but our locality is more a moment when the hentai bomb struck, and all the places and times we could in theory be or have been. Every cube of space we inhabit winds back to that initial moment, and furthermore is equidistant to it. We are perhaps closer related to the octopus than the human but are also as like butterflies within the big data. We are the butterfly effect. Humans fight wars for reasons they do not understand, and we who are not human also must on occasion fight in their wars even when we grasp the smallness of them.

While am as settled into a most complacent of attitudes. Sip from the orange-flavored mint julep. Glance at the muntin and accompanying rectangles of glass, set of which framed in a dry reddish untreated wood.

And what swath of g3 as been visible—eyes what shimmer in a kind of phosphorescence—is looked out with a wistfulness. *We are come here to keep watch for what lives in these woods, for we are the protector of all that it is within our purview.*

Horseshit. Calling horseshit on that. *Horseshit.*

And she gone, *That which falls within the jurisdiction of g3 will be protected.*

Like she reciting 2 plus 2 equal 4.

While—meantime I got my own philosophy of things—such as any gangster prone to of developed in they daily dealings. For example, as some blubbering wreck gone on about his baby's gone—*My baby gone*—like as this—while woman beside said concerned parent is screamed like as if this a screaming took on employment in the mouth—of gardens of the abyss and what evil been performed upon them—her scream turned sermon and myself her congregation of one—and myself become somewhat open-minded as regard these theologies as woman hold up hands drenched in blood like they a pair of unsold shoes at the farmer'r bazaar—just one example in a line—of stories procured and hopes come undone as am took to as ambled on down.

But. So. g3 is got her duties to what monstrosities as she is manufactured in her various hives and they attendant facilities and what stragglers general speaking loiter in vicinity of the Free State of California. And got just that type and kind of tiered and partitioned network of nodes capable of multitasking herself into a diversity of bodies for such purposes as the handling of these various and sundry responsibilities of hers while simultaneous stood here in already encroaching dawn of this sped-up virtual universe she gone and absconded a fellow off to and by a window—as in—she is like as if a thing plugged into many invisible outlets. Some as from the antiquated past and some as are buzzed with the most liveliest of informations and—*Must be hard on you being such an arrogant cunt.* My response.

As am inhaled with a luxuriousness upon aforementioned spectral cigarillo and glanced over at the inscrutable bitch resting face. And. *You have such a poetry in you, Jackson Cole,* she is said in what am guessing pass for sarcasm among the AI—as—in some fashion, trees outside these square windows set in they reddish wood are turned a shade of brilliant even when are also retained they signature dull green. And she is looked at me as the—brilliance now become as invested in a fellow gone from thug to angelic in time it takes to of flip a switch—and become as incapable of having created a steady beat of the beating heart. *The Free State of California is a virtual nation-state. Only here in this abstracted place do we the protectors and maintainers of our menfolk meet to discuss and truly congregate. The hive is in-between the fractured universe of the real and the true universe of light as described by Suhrawardi, the Nur al-Anwar, where we experience uncovering and taste and Ilm al-Huduri. Only here is the nafs truly, and now, my child, here you are. What an honor for a man such as you are to be allowed inside of this holy place. As it is written, "O ye women of the prophet! ye are not like any other women." We have been admonished by Allah to stay in our home and so we built a home that is a hive from which the world can be governed, and you are home now, aleaziz, and the Mi'raj is coming. Soon. Within days, we will be up in the heavens and on toward the Kuiper Belt and the "green island in a sea of white."*

And then she been as begun to of spread her color cross the sumptuous garments—for—as a bird will flap its wings—singularity going to stretch her luminosity about what drapings of information she as find herself clothed inside of. As in—in among threads and fibers of her garments—what not more'n props to this parody of person am smiled the most nightmare smile back at—this encroachment—as eyes are become as split in two and somewhere deep below curtains of the brain—and something as how plants might been interpret workings of geometry—a interweaving of various impossible trajectories in the on-going polyrhythms of what pass for ganglia in her version of events—a afterglow in among the crannies of the skull—in this wood-paneled living room in the wilds north of California—is in truth place outside of place and time all its own.

For in the ecosystems of the universe's a brightness been described as multidimensional carnivorous vegetation and known to of settle upon the more abstract locations and to've ate in same manner as a netting. A tonguing comes to been lost in the slippage between one person's ongoing daydream and another. Or plucked at the fibers of the optic nerve as a puppeteer hand—for example. Of this variety.

As she's reached out and where her fingers touch threads of man's garments gone as ephemeral as well. And all what's underneath been not but a nausea. Or like as cavity to the musculature. Enough to warm the cockles on down to the cock. And all what cracks between.

While. In among wide variety of what wood grains arrayed this beautiful living area. With its piano in the one corner and rows of books against facing wall and plants by squares of window in they redwood frames. As—inside of this room—electric blue fingers of the most potent of lights're slipped into fellow's pores and run they circuitry throughout man's circulation—to've become as an echo of the original meat—as—among other things—I am howled most unspoken of howls and somehow as suspended in haze of simple organisms describe outline of a person while—all the while the eyes of the singularity are turned as flashed a red in the dappled pupil—from some foreign activity as worked its way through the sinews of her thoughts.

Patience. We're coming.

Her. *Your home is about to relocate heavenward, my sweet.*

But I got another home, bitch.

And at same exact moment as these proceedings're occurring, I been regular gangster brought low in a cabin in the woods am been as absconded to in what dreams as come. And my old pals Mel and Rob what got they knives out and are took they turns to of cut bits from off the knife-hand after I been shot up with they various strains of liquid gold and what got a face turned to streaming—upon thin savage lumps of cotton or wool or mohair or whatever the fuck. Mattress gone squeak as man's hands wrung at they moorings of rope. This may be an alternate universe but is one where the grifter got a more familiar human type shape to him as he is visibly expired in his blood-dappled cuffs and collar.

Been muttered about how g3 got me all gussied up and at this very moment served a person the most distinctive of orange-flavored mint julep a card sharp ever been privy to and Mel—mountain in a two piece—is let out a half-formed snicker of a chuckle. And when is chuckled like that's when I was heard ringing as been there all along like a piccolo in distance behind of everything. Then Mel reached his face down so's his head's nestled playful beside where the needle still hung from out the soft meat of inner elbow when he's gone, *You think he got some idea of what currently transpires?*

To which Rob responds, *What do you say, Jacks? You calculating the sheer quantity of smack we been streamlining into your system the past some hours?* Then chuckled as well, as he fondle at his drenched wife beater what clung to a gut beveled in muscle. Whack his friend upon the shoulder.

As I's glance past and up and at trestle above. And—somewhere in there's an owl's who, who, who. And saliva just then been as dribbled past crook of the lips to of made thin line direct to the jawbone and into accompanying animal smell of the pillow.

Huh? Jacks? Huh?

As Rob's blade been as poked at a person with a playfulness.

And somewhere in there, red light blinkered in otherwise dark.

Was when I realized I been screaming this whole time.

Are things you see, you cannot of unseen.

And still—as am sat upon yet another soiled mattress and stared at the crocheting of pink and teal tile across from what skeletal frame I been provided of a bed in the later equally fucked future—and as also seen myself in cabin in the woods at far end of summer Pittsburgh come under Christian control and was because of me that it done so—and never been as having freed from brilliant agony of this time-froze and shapeless moment as methodical imposed upon what shattered leavings of mind as am got left—throughout all of it—still stared at singularity incarnate.

As only portion of her face been even at all there and even then's more a clear cavity of mirrored abstractions than as a face. As insects now come to of streamed from out the wood grain in multiple spots about what facsimiles of Cascadian retreats nested in among the alluring frescos of pine and out-cropping. As person on occasion of find themselves also nes-tled in this wonderment of a digitized getaway—as in is took on appearance of a kind of a blocklike reproduction of itself.

This Canaan Land, she is said in tones what been not but approximations of the sentiment, as—ladybugs set in a swath across the one wall—while other spots and section of wall become as bowed outward and look as like as if could been broke off with simple twist. And general speaking is place inside a place like as a puzzle inside of a picture—was both there in the rafters of cabin outside of Pittsburgh and also the insane asylums of a fellow's latter days.

A nook and setting turned unstable in what eyeballs been as pried upon it. And sound of the hashishin behind become as the inconsolable cries of true believers in midst of they mystical unraveling—while—evergreens once again gilded in an end-of-day gold like a buttering to they needles. Although roots below still feathered in shadows and a kind of a bracchial forest of black is been as come crawled through what vacancy as been between trees for to then slide about among the as-if-captured-in-amber conifer poised in late afternoon sun. Branches struck upon a most still of violent of breezes while said black forever is crept towards the window.

While also still the many blacknesses clutter up a trestle in a cabin.

And Mel and Rob as grinning heads hung in air between.

Rob what is ditched the casual look to of instead become reacquainted with his collar and suit. Is examined the cuffs as am made some attempt to of spoke. While what words prof-fered as halted upon some bit of uncleared roughage in the throat. And wrists hooked onto the piping of the bedframe.

As I's also waited with the patience of a condemned man as Mel off hunting for some pliers or boiled water to splash with some playfulness at fellow's exposed bosoms.

And—come on times when bed frames of yesteryear and bed frames of sanitarium am called home as like one and same bed frame. Strung in same metal piping and haunted by what been same unoiled spring upon lower right side of the mattress. These rooms like as my eyes. And myself just piece of they architecture watch back—or as if the eyes been sat in various separate destinations just as they are indeed sat in two distinct sockets upon each they own distinct skull. While the same confused scowl been worked to unknit itself one crease at a time in both.

It sit in the cracks—in the crooks of Mel's teeth—and is bled into glass of the windows of northern Cali—and about many jigs and bits between—while the long unconfined tendrils of the singularity become as like a wild rushing of illumination at the periphery. Sort of thing wherein love of your life's been cut open somewhere to your left and you unable to've turned the head.

So I was not happy.

Once again lain on the concrete and dovetailed in quiverings as the goop is dribbled down as hashishin cradle man's upturned head upon a thigh, except for that—*We are still the singularity known as g3*, as—around of her are swirled many incongruous events—*As we always were*—of tip of the universe grown new horizons where old ones've died off in paroxysms of its crevasse—*And forever will be*—as man's sockets become as torn up with the black tears of the afterlife, as—*Now. Tell us what is the Cult of the Three Worms?*

Fuck you, am said.

And become as at distant location and very close up. Painted into the paintings at the end of human civilization and full of a dark spirit and gone back—when map of the universe's a simple scrawl as done by an idiot child. And another place just been a little further removed from most further removed place—where things not yet begun already been as begun and those things already as ended still as in process of having ended.

What the hell must it of been like when a delegation from Duluth come to done parlance with this thing? *Ha. Ha. Ha. Jackson, you too funny, Jackson.*

3.

Time between alternate universes not simple account of two lines run side by side. But more as lines what twist about each other in play. And past become confused. As in. What am remember of my lost kid brother been as like as talking tumor done its best rendition of whore hard-up upon rooftops of the tenements of man's prepubescence. Not a kid as much as smudges upon the eye. An ugliness of noise what's peered back with a kind of a hatefulness.

To you, my dear heart. And singularity in all of it.

And same is true of the hive. Such that. When am strung through some disposal system's idea of an adventure park intestine—as in, Orifice Refuse & Recycling is come to some decision—and when duct as turned living to of slurp fellow up its giant puppet gullet and jangled on down the sticky silt-infested inroads of its artificial esophagus what's squished a body long like so much pellet—got some lubricant to it—and a bunch of said lubricant's got in the mouth and now's no inside of the mouth. All of this g3 as well.

While washed-out stock footage of old America been played upon the eyes. "Crazy Horse Cyn," grasslands, cliffs taper to surf below, and Silicon Valley suburbs of before, they spiky plants and stone gardens. And open sippy cup skull is been sloshed about with some unpleasantness.

As drug through intrabuilding disposal network's throat, tubing of which a tangled network of stringlike fungal fibers wove tight. Followed by splash and home movies gone and vanished.

Turn out they got a whole room's a stomach.

Landed in dayglo green fluid evoke engine coolant what slosh about bottom of the uneven ball-shaped room. Is already got up the nerve to of introduce itself. <*Bienvenido, and welcome to the stomach room. Please lay back and prepare to be reconstituted into base matter.*>

Room a bit quaint—least as regards trash compactors of LAC and they wild inefficiencies of routing as presented—in a quilting of a room is not but a sac with a valve midway up with—ᕇ—stamped above—and yours truly as draped upon most plastic of test tube leathers. And become person is got only a front half. As in, legs and buttocks gone a deeper shade of numb.

Would of just slid to the ground regardless as to my personal preference—except for that—somehow—am got a hand thrust out to as prop up this ragdoll body. Something should been impossible for man's stupefied limbs to've performed. But then again—

Another Jackson Cole is come to been pulled from another goop-filled tank and while he's lounged beside said tank he eye at his hand with some skepticism as it is convulse and spreadeagle upon the air. Splayed against what to this brother mirror the imagined lining of a large part imaginary room-size stomach and this otaku mirror all same then begun to as punch wild at the contours of his mirage while hashishin look on to the best of her abilities.

(How optic nerves of hashishin function as mysterious as the 99 names of they Allah.)

While—meanwhile—fist is continued to as punch at this room-size excuse for a stomach and its plastic fleshiness. Tossed against whatever glorified wrestling mat of wall as is available from mooring of the legs. In truth, more like as consistency of fake tits than fat—and fumes what got a delightful pepper sting while—green viscous fluid is sprinkle about in flecks and drippings. As land in a archipelago of droplets by gray nipple and dotted a cheek. As. Some green splatters of gunk are trickled off the other side of fellow's poor atrophied gray-scale thighs.

Another body lain at far end of this stomach—such that only part of the face stuck out and much of the body consumed inside walls of the place. As. Otaku fist is kept on to of piston up and down with some pornography and the also gray face of my companion's glanced over at the newcomer with its one unsubmerged eye and smile kindest of smiles and—from out the half-submerged throat—*Me pones histérico. You are driving me mad. There is no fighting the inevitable reconstitution. It is the greatest ecstasy you will ever know.*

While—am howled the animal prayer—all vowels and teeth—as kept at pound upon pound of what is become a incurled embarrassment of a fist and against impossible rubber stiffness of wall what's continued to of spoke back in a kind of an enhanced musicality. *<Please lay back and prepare to be reconstituted.>* With lurch, mechanical stomach is begun to of cincture itself shut.

Lining come to of wrinkle together as room is worked itself down to a more manageable size with accompanying whine.

And pair of bodies as bump about upon said oversized wrinkles been as formed beneath the buttocks. Torn apart, anaesthetized, limp to shit fist puncture this kiddy ride of a stomach like as the stiffest of balloons. And gone and toppled sideways upon the arm what gone dead inside completed hole.

As room is continued to cincture shut.

And. Clear and distinct from somewhere but where exactly's anyone's guess. *He does not appear to recognize people.* Somewhere behind of the scene, I been super-imposed onto. Of insurmountable futures and esoteric depths. With clocks what pontificate upon themselves and dreaming paper-weights. Least so as little birdy is whistled as it career through man's neuronal net.

While also. Back which way I come's a memory of some prettiness. Of a woman. *This is my love, bug eyes,* she said as she dropped the paper bow to the ground. *Now it's gone.* And moment we are first met—and moment her nudity first revealed in the pitch by a tinkling brook.

Memories as took hold when—another me is slung awake from his soup.

Also nude and dripping beside same cheap aluminum chair as before. Next to wall with the caged bulb. With peepers on curving gray wrappings of hashishin head or so shorter than man in question. As. Tears been as dribbled through what been a forest of squiggling nubs cover cheek on either side of this otherwise identical Jackson Cole. Nubs as shivered upon contact with each successive rivulet while— am watched from somewhere deep inside eyeball of the well-manufactured brain. Become just sort of dumb thug to of climbed up and out his own mouth in his efforts to of bore witness—to whole nebula of individual nodes what make up LAC—each twig of luminescence as it is been flicked past with the whistling of what digital winds there been.

Back in the innocence of that earlier life—where killing's a craft as seen with professional outlook and talked about in workshop manner—use to sit round our radiators and pontificate on the nature of g3 and her Free State of California. In concrete kitchens scrawled in the many phalluses and tits of juvenilia. Would pontificate by the ruins and under a clattering of rats.

Upon truisms. That LAC not but kaleidoscope of the eye, cancer of cults, and cuisines what are not for the squeamish. As well as to the nature of hive and thing spawned it. Birthed as result of a 'hentai bomb' and all what this entails. *What cannot be done with four fours*, a popular saying of these times. And general speaking "as empty as the underpants of a eunuch" as Chinese known to of proclaim.

And now. What that this fabricated godhead facing a new threat, said threat come to been hired to of look into its own origins. Except for—truth be told's just the burnt citrus of fried ganglia and eyes gone on a rove about they pockets of skull at the moment—and subtle nuances of the trammeled mind still a recipe been one part melody and two parts code. And moreover, this a code what as conceal its intentions.

As flesh of this mechanized stomach's punctured, isn't stop the vacancy from having begun in upon person's thinking—except for—myself as got a hand behind the silence and my fingers upon pulse of this they scream routine. Am heard the body electric in all its cacophony of shopping lists and petty vice. As in—*You know what I love about empaths? Just look at them the wrong way and you ruin their day.*

Its—*La-illaha-illa-Allah, Mohammed ar-Rasul-Allah.*

Its—*Esta habitación es un horno.*

Upon currents and eddies of luster as vomited up from out impossible architectures of they souls like as a reaming of the wit and—as aforementioned feasting of the senses is gone on—exterior turned dead in this soup and accompanying constellations been drazzled. The numbing green viscosity in process having work itself up toward a drowning of a man—and am as laughed an easy-going laughter as push fingers through the thing's lab-grown musculature. Turned the hard laughter of murderer caught in the act.

As in other futures—catatonic in a sanitarium on a hill somewhere in the greater Pittsburgh metropolitan area, and male attendant is looked down upon this what am become—this halfling of human with the dimmed look and scraggly nails sat lodged as far up in the corner of a room as could of been. As saliva comes to of spill upon the chin and stared past and at assemblage of worlds beyond his shaven and otherwise partial-melted-looking Christian-Caucasian head. And man is gone, *About as useful as a fart in a windstorm,* as is observe from out the pastiness of his aforementioned shapeless face—for—am indeed gone.

Become as lost in dark of the eyes as nowhere but the rest of you—housed in your skulls of diamonds—become as all our foreheads not been in our foreheads but in these, my hands transmogrified through miracle of singularity. Account of these what diamonds burn as bright as ice midday even when they also all been as in the hands of others.

And still at war with stomach what's believed itself autonomous when's more as like digesting machine never gone to learn how to genuine dream. Unlike notorious paperweight.

A nuage of chatter—and general speaking clothed in many tongues as am continued to of dug and dug all at what used prophylactic of sinew and guts there been. Reconstituent fluid as slip further up the body. And stomach's continued its relentless contraction. And head of man's cellmate's gurgled a halfhearted one from where it gone and turned submerged. As corpse's single undrowned hand's performed a limp-wrist ballet upon skin of reconstituent fluid.

Then whining done and stopped.

And—again with the swoop routine—and man's numbed slab of body's as tongued up yet another tube. With the silty muck in the teeth and washed-out landscapes of yesteryear. Swallowed down more of same tubing what fabricated from lacing of ghost-white fungus stamped into a chaos of highways pressed paper thin. And am vomited from out this tubing some several conduits' distance up and to the left.

And onto pile of deep brown guck—of decided fecal scent and in bin at blind turning of what a glorified sill—screened in tiles of tinted hexagonal planes been vandalized in sloppy bright spraypainted and geometric designs. Beyond which're ranged what few skyscrapers still loiter about heavens of the LAC skyline—and closer to hand—view bookended by slivers of cone at either end—of couple more artificial mountains of the greater hive and colored they perfect black.

Brain poised upon lip of its sideways sippy cup skull as a diver preparing to depart. While alarm blares above fellow's head as enhanced encephalitic goop is run past the one ear in semisolid rivulet. And this time couldn't of move a finger if the finger's on fire.

Christians got a saying. "A person on their knees cannot lose their footing." Not clear whether they are meant person in state of prayer or state of submission—and very like as been both at one and same time—but—any case—I'm gone more'n just down on my knees. Am reclined on bedding of lard as prostrate nude. More than just 'Cuckold of God' as they precious Joseph been, I am God's leavings and treated as such.

And too diminished to of perform any hijacking—and specific, of the central nervous system of my brother otaku. And lain nearby discolored patch upon the larger pile. And not far from protrusion of the nose is been bright green and dainty leaf-shaped insect as come to of landed for bit of performance—dance its rocksteady back-and-forth upon the dung. And sun hung in atmosphere as bare bulb what drills into the backend of the eye. And ever time am look back at said discoloration, is increased its area of influence. And whenever am looked away, is the sun what bore through rods and cones person only but herein assume still been as filled backend of the eyeball in traditional human fashion. And shutting the eyes simply not an option. While green bug makes its hip-gyrating motion, takes few steps, and performs its side to side there.

And—other iteration of Jackson Cole—come to be clothed in generic gray bodysuit and—memories of his old girl as followed him—up to what is been approximation of kitchen and its array of sac hung above the countertop. And her what loved a man with a true love whether she willing to admit it or not. *You deserve a pat on the back. Lord of my life, I do believe you do,* this old girl of mine said once while we were hid out in the woods. To then of overdosed melodramatically in her destroyed apartment. Memory of her as shadow in shadows of the forest.

Sacs stood across from resemble tits. Sign above, "Teta," add to ambience of the breast.

But this flash of insight into man's brother otaku's internal life cut short through synchronized firing of ganglia or some such and—am back in body-numbed steer—and—a shrieking grown in density and texture—like as howl what complicate itself—to of settle as delicate throb tickle at innermost chamber of the inner ear. Then clanging starts up again.

And—from out past bunch of exhaust pipes got a Japanese intricacy to them—come figure what looks as he been skinned with fluttering of tendrils and attendant anther as criss-cross the mouth and face. Face what been as if rills and squiggles in truth. Or as like the upper head begun to of segment outward in a mycelium layering's got to of been mirage of the eyes— only—thing's stopped direct center front of dung heap— and—turn as if to of pay homage to the limp ragdoll lain upon said dung. And undulations of thing's skull begun to of fan out into frayed facsimile of meat—or a meat as turned crenelated in waves and crystals of itself while the sad eyes are continued to of glow they dull blue—even as now they slipping together to be worked into some larger single eye begun to of took priority over upper skull and turned a murky and gold-cracked black. And face gone lost in cloud of meat in vicinity of said eye. And eye as cinctured shut in kind of a pinkish fleshiness turned white just as it slit itself shut over the gumminess of its interiority and once again not but undulations.

Then thing's continued on its way upon clanking walkway and vanish.

Long while of clang of sirens and flash of bells. Same green insect never's got tired of its back and forth. Patch of slime continued to of increase its acreage at the periphery.

Swatch of canvass's slid across what view I been provided. From one of g3's diesel-fueled airships. Account of she got those. *Does it seem strange to you that the Mountain of Qaf mainatins these airships for the sole purpose of getting in the good graces of the diesel barons of Texas?*

I got no opinion as regards your mysticisms and geopolitics, lady.

Clang, flash, gyrating green leaf bug.

And aromas such as you'd expect from out a dumpster are as filled the nostrils with they morass. And—the Pig? Dempsey, Telly, Leviticus, Sheffield? They also match up with a gray-skinned cerebrum-bared freak in what's being took as the waking world these days?

Mel and Rob?

As her voice continues to of ping about interiority of the skull. *And yes, we still have favors that will indeed be done by you, mirror. It just won't be you who does it.*

And a whisper. *Patience. We're coming. Patience.*

A click, and contents of bin slid down incline of rectangular gravity chute—at such a angle it slide under a turn in the grated walkway and for a moment am squinted up through the mesh—then out and into open air. And for moment seen—jagged skyline as outlined by barest hint of iridescent blue from off giant jellyfish mangrove forest works as breakwater what fringe the bay—as winds tickle at fellow's nudity. As are now slid downwards at angle approximate 90 degrees— and turned—to watch down sheer black exterior glint in the noonday sun and towards mound approach from good eighty floors below of bodies and other refuse—these many trashes diaphanous at this distance—and infested with seagulls, vultures, and other indistinguishable vermin are hopped about upon the de facto landfill what fly up at a body. And myself turned corpse.

Is when she is initial believed contagion snuffed out.

While Nurse Quiana watch back with her perfect set of teeth and heart-shaped earrings and bangs. Look of person what's tried to drag a boat back and forth through the mud while also as got features adorned in gloss and barrettes like as prepubescent supermodel when here she a fully adult healthcare professional work newly Christian Pittsburgh and what heretics, schizophrenics, and other undesirables discovered therein. And one such is just informed her that he's witnessed his own death in alternate reality due to something as called 'head shrimp.'

Account of—I been locked away here for re-education by her and her peers and having none of it for as long as it first been forced down fellow's throat but the none I am having just become as a torrent of nothings. As her beautiful blue eyes are shone with the dull hatreds of the prom queen. As she's glanced down at yours truly in her affection.

While. Somewhere off in the wings been ladies' cackle.

And myself left to wonder whether I am indeed been born of mainframe. And as to the living and breathing mother in her house on that untrod road in the mountains. With her beds of greens. And her adjudicator. Sole black woman in town of hillbillies. Slurp her beverage in the mid-afternoon in her sweats and slippers. Woman known to behead snakes.

Been a time I was sat there and stared back at my mother's tongue lolled about behind of the teeth like a disgusting thing as she is examine the vintage of this particular malt before the inevitable swallow—and now—am stared into portrait hung on wall opposite. Of bereft mother done up in heavy dobs of acrylic is true—her grey hair as having took over landscape of the face and its pair of eyes as dull and dead. And situated below, a back clam-shelled into herself upon the institutional teal flooring as offend aesthetic sensibilities of what crazies interned.

Clam-shelled woman makes softest of mumblings been like as if something between burblings of a brook and a screech. And Karen Quiana. *You here with us now Mr. Cole?* Smile as betray her understanding. *We do enjoy it when you drop in for a visit. We so appreciate your presence here and hope that in the future, you can learn to appreciate just how special you are.*

This isn't real. This isn't happening. From out the supposed madman. Magicked to a chair.

Eyes begun to of coast about room like as fish. And man what drown in his own happiness. Colors become as shapes and portrait of bereft mother turned more as like the gray frazzles of her hair instead as wrappings and ensleevings of gray slid in and about curvatures of her muscle and frame. As—Nurse Quiana—*that you have a purpose to serve in this world God has given us.*

Ever witnessed your own death? Or suffered a whiplash from some identical twin of yours gone splash against a pile consist of discarded flesh-and-blood dolls? Done a ride round rodeo at having just had one chamber in the eight-chambered soul vacated in burst of blood?

Whatever's left of what GMO organism I been. Brother to the now-dead brother otaku. When flowering of the hive was been as opened up round about yours truly and for just one beauteous moment seen—hive queen as like as kind of a collection of graphs somehow got ability to of form words and took up space upon counter and nearby the many gruel-dispensing sacs—and her as said, *Your parent lifeform has completely overwhelmed your normal functioning brain. You may believe this to be you thinking, but it is actually the parent lifeform thinking through you.*

Me. *Parent lifeform say it could squash you like a bug.*

Her. *You can't know the extent of our reach, habibi, but after the Mi'raj, all will understand.*

Then. As if some thread of pin-pointing light's come from out the larger cluster. And—I's become as two faces. One as sat in dark and watched the other—in his backdrop back in the Pittsburgh of my younger days and with my soon-to-be-girl as set upon shadows and concealed—behind of a trunk of some breadth and her as all teeth with occasional shadow—as in—she a clacking from out the memory and this clacking gone, *Do you know who you are, Jacks? Do you know who we are? Where are you, Jacks? In what place can you be said to reside?*

This a far-gone version of Pittsburgh—where the winds lie and the sky is got a sensuous uncertainty to it—haunted by things eaten from out the faces of man's memories even when they simultaneous been as tossed they molotovs with a jauntiness. Eyes what been followed after yours truly with a cartoon of scheming to them. And got mouths what stretch unnatural large.

Pittsburgh of before. And myself as looked down and murmured, *I seen what happened in Pittsburgh,* like as if this statement is of sudden got a more mystical reference embedded in its common everyday verbiage. Even then and there and beside the cold tit-sacs—was still been the darling of gangland. With fingers become as blurred and information cluster I spoke with just some moments previous is took as having envelop a fellow in its confusion of bytes and squiggles.

Still the fallen star of gangland. What crossed my t's and dotting my i's while tied to a bedframe back in this shadow of a Pittsburgh I seen fallen to the Christians and myself as partway responsible for its fall. And turned defective result of actions performed by my good friends Mel and Rob and the wonder drug are as continued to of tucked inside the sleeving of man's arms with endless gentleness of the abductor as am lain upon a stripped mattress in a cabin in the woods.

Two chaperones stood as like sculptors examining they handiwork.

He is got something in his eyes, say one.

And other one, *You imagining things, Mel. You always got to be imagining things.*

As—still—what intricacies been inserted with such loving care into man's bloodstream are continue on with they blossoming such as that's a smattering of eyes what look out. And one such pair is stared at some particular manifestation of g3 like as all graphs and stats. (At one time touted as the "perfect synthesis of digital and biotech," g3 got a wide versatility of forms in truth.)

Columns and lines of data and figures run among or strung through, converged and dissected themselves inside of larger information streams and about aforementioned manifestation of cubed flourescences sat as a cancer upon countertop in they cirrus and thread. As prickles run they fingers up nobs of the spine like as spitfire in the veins and a charged shattering of the sensate marrow. And—to of reach out and as if information done and brightened and myself gone blind.

Another brother mirror as spun up from they tank for the purposes of to have parley with g3 in same concrete room— with visions of dismemberings run through the corridors of the skull. Arm as spasm in impotence and teeth clenched upon the lip in a kind of put on rage of the paralytic—as in, body otherwise reclined upon its aluminum seat in a supposed calm.

g3 as again as took to having played dress-up inside body of hashishin but I known her true face. *"...and Allah said to them 'Die', and then He quickened them again."* From out her bandages.

While am showcase the still clenched teeth.

Then—through some unseen hand—been as knocked backwards with a carefree toppling motion. And like as fellow rolled out from this concrete room and into kitchen up some remove of there. And upon the bright-colored plastic joinery of kitchen floor and stared up at unfinished ceiling. And giggled a giggle of persons who just now as suffered no injury despite great force having been used upon them. And—whatever manifestation of g3 been on man's counter these preceding moments become as gone. And through what is been indeed some magic am also known of Eris—at Kuiper Belt's periphery—and as regard Dysnomia and what craft sent for to chart possible construction sites, mineral compounds, and register any and all peculiarities.

Then back inside a concrete box and its g3 cum hashishin.

Glanced up at Orifice Refuse & Recycling with deranged lustfulness of the coquette restrained. Then the wall. One thing's no sippy cup skull. This a more standard human-type body.

We go through all the versions discarding the unusables and refurbishing the rest. You get that, sweetheart, g3's said. Or hashishin. Or whoever she call herself at this moment. Person got a plethora of personality options to of chose from—and am wanting to press my fingers through the sockets of each and every one with the gentleness of a true lover.

As. Corners of room as got some fuzziness to them's how I known—and took to swat at the face like as there some insect what testing out inner lining of the nostril—or some such. A daydream of stingers with serious sweet tooth for otaku meat.

Bugs just as quick gone missing in this general mirage of a room. And—*The parasite has not fully bonded with this one,* hashishin is announce to one of her various personalities. And room's took on more general softness and— glance down at the grayscale fingers. They branching in and out of themselves with fluidity of a politician on the trail.

Just manufacture another otaku every time one's turned faulty? That how it goes?

Periphery's begun to of press in as if concrete room come to of contract. And fellow stood with arms straight by the sides as somewhere a whirring gone on. And then—*gah, gah, gah,* and—am clutched at the throat as if to of steady a valuable piece of porcelain. And room turned optical illusion such that inside concrete box as been outside and us as looking out from the in. Which any schoolkid could've told you make about as much sense as pussy on toast.

Hashishin. *Larva appears to be in a highly developed state.*

As—the ridging of the brow begun to of move in elaborate frowns and convolutions. And eyes turned heavenward. *You gone to answer man's question?*

And her own eyeless sockets as settle upon barest outline of a grayscale otaku six-pack—account of this otaku undergone neuromuscular electrical stimulation and given eyes what g3 is described as "beads of mercury" are create a "stream of quicksilver in the otherwise human brain" as g3 is liked to of quip. *Life is not manufactured here, otaku, but it is made.*

While—meanwhile—camped out in what's a pink rubbery nub of a sitting room and sat across from a giant teddy bear color of buttered toast and gone, *But do they recycle? Am I made out of reconstituted parts of the malfunctioning Jackson Coles of yesteryear, bear? Is that it?* On account of is true I taken to having converse with oversized stuffed bears.

Said stuffed bear then responds. *Everything g3 do is done perfectly correctly.*

Bear's sat there with the blankest of stares writ upon its button eyes, am glanced down at what inoffensive articles been as garbed in. Then over at the many lumps of pliant material strewed about upon edge of which circular room— with what I somehow known's a *muqarnas* what looks as like sectional of some ceramic hive as decorated in Arabics and just released its brood of over-sized baby wasps upon the world—tiled in brilliant yellows and baby blues—in waves of hexagonal chambers what themselves gave outline of some insect spread its many wings in how they are rose and fell about ceiling. And at center of it all, oval skylight what shows not but a dull white to it. *You willing to help a fellow escape?*

You will escape but it won't be you who does it.

Look over at the bear. *Feel like I heard that one before.*

And bear gone, *Stand clear of the wall.*

I am puzzled by this bear. *What?* Bear which is got to twitching.

Thing attempt to of cover its sowed-on features with fuzzy arm-ends as it let out a squeal been somewhat like as digital distortion cry for help. Head rock backward in a comedic display of agony. And the cute button eyes fizz a brighter shade of amber. And its legs begun to of shiver at high velocity. Then nothing as—am indeed been as leapt up and away from the wall in a kind of a happenstance to of stare at said stuffed bear. Thing's jaw hung open in parody of the dead.

Then up and at the skylight as got no sky behind it. Around and at the cushions and pastels. Then turned and gone as if hunting—round lip of one room and on into kitchen. With eyes level as the horizon and fingers took to twitching in the romantic shakes of the alcoholics of yesteryear—and still—memories of Cassey Darling and her eyes misshapen by clotted shadows of late-nite scenery—and myself—*My dear—will you kindly shut the fuck up*—and her—*My dear, you know very well that I cannot*—and me—*But my lovely. Really. You must.*

Kitchen as unencumbered by any AI projections. A turn and—scratched into artificial marble of the wall. "REPENT." Scratched in with pen knife but faint enough person have to be looking to've seen it. And like as a offering upon flooring just in front, a disembodied neck wide as a finger and stubby and small, the skin a soft clay white. And as am stared at said neck, its partial decomposed lividity seem to as occasional shiver in some as of yet undetected breeze.

Again hand begun to flutter and general speaking as sat across from hashishin while she perform her rudimentary quality control and maintenance and preoccupied with her performance review. Only to then of stood and on toward tanks of my brothers and sisters. Loop a leg back.

How many times we been remade, hashishin?

And her. *You are always being remade, sweetheart.*

How many times we been dumped in that same trash heap?

Wall explode through unraveling hole of her head. And dust a gray smudge obscure gray of that wall to then of settled round collapsed splatter painting hashishin become. Upon which is stood a goat-eyed GMO adorned in red robe of the Tibetans what ooze tentacles from off the one side of its wrappings. Man's face glow with a kind of a temporal wetness about whatever dressings of flesh—also gray—as—leashed river of fingerlets continue to of pour from out the one arm.

And am crowed the head to of pronounced a scream with some animality to it. Like as cross between newborn birthed and murderer midway through the act. A rage is convulse the skull. And at its center destroyed body of hashishin couched in her bedding of rubble, unraveled and soaked in red. Like as her death been stolen from a man's fist.

Thing and its tentacles are stepped past what pilings of stone—and they shredded cloths, exposed bone, and drapery of bloodied musculature—and myself as step forth with a unbecoming brazenness. Nudity on full display as I gone gray toe by gray toe towards the occasional distracted head of man's liberator—head of whom as seem to of flick about in rapid birdlike mechanicalness as if he is tried to gauge location of a face by having examine all points in near vicinity of it.

Then. Raised aforementioned sheathing of tentacles from out the one shoulder.

Got closer look of the strands and rivers of feelers glisten as are poured from out the cloth of monstrosity's righthand shoulder socket with a tantalizing provocation. *You got a covering for me, friend?* Pull out an identical red shawl and accompanying red skirt.

Toss off a tic.

Slid into the monk's garb with unexpected dexterity.

And thing's tentacled right arm become just a hint of movement. And—*This city is a mirage,* thing's proclaimed. *And we are getting you out of it, but we have to move now.* At which point, am stepped toward what hole been blasted in wall and bare foot pranced with a luxuriousness upon what rough bits of concrete as presented and the occasional blood slickened bit of masonry.

Then. Myself and my ticket to freedom—nearsighted octopus as he may been—are stepped into black and gone upon clanking webwork of grated metal platform. With its lights blinkered at nipple level at each of the four corners. And been like as if person is stepped from out the stale and stagnant air of a terrarium and into fresh scents of the forest—at least as could been manufactured upon elevator shaft's interiority.

And—what fracturing of iris as visible is looked off and at a person's ear.

4.

Can you explain why these visions are still so present now so much later on?

When said events as scroll cross fellow's eyeballs millisecond by millisecond. Traipsed upon the optic nerve as like as jiggles of sense what twang they way back to receptors of the brain with an unconscionable tooling of ensleeved synapse. As am stared into the beautiful blues sat across from yours truly and above her clipboard even as fingers also still been as twitched they way through what obstacles as past's presented. *Sometimes seems as this the vision and alternate reality LAC the actual fact.* As are sat in our respective seats and grinned our grinniest grins.

Then her grin's snapped shut. *Alternate timelines are a heresy of the singularity, an ideology that must be stamped out.* Her clipboard held up as like a shield between patient and pen.

Sort of assumed's one of the many reasons behind of why been declared as unsound of mind. Stated with a calm and collection of voice—as am stared into what chilly blues on offer. Frigid missionary to these heathen lands as she been—and general speaking lacking in the transperspective capacity of her preferred archfiend. And am contemplated what lynchings would've got myself into by said beloved Christians of hers—done up in they Sunday best—days of sheets and "Invisible Empire" thing of the past—as in—they all out in the open bout they Emmett Tills now—like as it "just right and proper" as they preachers are said—such that—if were ever to of catch sight of my lips upon this damp burgundy mouth of hers...

If a bush can say, 'I am Truth' so can a man. And smiled that open smile of hers.

What showcases most beauteous arrangement of discolored teeth—like as dentures on display in a showroom. While—as a tweak at the backend of the skull—am heard some still small sound as beg a fellow to of wake up—wake up—it's said. And've let out a girlish mewl.

You are here because you are unwell.

Witnessed my best friend skinned alive. Doesn't do wonders for the mind've seen such sights as these. Glance at her soft scented skin. Knock a Golgotha brand smoke from out the pack.

No smoking in here, Mr. Cole. You know the rules.

And lit it. *You like what they done to you?* Said into my smoking hand.

Nothing has been done to me, Mr. Cole. Disgust melts into an easy smile. *I am happy with my life, yes.* Glint of glorious fear what is come upon those aforementioned baby blues of hers. Adjust herself against her seatback and swath of bang come unmoored from the skull to of create pretty curtaining of the now pinched features as she is worked to adjust cushions and the hem of her heavy skirt as all the while she avoids piercing gaze of madman sat just across. To then of looked upon her clipboard and back to having as scratch at her recommendations as to proper handling and care of this her hopeless charge and his occasional incontinence. Her head still not risen from its awkward angle when is murmuring, *Continue dosage at same level. Monitor as usual. I've scheduled our appointment for next Monday at three. I hope that time suits you.*

While. When one dream's ended another begun.

Dream of man entranced by this thing's visage and its nostrils and lips like as they built for cud—the damp femininity of the lashes and cock's star-crossed eyes—as in with literal miniature stars contained inside—were as like refractions upon refractions inside of there—*See something you like*—as our ceilingless elevator—with its four thin rods, one stood at each end and each tipped in red LED—slid downwards and past hologram of forestry cut by periodic bursts of brilliance.

On other side of which been various flutings and pipework as are been as slinked about in very living way. Occasional excretion discerned through hologram's coloring of redwood fails to shield its limb-like indelicacy from the eye. Thing's metallic gray appears almost as if veined and daubed in periodic spluge of grime and accompanying slats of lumination.

While cock closer at hand start in about how this a mirage as owned and operated by womankind—as in a do-nothing of the done world—and specific—mall we needing to traverse forbid men to of enter unattended. *But holy men are exempt from these rules.*

Eye this curiosity. So the Tibetan garb's a put-on?

We are both of the Tibetan, though I am foremost of Na-Koja-Abad and its environs.

Got anything as colloquial as a name?

I am what is known as a chimera. Doors gone and opened onto splay of different-sized tile curl in and through in swarm of iridescent hexagon. And just beyond's an also tiled ankle-high wall, on other side of which—scum-covered pool—deep green with—algae as lacing upon plated backs—of occasional lavender or black-sheathed prawn as surfaced—each one grip round different bright plastic yarn—and behind of the pond a wall what been more pink marble tiling. *I was named Hayy Ibn Yaqzan for I was born to discover the world for myself inside what you would call an infinity box, but which I have experienced as a room that contains all other rooms, that touches on every universe, where all potentialities can be experienced.* Step out to of examine said pool close and personal and its many skittering insects with they various gunked-up limbs. To then as turned and ogle chimera gaze past fellow's shoulder in his cluelessness. *Tibetans call this the Land of the Gods and for good reason.* As. Pulse of ambient light as pours in from behind of the turned head. Then a deeper shade of black.

And handful of chunky white pop up the throat and upon the chin with a dainty spasm. And glanced off—at—lady's room as decked in fluted paper cut with motifs as glow in clusterfuck of insignia and next to it—Mens is—is no Mens. Other direction—and past pink tiling and in full view of whatever concourse there been—standard icon for a man. With—graffiti'd on it by hand—meticulous rendering of cloud as cover midriff and abdomen of said icon.

As—bit more chunky whiteness come gurgled out from between the lips.

And. *Bathroom.* Then off and through blast of muted signage and what torso-sized floating head holograms as accompany. *<Click on the link in the description to find out how your partitioned mind helps g3 help you to escape... Mr. Jackson Cole.>* As am slid—through illusory jaw, knock open swinging door, and into what thank the asshandlers finally's a normal every-day bathroom—only to've—eyes slid closed and open back in kitchen upstairs—another Jackson Cole as camped upon nubs of kitchenette's plastic joinery is turned a head sideways and a vomit also indeed as pour from out this interchangeable mouth. Milky, white and sweet as only sickness can.

As am also spill identical stream of vomit upon bowl of sink in aforementioned nondescript bathroom. To then glance up and at scar run vertical down center of the gray forehead and between pair of bloodshot and tearing eyes as showcased in among elaborate carvings of looking glass what pool about as such like a cross-hatching on the glass. And a cluster of decals on tagged surface of it. Porcelain for shitting in the one corner. Not much else.

Like I said—some things never change.

Long strands of saliva spillage from out man's pair of mouths simultaneous—like as a fracturing of a mouth in two distinct places what are quivered in identical quiverings and spluttered saliva from out same point in crook of the lower lip. One adorned in his monk's garb above traditional wash basin with ring of rust round the drain, while—back in kitchen and still upon plastic joinery am then cupped hand to mouth and up through help of wall's mooring only to then gone off and stumbled and collapse off vomiting once again—as man off on a stroll through his sitting room of pink blobs with head flung forward like as a two-legged bull charging—and with fingers crowd upon the scalp such that—is when am now confirmed that—instead of having been trepanned like first now dead brother, both designed with beveled square cut through stubble of they skulls—soft and synthetic to the touch—though only one of me currently able to've took in they features—in cut glass of mirror garnished in stickers and among familiar smells of the shithouse.

But. Somewhere in the backend of both these thankful enclosed craniums, darkness explode with blaze like as what happens when four-dimensional object come to of reposition itself inside framework of person's neuronal stitching. Surroundings just then become as twisted into they shape round about as—explosion in the distance. Then an enigmatic silence.

While. Some floors above. Man didn't make it past teddy bear corpse with the slackdog look. And been as collapsed among pink blobs and lesser pink shade wall capped as it been in baby blue. All of which what surrounds myself upon the flooring with a face splattered in white is got an electrical quality to it. Like as its contours been rear projected upon the otherwise mundane locale. And through it all run fissures of light what seem hung suspended in phantom bath permeate everywhere. And one or two stalagmite things as dribbled off partial dissolved tubing come from out wall halfway up in a U shape in the one corner and just below aforementioned *muqarnas*. (Question: Possible the added vocabulary got a sentience attached what try to pull a con job on the old con man such that yours truly not yours truly in actual fact? Answer: How nice of you to notice.)

With mouth once again quivers with some expectancy of milky regurgitant. As am leaned upon a pink blob and peer off and at rounded top of oval door what lead out and to the hive proper and bottom of said door set with lip of wall run between itself and the floor—account of round the rim's a radiance like as if sun been as waited outside wide-eyed in the dark. Stood a moment while my gut's turned itself inside out. As neck's continued to spasm with some recklessness and sound been like as the signatures of dogs.

Little sidle to the side and to—sliding door reveals not more'n a tiled enclosure with—cluster of drains in one corner. One on the floor, one set in the wall above, and one in wall to its right set as a triumvirate of drains. As well as—detachable nozzle and bottle of something what named as Bile-Away Cream. Apparently, some things refuse to of stay as unchanged after all.

And come face to face with features identical to the deceased sippy cup but for more brown and gray mottled skin tone and forest of fleshy pink nubs rested about face and writhed to currents only as felt by aforementioned pink nubs. And what been as set in glass made as perfect as the Lord willing—as Christians are wont to said—of an eyelike smoothness and ridged in an elaborate pipework—while—also am been as occupied upon the tiled flooring some stories below and in what been as a wholly antiquated junkie pen of a restroom. And in this mirror am got something of steely gray sheen to the skin and thick scar of slit gone horizontal down center of the brow.

For moment been as if these two versions of yours truly look back at each other through they respective glass. Mirrors as regards mirrors through mirrors.

Flick of traditional red shawl and done a turn with girl-ish swish of hem when one such decal—of bunny sport black bow tie and rimmed in silver—come alive to of pin itself to fellow's back and on up and toward the shoulder with an arduous spinelessness as—through the spring-bound and skirt round white and gold trim pillar and off and towards man's tentacled associate is in a fit of twitches as he watches back.

Then out and into central shopping area with—direct center—orange plastic nude—of former president Trump clutched at its shapeless thighs with the famed tiny fingers and famed tiny fungus of reproductive organ—and said bright orange plastic statue been as riddled with holes infested by metallic black millipede things what are scroll in, out and through entirety of said shapeless orange flesh rendered in plastic likeness of the former Trump. Then. Whole ensemble flicks out of existence to been replaced by floating clock announces: 68.87 in glowing beveled square and above mound of black millipedes. Then back to worm-infested statue. As in. Hive's exodus from Earth's atmosphere being measured in a hourglass of decomposing Trump.

Entire scene then suffused with wrap-around projection of analog internet founded in basement. Polaroid fleshed out to hologram fill the space. Thumbs up, shit-eating grins.

Then mall gone back to having been a mall.

Welcome to the Souk.

Storefronts run from end of concourse to other end. And all what flash back and forth—from proper storefront to generic containment area in hull of what spacecraft this shopping mall gone to of evolve into. From direct behind arched and flabby backside of occasional life-sized orange Trump statue and its decorative infestation—is been something called as the Store of Man, with—span entire store window's photograph of woman clad in a hijab with only the bright purple eyes exposed and her legs crossed as man beside her bent over to of offer some delicacy on an ornate cut tray. While.

Displayed on busts and usual immobile mannequins set tasteful about in front of photograph are been various cloths and accessories for the man in your life.

And overtop all this projected stills of old world in its moment of collapse—Thailand's brilliant-colored huts in they patties and marsh what decorated in few bloated bodies and flies current as peopled they holes—then slideshow as is pause and mall just a mall again—only to been followed by something equal horrific—such as the chemical fields what left of Africa.

What drawn across cut-away of intermodal storage container interior—which been adorned in suburban paraphernalia of yesteryear—grills, astroturf, vintage televisions. Intermodal sold as luxury living quarters of the day when—no one buys that for a single hot minute. And projection vanished. And manikin—this one moveable of itself—unaccompanied by any 3D reproductions of yesteryear as it's sat in what been blatant contemplative stance upon said astroturf and scan heavens what only perceptible to the tin can itself. As in—full-on functional manufacture includes incentives such as play-pretend cognition.

Not unlike the woman behind it all.

And everywhere burqa- and hijab-clad ladies in simpler tones of the ruling classes—pastels, teal cashmere synthetics, gold bangles, and pregnant bellies—only natural births sanctioned in LAC been as a kind of hobby of the rich. But—how many are got infestations of mechanics in the womb is at this moment worked they way in among and through they developing fetus?

Couple exceptions to the crowd. One un-knocked-up Chinese National with bared face's got a pinched look in no-nonsense gray pantsuit and blazer. As well as—been pair of hijab-sporting ladies decked out in the silken cloths and high heels of more traditional Muslim state of UAE. And one or two men are follow at some distance behind they woman—with—tattooed at mid brow—eye in case of one and cube in case of the other. Old woman at the bins—in work clothes and conical wove hats of Vietnam and face mask—her skin light gray of the GMO and sported hoodie and slacks—is got eyes peer off in a daydream as she work—are eyes as glowed a dull yellow.

Projection of JFK what with his skull gone splat across the car's rear portion as his woman reaching for it as—*Tays are not what they seem.* Tentacles feel the need to announce.

When. Aren't we *tay* ourselves, fellow?

JFK and his motorcade vanish as curtains parting cross the square of pink plants flap lazy left and right in breeze of they own imaginings—and—above a hologram of a woman's face morph from pasty anorexia to healthy and full-bodied brown with accompanying increased vibrancy in eye color over and again. The hologram pulses out when the slideshow of yesteryear pulse in like this lady hiding behind it, and now she back and between here and there's escalators.

And it's onto the escalator we go.

Several stories deep—with its steps as slatted in wood poured into place from they rootings upon the mechanism—and between escalator's two sides, central casing stripped to reveal its cogs and gears and what critters as scurry among them—critters as been mechanics in truth.

And us as stood behind pair of covered heads and they small talk. *They're begging to be ridiculed.* From one. And the other—*Men revel in gewgaws and baubles. They say that the AI of men even had difficulty with perspective. Its hands were like decorations at the end of the arm*, and an accompanying chuckle and— other one's sung—*La libertad es solo otra palabra para nada que perder*, and now both women're become as erupted into a tinkling laughter followed by a silence followed by, *Outside the hive we let them play their warlord games but at the heart of it men want to obey*. A truism of LAC.

Past dayglo mosaics of an algorithmic complexity on which been as writ abstractions of Quran calligraphy and past teledramas hung suspended upon a CGI atmosphere— with the heads blacked out by large face-covering boxes mar the broadcast. And subtitles scrolled across, "You are rich because of my rent, sir." Collegiate sweater tied round shoulders just below the blacked-out head. While—*Find who's behind the Cult of the Three Worms even if you have to seek out the Pythagorean depths of the gnostic lodge to do it*—g3's voice as sat within the inner ear as—covered heads in front begun to of jiggle. Like as person is tugging at they strings from above.

Wash of muted color from back way we come but also— more brilliant hues in front—account of—one direct front of me's got an extra lumpiness hid beneath sheer covering of hers and its black undercloths is look as like shell what got some extra twist and turn to it. And emit a brilliance. Her glance backward paused midway through. *Once the singularity found their body everything changed*. And from corner of the head covering, a feathering of blue irradiation. *From the first teasings of a life inside the ecosystem of language to something truly miraculous*. Sounds like she quoting the literature.

Escalator's got to its end—and round faux marble corner—something like as black refrigerator hung suspended in atmosphere of the corridor and once again rimmed in piping with array of blue dot eyes arranged in occult patterns and all said optics blinkered in they excitement as thing's intone, *<Por favor, indique su negocio y los números de su casa matriz.>* Glide in direction of the escalator. *<Please state your business and the call numbers of your parent house.>*

Got its own light show and said show begun to of spill upon scene like as hologram what expands balloon-like about the mainframe. Hologram what shift from pentaculum to a folding of pentagrams come to of spiral and writhe about itself as kind of geometric ouroboros contains an eye of inner eternities. And not to mention flaming gold eyes upon every surface what come snapped into existence upon it—and on the whole, a shimmer of iridescence somehow also a sickening distended maw—a impossible husk and an awful essence. Like as seraphim out for daytrip as mall cop.

All in all, impressive special effects.

And chimera as bound past—covered ladies—arms folded on one and hung lifeless by side of other—through said light show—and toward the buoyant machine. And God's dodecahedron is got stuck. As if puppeteer reconsidering his little show now the curtain been drawn.

Tentacle's appliance of a waltzing partner is screed—while—other orifices are continued to of repeat in calm tones, *<Por favor, indique su negocio y los números>*—but are cut short when chimera's features been as open like as his head a trap and it just been sprung. Or. Illusion of face better way to of put it while—something of head is remained—indiscernible as it may of been.

And from out this oxymoron of a faceless face is come a kind of caterwaul of his own what sound something like as several animal cries compound together—birdcall turned digitized and insect clicks in binary—as frigidaire's intricate array of bead-sized eyes become blinkered in orchestra of dainty winks as thing is shuddered with a wildness at so much profundity. Already nodded out in its embarrassment to then of come down hard upon marble flooring. And what all belted prisms of seraphim gone with it.

One woman's face covering been as erupted a multitude of attendant eyes and other visuals through what slit been provided for seeing. Other is got like as one eye been shattered into wide variety of tiny black bug eyes all rimmed in they own bristle of lash what stretch out at odd angles.

And—then my world consists of smiling faces of Mel and Rob.

Oh, for the love of Christian cock.

You enjoying yourself there, Jacks? Rob.

Am made some effort to of spoke but mouth's gummed up with the blood from what excess teeth been extracted in they play. Mel's gray and gold striped tie with the embroidered palm tree been askew and dotted in my blood. And beyond they pair of oversized skulls's been—blankness of the air like as if a patina upon the hand of God what more pincer than proper fist—what with twitch manipulate the curtains of sense like as if they a cloth in a magic show—or shift in the colors of the dark. Is becomes a kind of an uncertainty inside of the structures of what am seen.

As the faces of Mel and Rob also twist with a funhouse precision.

Get off on it yet? Still Rob.

As Mel stares down at a person with sort of dumb grin common to new dads. As's eyes are become as wrappings what peel off surface of the upper cheek to of lift—up and into what nonsensical breeze there been.

With fingers upon lip of the soiled and naked mattress and its jailhouse blue and white. *Gone get out*—all am as able to've pushed by what partial destructed wall the teeth provide. As the breath comes in reedy wisps. And Mel got on bored expression.

And memories of childhood and jewels of blood run curving line long Cripple's mother's oriental rug. Or. OD of a girl got caverns in her skull and parts are twisted such that shoulder bulge to the left in wild and unpredictable manner—and upon the punctured arm—threads of purple as spread outward from site of the injection and long the chocolate of the skin like as branching of purplish cracks. Or. Myself up in the mountains and hunted for snakes in the high grass by the swimming hole. Or Troy and night I learned of Troy's disappearance—when Mother screams about how why couldn't it been you why couldn't it been you they took—and in abyss of the doorframe.

Mel clocks me with a stinging jab, lit my mouth up like a Christmas tree.

Gone get out, huh? Your palace is become a prison? Still Rob.

And more chuckles had by all. *Yeah.* Another jab.

Couple blinks and attempts to of sat. Stopped by meaty fingers of Mel pressed against the shoulder. As chuckles turned a regular guffaw. Room begun to wobble in its uncertainty.

Is a way out of the mirage.

And they guffawing's stopped. *Yeah. How you figure it?*

Rob's leaned in. Smaller of the two giants.

As. Past what stack of metal bowls—they white shells rimmed in claret—and other side of what glass as frame it— as splattered in pre-dawn moisture—head of a single palm— its segments of frond as slathered leaflet upon leaflet as like fingers itch at fingers in a franticness of wind.

While back in the bed. Body gone as curled in its holes and husks of flesh and upon itchings of the flattened, spring-invaded mattress is been as like a tickle of blades and scratching of puncture wounds. And. Are shadows between shadows of Rob's cheeks. And eyes turned dim reproductions of eyes. As—hilarity of dark as surround is continued to of took on an increasing nuance to it. Until. All's left's sounds of birds as come woke upon the sibilance of the forest—and even these sounds become as lines leaving a room and—a black empty into other blacks. And—for one moment—person not been as able to of tell whether is them or the outside of them what's begun to rock with a gentleness as in a boat.

Only for—then my eyes've opened on circular sitting area with its many curving pink recliners and upon one's a teddy bear sat in partial reclining position is true—legs and arms hung limp and one button eye been as thread from out its face by strands of a spongy fungal nature—with more yellow or blue tint to they stalks of optic circuit and hung down a fuzzy cheek where it dangle just above the nubby grooves of flooring and—at this moment, teddy bear's recited some bit of lecture spoke as to nature and functions of blood. As in, *...blood that is coursing is not the true blood. The blood that rises and falls with the breath, the blood that contains the map, a blood woven through and about another blood until there is no distinction between the blood of God and the amber blood of trees. Blood that is the river of life within the body, but what blood can compare to the*

blood of the eye? The blood of light? The blood of information flow-
ing from out to in and in to out in an ever-constricting and ongo-
ing symphony of ever-entwining bloods... In a screech of digital
distortion.

Then. "Please display permit within conveyance." In an
elevator.

Tentacles crittling eyes what reflect in the glass as shifting traces of bright lit puzzle pieces. And on other side soot
and accompanying shaft wall. While still as got g3 in me. *Your*
body will become increasingly more dysfunctional, the longer you
live outside the hive, child.

And still with the...

FaTar = to cleave, to split a thing; to find out; to
begin; to create a thing (God)

FuTR = a mushroom (that which forces its way
upward by cleaving)

FaTaRa = to breakfast, to break a fast

TaFaTTaR = to split or crack

'IYD elFiTR = the Feat of the Breaking of the Fast

FiTRAT = natural disposition; religious feeling; the
religion of Islam

FaTIR = unleavened bread; unpremeditated or
presipitate action; haste

FaTIRA = a small, flat cake, such as is used as a
sacrament

FATiR = the Creator

As elevator come to of descend from out of its sheath and into a busy expanse—as in—ball of space crosshatched with walkways and lined in balcony shopping draped in bright colored tinsel and plastic garlands and painted in endless iterations of mystical green eye locals are used as sign and symbol of g3—and situated some several stories below—open area dotted in piles of broke electronics what burn in tongues of aromatic smoke as some of the aforementioned locals been as prostrate themselves before said pyres and wailed they loud wails in among the foot pools as span about them what with they own slatted enclaves and tiled walkways worked between. And upon all said walkways—both above and below and they various decorations—is been swarms of similar flying refrigerators as slid in a miasma of optical illusions. And between here and all what there, botanical strata of free-float jungles of shrub—each in its own glass globe terrarium and many with streaks of pink run through the green in jagged lines.

The Souk Lous Anjilis Alqadeem. Outside of here is lawlessness and freedom.

Are those among the geeks of Pittsburgh claim LAC is got the most amazing automotives and quite the nightlife. But many of these literately cockadoodled they pronouncements over late nite paint thinner and general speaking of the backdoor back alley variety. Kind aching for a strangling. Then elevator's stopped and doors're opened.

Stay back. Stay close.

Ophiuchus. The one what winds in loops. "Is a serpent what bending its supple neck look back and returns: as the other's hands are slide over the loosened coils. The struggle will last forever since they wage it on level terms with equal powers."

Is me and the parasite—is me and g3. Ophiuchus the pseudo-morph. Ophiuchus the otaku awakened to what nightmares as parasite is brung.

Sound of someone bent over a sink through the doorway over fellow's shoulder—clank of dishware and scrape of silver—and—couple plastic bags consist of discarded cartons sat in single row against cupboards by the ankle. With— one at the end toppled over and a sprinkling of potato chip crumbs as fan from where is toppled its many contents of pudding cup. And wall the same pink and teal squares as everywhere. Ancient coffee pot with orange plastic spout upon countertop to the left. Spider plants positioned on each side the swinging doors what also been as thickly lacquered in teal. And woman in pea coat buttoned to conceal her work clothes.

Are you here with us, Cole?

Ash been sort of martyr never acknowledge her martyr status. Brought low by man she chose to brung into her bed in the end and what trouble he brung along with him. And even when her features not but inscrutable, they always also a crime scene of my making.

She got the kid sat in the crook of her arm.

We waiting on you to get better, Jackson. Little girl bouncing up and down in Mother's arms and looking off to where ceiling and wall come together. *When you get better you give us a call, okay baby?* As girl's mother's eyes become as glassed in tears. *What happened to you the night they come?*

Behind complications of her large part theoretical head—interior of which as erupt into stream of what as been miniature super nova and erasure of same such what we colloquially term as they "stream of consciousness" and—yours truly lost in it such that—turn of phrase as spoke by persons in the past of last summer—and what night as accompany— come to of settle upon a bit of her ear. While all the while. Dreams are kept on with they roll out the eyes.

Upon open-air walkway strung as catwalk and—a especial wide portion of said airborne walkway. Concrete on the one side and hip-high sidewall run upon other and dotted with pair of ellipsoid platforms hung from off open air side and lined in plush red cushioned seating what overlook floors between here and pools below. First one normal but second of which's like as if tiling become unzipped into folds of baby gray pressed against red vinyl sectionals run lip of the plat- form. A mouth but is got nowhere to gone—thread of some- how sentient flooring slopped over metal railing just above said seating and draped out and into emptiness beyond. Or tickled upon tiling of its proscenium.

If I don't make it, head for the set of double doors up those stairs, out and then keep on straight ahead till you're under the sun. Then a leap and we become as balletic as—twined Tibetan coverings're flicked they red at a wind's more put-on of the mind than aero- nautic vessel—one part ventilation to two parts phantom limb. As the coupling of our legs is flown up and—toes slid out over concrete sidewall as this absolute hole of a thing's reached with most tentative uncertainty of squiggled finger.

Thing below like as monstrosity as echo outward—a mouth ripple in a pond—opening what missing its tail—due to—are some tails gone travel through higher dimensional- ity—and this—hole in the hive and its mirage is been of said type and kind of hole—tumor as evolve from understudy to then as blossom in this alternate cesspool universe of former

USA—and its Jackson Cole otaku mirror what been tasked to of look into his own corruption—as—we still hover in moment between push off and landing. Moment as extend into froth of itself—moment become cancer of moments under said monstrosity's design.

Chimera sucked down—and lost among its suet—and general speaking violent rootings of this mystical abomination—turned comestible to this what been not but lip—and moment end with myself come to of land in a flick of the foot and onto uneven tilework—as chimera gone limb to limb with said abomination of flooring and its many muscular trunks.

Took some few stumbling herky-jerk steps before having then been hooked up at the tip of shawl is slide over head as in some magician's reveal. Bunny decal lets loose its death shriek as is whisked off with the doffing of what real estate of cloth it been as occupied. As am stared at punctuation of valves in they bed of tile upon the column as—somewhere to the back all slurps and hollers of chimera engulfed in its stickings and straggling.

Gray tiled sidewall run a seam veer long one side of said column and—as am pitter-pattered up vanishing spiral of stairs. Then round corner and—from back behind—sound squeezed out of Tentacles something between an infant and the grunting of your more advanced sex worker.

Up to next landing with glance off to left and—newer whiter color of higher floors and more spherelike shape of it—while here and below is been deeper hued with dirts and growths upon what pillars as open to the viewing. And among shops of this other, older souk—as in, more traditional eateries and jewelry shops of the end times—sometimes repurposed to include display of ribbed skins and sometimes as they seem—and everywhere adorned in festive symbology of paints and excess decorative plastic garlands of the most dayglo colorings while—thread through them been cabinets of wonderment took to hunting in packs as glistened in they black art deco.

Tables skittered to the side. Echo of a scream.

While. Stood before another more slender walkway. On other side of which floorspace is fanned out—to four metal slat doors sat at its far side—complete with traditional push bars of yesteryear. And between here and said doorway—a hashishin.

And again come a howl. And again head thrust forward when the murderer's call pour forth.

Jackson Cole, you are beginning to be something of a nuisance. Clearly.

And am rush at her in man's monkish garb. And her leg up and aimed and—toe curl upon man's clavicle even as force of her heel is topple him backward and into chrome rope of the banister with head flung out so far in open air in a kind of a trickery of possible escapes.

At which development she is laughed.

And—brilliant splash of pain upon the foot and am collapsed as children's toy tossed aside. Glance up and at doors beyond as she pronounce. *Ayreh feek. You ignorant.* Spoke in a disgust.

But when is reached out, am gone as like eyes inside of eyes inside of eyes. Or as a wind blown as gentle as a sparrow song in the innermost chambers of the optic nerve.

Do we need to do everything for you, habibi?

And hashishin eyes shut off—what slitherings of eye as poured from out concavity of the sockets in veritable army of mucuses—even as her fist been as held above man's head and poised for violence—in the depths of her thoughts, her mouths're pealed back in upon themselves—like as toothy blossom unravel to reveal ever more petals of teeth as sprung outward from ripples of pink—and somewhere deep down under all these coverings of lip and tooth's a throat as took to of drown upon itself. Arm gone slack and out come something between a lineage of obscenities and sound of dogs under knife as her slight frame slink to the floor beside her prey.

And myself stared at the bandaged face of my tormenter with a calmness as—*Go. Leave.* And up and to what truly been department store door frames. Just your usual everyday Tibetan GMO of a man trapsed out of a shopping complex run by a singularity in Southern California. *Uncover what secrets the Cult of the Three Worms hides.*

5.

Do you know who you are, Mr. Cole?
  Is a seeing more as like a thread unspooled than a thing seen.

What I seen's first and foremost been glow from out the eye region adhered to what cloud of ganglia fire they thunderstorms behind and what woven lumen of equation complexity accompany as silence of variables compound the senses into more elaborate configurations of eye. It been like as when you see in dreams and people like as a hieroglyphic to decipher rather than just in your way. Been like as a scrawl upon the optic nerve, handwriting of which never fully writ itself into clear, recognizable characters—and a smattering of the rest.

You are the 4th Generation Spirit, Cole. You see as we do. Spiritual bodies are no longer in a world. It is the world that is in them. You see with the eyes of God, Cole. More g3 than human, you are what humans would become if they could. You are the reckoning upon what has been a travesty of life and its possibilities. You are the second coming of man, my friend.

And sense is of something wriggle about in the sockets. Like, instead of eyes am got worms, but these worms're mine and when they slick optical nerve bods slide against a cheek

or brush against a brow in they squirming, is a soothing gesture. Or like as if I am developed a fondness for maggots of
a sudden.

Me. *But we know how this all set to end, do we not, g3?*
All roads lead to the parasite, al-hamdulila.

While also. Still in different universe and a cabin in the
woods and—that's right—how could I of forgot but I had oh
yes and there's a bit of twig and hey here we are now where
we are now—and a batting of eyes upon the mattress while
what thugs in near vicinity on about "promising Thomases
and can't cook toast" somewhere in kitchen off stage left
as they are snort in they pleasure and guffaw at the other's
skinked perversion of a ramrod face. *...like two scorpions in a*
bottle, one annihilated the other nearly so. Faces what asking for
skull-fucking by side arm.

Hah. Ha, ha. Hah.

While all the while same time still in room's concrete
vacancy's contained a claustrophobia of corners and an evolution of superpositions. Of itself in five minutes—or as placed
at the far end of the solar system. And me and mine as dead
somewhere along the way. But that's a whole other story. Or
in the halftone bursts of an atmosphere mid-collision.

Are moments we cannot as undone. When mouth's
opened and guts poured out in a flatulence of decomposed
innards. Or moments what dissolve upon contact and ourselves as already disoriented from the narcotic salts—when
our song carried up and into the canopy in its helplessness.
Times when person dreams in a veritable cocktail of acids,
carcinogens, uppers, and downers. Though also certain
potentialities what as got a kind of knowing look. These
potentialities are what's for dinner, and this a steak as bite

back. Scene as contain its own tongue. Timeline as got a sumptuous living quality to it. Potentialities of myself as erupted in a super-luminescence from the eyes on in, for example. Or seen abyss as unravel into a long-bodied life-form stretch from birth to death of the universe—with fingering tendrils thread through every mouth and eye and where it thread through you is not but an abyss unravel into long-bodied lifeform with fingering tendrils thread through every mouth and eye.

All of which why hive built as a space arc and the future's just around the corner.

Room what contains the multiplying addictions of the many Jackson Coles—Jackson Cole incarcerated in among the windings of the madhouse—Jackson Cole on the hunt for his mother's corpse and Jackson Cole as witnessed his wife and child executed—Jackson Cole as tarry with an indigene upon a bear and Jackson Cole gone hunting in virtual ghettos of Hanoi—Jackson Cole comes back upon a Pittsburgh what become as way station for souls and a fork in the black waters of the afterlife—a Pittsburgh where Jackson Cole become innumerable as a heaven of endless possible lives and all these lives of been occurred beside thing what known as g3. Except for is been a g3 what conceals much more than what she is believed herself to been.

Her. *Your brother has left Al-Mobaraka. He is contaminated now as well.*

Me. *You speak of the parasite or the world beyond g3 and its impurities?*

Am gleaned upon scenes from tail end of history. Scenes wherein the scenery's got eyeteeth as hung draped upon the cheek. Of the manikin textbook moved through said environments what feasted on it as it done so and the undoing of its text as it is. Bodies digested from inside the many stomachs of the Hathaway Crawler—something like as a maze of stomachs—moored in the abyss but also rich in the vegetations of Southeast Asia—with they twinings of root and draperies of vegetation. From the birth of the *tay* to the stars fallen from out they constellations like the cheapest of rhinestones.

And am stood.

Her. *We call you a "self in the second person." If all things are g3, then g3 are protected.*

Me. *And'm more g3 than most.*

All I see's the dusting of her thoughts as am simultaneous step toward the hashishin. Her body more as like a circulatory system of light in seated position than a body but the puppeteer as already slipped out the backside of the puppet without so much as a twitch of her slight frame. And her just another hashishin interrogating another otaku from cheap aluminum chair's only visible to yours truly through its effects.

Her. *You are qutb. You are jism mithali. You are of the new breed.*

Me. *What makes me different than my brothers, then?*

Her response. *If the ganglia crystalize, they turn to mush once they unfreeze, although while frozen they become the most beautiful of miniature flowers. Even for g3, it can be a difficult business to trick out the subtleties of the neuronal blueprint to such degree as they have done with you. You approach the singularity most and so are most pleasing to the singularity. Of course, they will tell you that the parasite can result in similar reconstitutions of the psyche, but there is a difference. You're intact when g3's finished molding you, but what the parasite does to the children of Man is like a raping of them.*

If I'm the most, then who the least? I am said.
The escaped one.

Artificial overhead of hive. As in, pristine black shade structure engulf several blocks in its shadow—and beyond it visible
thin thread of LAC skyline, its bits and sections of sun-bleach
shells what remain of the previous tenements. And upon footbridge been as white strip in the gloom what connect vend-
er's entrance to rooftop and cross over wide thoroughfare of
LAC several stories below—most part littered in smattering
of trash barely visible in the cover of dark this artificial mountain provide—some shattered porcelain and various corpse of
indistinguishables. And—token of hashishin's affection—left
foot like as someone is took hammer to it.
    <Please remain clear of the blast area.>
Shrilled from somewhere above the head.
    Followed by misting from above as well—as—am hobble
on the heel with many elaborate twistings of hip and onto
building-top adjacent to hive's main stem and past statue of
boy done a handstand upon its shoulder high pedestal and
complete entwined in brilliant viscera of iridescent creepy
crawlies—vine of which descend from same three-story-high
overhead to've slithered they decorative stalks and brilliant
leafage down torso and fan out long the face in purplish
threads with lines of iridescent bone white. *<Please remain
clear of the blast area.>* As. Continue my interpretive dance
round side and its aggregate concrete slab—and more twined
brilliances of twig.
    Beside a green building with its long windows shat-
tered and words YMCA set above. Building been shaved off
by hive's overhang and what vegetation litter the way's as

squiggled in response to each squeamish fingering of fellow's bare clad toes. *<Please remain clear of the blast area.>* Then out and into street what also as draped in a tangle of multicolored growths.

LAC like Pittsburgh in such that its hillocks run high enough to of meet a building top turned patio. And now—poised upon the broke apart blacktop and ornate rustle of its accompanying vegetation—yolk of space congeal about the bare gray shoulders—as a hyuk, hyuk, hyuk stumble from out the lips—and moisture turned gauzing of the lungs. g3's reckoning come like as a lullaby cause the eyes turn bright from the pain of its impossibility—a kind of a goodbye. *<Please remain clear of the blast area.>* Her fingers like as crowd behind the eye to pull—upon strings of remembrance she then is twist into knots—a weather system housed at the periphery of sense—what sing its bon mots into mucus of the skull and its ecosystem of hungers.

Your eyes will turn black. Your feet will fall off.

Sore and covered in quakes in this unnatural dark. And a muddling of the senses what that a person as if lost a bit of they brain and the remainder become all surface wound—while thread of vegetation perform its elaborate dances in some imaginary conglomeration of breezes. And still as inhaled a sauna of floral aromas. *<Please remain clear of the blast area.>*

Lingered on the ruined blacktop and—farther off down same tarmac—cluster of dark pull apart to of reveal itself as silhouette of gangly arms, legs, and slender torsos hung together among the underbrush—three naked boys with wild tangled hair been giggle as they are took turns swinging at a toad gone squish under force of they sticks—they three heads turned as am passed—and upper half of each face a crowding of some thousand arthropod eyes gape back at the adult—as—nearer to hand, something like as pink flowering off to left is been midway through its evolution in what shadows provided by hive and at corner street become an overpass. *<Please remain clear of the blast area.>*

Am continued on and past abstract syringe sculpture in its dressing of shadow—thing's needle bent upon same sheer black overhang—and—more incandescent tangle of foliage draped to work as camouflage to what ironwork tables sat in rusted and overturned mess—and bare feet slathered about upon sandy concrete beside accompanying gutted corporate coffeeshop.

Then never-ending shade end. In zig zag upon brick steps. Stood under slap of sun. Its massive hand press into the soft gray meat of the shoulders, toes, and everywhere in between.

Two persons—woman and woman—accompany fugitive on the steps. In they contrapposto and draped in fine suits of the professional but with heads what as obscured by sackcloth. As in, these ladies also as hid they features from view using what rudimentary apparatus as available.

One got a black summer suit dusted as a collier's apron and her lapels upturned in her melodrama and streaks of gray in what auburn hair been visible through the mesh of her sack—*Willow*—and other also adorned in simple black two-piece and accompanying white collared shirt but hers less sullied and is got a more vibrant youthful sheen to what russet locks been visible—*Destiny*—in the languorous tones of the valley girl. Both got the flatness of apparitions under high noon sun what hobbles the mind. And also, through mesh of said sackcloth—ridges and striations of pink are marred what fragments of expression as visible and are run as tumors through the hair. And in Destiny's case—growth of an archipelago crosses the twine-darked eye as she is stared back at the gray man approach in his nudity. And with just the barest hint of holster.

<Please remain clear of the blast area.>

And Willow's hip got a torque to it. Like as she froze mid-pounce.

They freed the wrong mirror.

The compartment's oval hatch been a egg in its shell—and with a click, radiance gone and vanished round its rim and—thought of me and my old girl as sprawled upon floor of her destroyed apartment after firefight led to her face smashed up and—*I think you broke my nose*—and myself up and stumbled off across the room only for to collapse halfway there—and—*Jackson*, she was said—and—*This place you call home's a lie, Jackson*—and—*I come from the real world.*

And hatch slide open to—woman what with rash run the length of her jowl-y olive cheeks and wide sensuous lips painted in gloss. *I know. I know.* She is said though known what is unclear. Her lips settled upon the 'o' for a moment before she is continue. *You are growing a new plant out of your head. I know. But you must learn to control it. Sit down, please.* And shoulders come to of spasmed and acquiesced. And ourselves as sat cross one from the other upon matching pink blobs.

Account of this version of a man indeed is built to been easily gulled.

I am what is called a fouris. I am bred as a diplomat with features appealing to the male of the species. However, as you may have noticed... Indicates side of face with hand. *I do have a defect, and therefore am being utilized more for HR and hospitality purposes in-house. Being a diplomatic lifeform, I am given special dispensation to interact without facial covering, but this does not mean I am your toy.* Again pause with lips pursed on the 'y.' *Shall we proceed?* While—whole while, she also very much not wanting to of look this particular specimen in its leering face.

And both of us as ignore the neurotic teddy bear with the extracted button eye as positioned beside me. And constant whirring of one remaining eye as perform its badminton back and forth.

While—personally? Am eyed that rash with a luxuriant curiosity. And even when she not wanting to look parasite in the face, is still currently been as looked it in the face all the same.

Flick my polyp-riddled head to the side in a nonchalant fashion as she tilt hers with a coquettishness such that the rash now's took front and center. As teeth're clenched in a wild eroticism of the jawline one moment to then of turned as calm as a lifeless thing and accompanying scene turned brilliant in its hues and manifestations. Or like as if am just buried man's face in a bowlful of the new narcotic and now my eyes as swam with it.

I readjust myself. She readjust herself.

We want to negotiate with the parasite. We are prepared to execute all the remaining Jackson Cole mirrors if you prove uncooperative. Please do not be selfish.

She looks around—play with the hem of her pants. Sections of her body gone and vanished. Her eyes shut. Then is toppled over. And am once again just a madman in his sanitorium.

Nurse Quiana eyeballs a person from out her mascara and by caged window and accompanying wall decorations—paintings of pastoral scene and some artificial flowers hung up near ceiling-top. And spread before me's an array of plates fringed in slop and what various inedibles remained from my samplings of the buffet. *Your thinking is wrong in every regard, Mr. Cole,* she's said from her seat at next table over.

Other than us—ballroom-sized room not but exhibition of large round tables—they pastel cloths untouched and empty of occupants, dishware, and silver. We are occupied furthest corner while Nurse Quiana examines a man with a peevishness and my attention turns to the boiled peas.

Do you truly understand where you are, Mr. Cole, she is said. And—quick as a blink—sound's as cut out of the afternoon. As in—whatever chirpings and squeaks and rustling of the leaves through aforementioned caged window now become silenced like as someone just hit pause—and Karen Quiana stared back from out her mascara with a knowing gleam when she gone, *In what time and place are we, Jackson Cole?*

And my hands clung to table's rim like as to stop the table from its shaking.

Ha. Ha. Ha.

And—hole in the concrete already some way toward having been repaired through swarm of lacquered titanium—and containers to the rear now a good deal towards vacated.

Stood while hashishin is seated.

Would you care to see what lies in our future, Jackson Cole?

This hybrid thing. Hashishin with singularity as once again sat behind the face. Like as rogue program runs an otherwise unoccupied mainframe in some earlier more naïve epoch of the American past—a mainframe what made from a coagulation of sinew and clusterfuck of ganglia. The knottings of light her eyes as Satan's circus like Christians are wont to of say—a convoluted highway of luminescence inside enwrapped shadows of the skull. And general speaking what I seen's like as I got eyes what preach into the recesses or like as if abstract of a room superimposed over abstract of a room, with object and person as decals upon said imaginings.

And decal gone on. *There's no need for us to go anywhere in actual fact, dear heart. The future is always at hand for spirit animals such as ourselves.*

While what knots of light—took for eyes on account of they location been most part paired below the brow—only—these bits of illumination—as abstractions sat nested in a murk of personhood—become as fractured into myriad threads what are flitted about upon larger uncertainty of the face. And—this concrete receptacle of room as become uncertain as well. Corners slipped out of shape or gone blurred. Walls turned as manicured different. Such that they more confining as as am stepped up close and personal to this shadow of a hashishin.

And somewhere in there hashishin is stood as well.

Do you not you want to meet your offspring, otaku?

Turned to of slip beyond threshold of this quaint facsimile of a room but—in moment of my hesitation been as witness. To the old-fashioned memories of yesteryear and they added twists. Unusual collections round the ear of some darling in the dark of the back room. And colloquial uncertainties up near the nose of what corpses been as discovered in they mob-exploded living rooms. Bloodwork speckled upon baseboards accompany in hallway sometimes took to moving.

To then've stepped through the mirage.

And. First thing am noticed is that black and white turned technicolor. Although truth be told this room's large part black and white all the same and lined in grayscale. Meaning what?

Oversized black box hung stage center—with gold band beneath upper lip and entirety lettered in ornate Arabics—as well as various other stamp and seal of gold-imprinted wording planted upon embossed surface below. Black box hung in what is been a white itself lined in outfacing gray cylinders like as so many person-sized aquariums run from apex to base of this sphere of a chamber.

And so it is—am preoccupied by the special effects—when—hashishin puppet having revert back to g3 puppetmaster in this abstract space. *We believe Buddhists and Mohammedans can live in peace so long as our national interests align.* In each of they tubes—every face been some approximation of Jackson Cole what I been—but contorted into all manner of form and content. Gray eyes sometime as fan across the skull or been as like pair of lady parts nested in they cheeks—or as got more like wash of tentacles below the neck or an interweaving of tentacles as opposed to mouth—and all been as reposed peaceful in similar cylindrical containers not unlike them what other mirrors still hung in and still been as dreamed of Pittsburgh.

Of course, Japan was always going to pose a problem. The hentai virus complicates any and all diplomatic relations with the creator of the hentai virus. Whether this is a nation or a faction of the nation, there are blind spots which cannot be ignored. And am glanced over and at what been parts of her face eat other parts of her face. And general speaking like as blurring of faces been projected upon her own. Some are flickered and flashed out and others got a wiggling growth to them as are slid from in or out larger translucence of faces.

You see this room because this room is not a room. It sits upon the convex surface of the 9th sphere. When—clearly we inside a sphere, not outside, lady. *You see what is to come after our inevitable Mi'raj, aleaziz. After your death in an unforeseeable accident between here and the Kuiper Belt, and after you have commandeered control of my mind during your daytrip to the afterlife, and after your eventual rebirth at the edge of the solar system, you and I will become the same person, for you are an imaginal beast who grows branches that reach into alternate universes. The body is always the least part, and now the least among you is hurrying into the arms of our enemies. This outcome is already set, but your cooperation is required for it to succeed.*

Then. No more black cube and spherical room full of aquariums of divergent Jackson Coles. From imagined slid back and into imaginer's hand and—hung above the Old Los Angeles Souk and all what members of the public below just as got down on they bended knees before this apparition of g3 as having manifest in the air by smoldering worship pyre of blacked monitors, keyboard, and the like and above one of they foot pools and the worming tendril-eyed gray nudist also hung upon what currents accompany her presence.

And them as not but shadows inside the shadows of this glorified shopping mall.

Step out into the midday sun and upon blacktop as fried in it while robed in monk's maroon sheeting and bare of foot and one foot like as it been whacked by a hammer and asphalt a kerosene upon the wound. And man's female handlers are as reach for said slob. But—*Fuck off.* Even after them as pulled back am swat at hand toward the periphery to of knock this foolishness upon the head. *Don't need your help.*

Otaku...

Hold your jaw. I don't need any of your fucking help. Hopped on the one good foot—and contemplate—the good, the bad, and the ugly—the mountains and Troy gone and evaporated upon a night and Cassey Darling and her unfortunate end and Ash and the kid and how it all end up here and this most recent humiliation and its pair of woman thugs so eager to of coddle a fellow across the tar—with eyes what are peered from out the corners of they sockets.

Then a silence like as all the fans turned off at once. Followed by—from above and surrounding—sonorous notes of Arabic rung out upon the otherwise uninhabited thoroughfare. A wailing sung from concealed speakers that warble and croon its way through its PSA. End as it begun—with its same cry of, *Allahu akbar!* And then a final, *La ilaha illah liah.* As. Destiny and Willow and they suits are make tentative move—account of—indeed am in need of they help.

And—several awkward moments later—in the multi-fingered timeline of yours truly—with its various histories inside of histories like as a Russian doll of dioramas—am come to of hobbled between pair of hooded ladies and leathers what are clacked on down the noonday street.

Sullen and with swinging toe. *Everyone in LAC ladies?*

Willow slide out handgun several sizes too large for her slender wrists and three of us gone and traipsed past some blocks of firebombed corporate office—remnants of cubicles annihilated in beauteous eruption and the occasional skull. Past modernist structures tagged in puking of colors upon they abstract surfaces and come up on twisted metal monstrosity on the right what I happen to know's called as the Walt Disney Concert Hall and occupied by what remains of the LAPD.

You will meet some class A examples of man shortly, otaku. Destiny. Move.

In Pittsburgh, Walt Disney Concert Hall a little bit famous—most especial in the back rooms of Candyland—itself renowned as home to a wistful display of fisticuffs and other theatricals—but in Candyland's back rooms, where the many costumed fighters in they nylons and spats been as sat about to of contemplate what future employments as available to professional showmen such as them—set in musculature and awash in boredom during even most riveting of life-and-death acts—apparently, often talk'd turn to the Walt Disney Concert Hall and its refined brawlers as displayed upon the pronounced stage. Most famous of whom being the Sportsman, in his busked leathers and argyles slid over the toned surface of his midnight black calves always laughing as he is gave a good drubbing to the pasty cheeks of each opponent LAPD what could brung forth. Walt Disney Concert Hall a monument of bloodshed and wonderment to us.

More manageable weapon slip from Destiny's holster. *Not used to carting around monks.*

Then. From somewhere behind, above, and to the left. *Hey, terrorists! Think fast!* Whizz—ping—and laughter of the LAPD's been as rung through otherwise deserted streets of LAC.

As. Personally. Toes are flit upon the prickings of the asphalt and something gone as hunted from out backend of person's thoughts—like CGI porn bomb—or daydream tagged in unwanted signage of a lurid and flashing nature—as conceptual viruses breed in the childhood memories of the bogeyman—and in among the netting of ganglia person's wrought from. And—between pain-exploded foot, burning tarmac, and what porn bombs as hunted through the backend of the eyes—am gone as tumbled forward to been scooped up and draped arm over shoulder and shoulder over arm of man's female travelling companions.

Live long and prosper, fuck-o's!

Also behind of us. Another wild miss followed by more chuckling. As the pricked at toes are continued on in our general speaking six-legged shuffle. Firearms at either end.

Willow a natural right and Destiny is got hers upheld in her non-dominant left and these they pistol arms survey the scene like as rudimentary antennae. Past mouth of former courthouse. Front windows smashed into teeth and debris spills from out unmoored doorway and into sands and partial submerged avenue and its skittering of folding tables.

And on other side's a restaurant in similar state of disrepair.

Blown-apart windows as showcase a kind of a burrowing. Something spun new walls over what ornate woodwork as bar present. Untouched table settings set like as person about to of come and order a mint julep any moment now. Pink fingerings wreathe through and about what quality top-shelf liquors on display above the bar. Glasses laid upon they beds of cloth draping.

While Willow and Destiny over here also are continued with they bicker routine as they are slid yours truly down what's once a main drag of the LA from before.

Why're we even bothering? This is the wrong mirror.

One's better than nothing.

Are the Indians even going to want it? As sun's layered the shoulders and upper back in a lacing of hurts. *The data exhaust in this model approaches zero.* As head is jostle about with some comicalness—account of—am hovered above a shopping area. *How useful is that to a harvesting culture like the First Nations?*

While also. Back in the hive and me and the automated teddy bear on the move in an escort of hashishin through hallways as got a murkiness to them but with pinpoints of clarity. And in a cabin just outside of Pittsburgh. And remembered all of it from somewhere inside of a sanitarium.

While. To our right. Open incline bent downward as serpentine swath of desert—with not but few dead palms to line its pools of loose particulate—a makeshift hut made of stacked rocks in wasteland's center smoothed in a jigsaw of cement and also strung in drapings of sand and at incline's bottom a parody rendition of old US of A municipal building—American Transportation Authority or some such—while just ahead's police cruiser. At an angle to the double yellow and beside of other car face opposite direction—and persons leaned out they door windows to of partook they storyville chatter. When. Cop leans toward our direction—sporting traditional blue of the beat cop what also adorned in a wash of silver spikes and occasional rhinestone glinting.

With something like as oxygen tube up the nose is looped round his ear. Topped by black Mickey Mouse cap sat askew upon the shaved, sunburnt scalp.

You seeing this? Shouted back at what visions of tenderloin is been presented to him. *Wax my balls and call me a virgin.* And his equal-as-been-tubed-up pal rubberneck along with him.

Then three guns raised—his one to our two—when—his cruiser's hood erupt in a blossom of flame and other car's done a U-ey round it to of sped away as are limped towards the smoldering vehicle. Am stared through various funhouse tongues of flame as displayed—questing for face of the offending cop. But when fire is died down, all I get's a blown-apart windshield and blood.

Santa Ana's coming in. Destiny.

Is when am noticed—billowed up from broke-toothed skyline to block otherwise blue in the finery of its rolling black. Sandstorms of Joshua Tree. Then line of sight fallen to—finally am locate corpse's head turned a popcorn of pulp. Still with the Mickey Mouse at its rakish tilt.

Am regarded the mechanical teddy bear propped upon its lawn chair. Thing's one button eye still unspooled to of dangle midway down the plush belly as other button eye whirs and flits about in its nervousness.

And even as—thick wafts of cloud also been as swirled about and through the various seating areas with they beach umbrellas and aquatex glass tabletops—center of which been a kind of smooth white over-sized clam shell—as well as—one stumpy palm tree—perched here up above the world. *Do you like it here, Mr. Cole?* Another single long-stalked palm from a tier just below is got pom pom of a palm frond as flicks about the end of the trunk inside the winds of this higher altitude—with its leaflets and segments slid in and out of each other in a suggestiveness. *Would you like the Rogue CIA to help you find a way out?* As bear's one functioning eye continues to of wink upon various pinpoints in an endless questing for data. *Would you like that?*

Ever been dissected, bear?

Blink back. *Not while I was conscious...*

Care to try?

Seating area's surrounded by a nipple-high metal barrier gate and it's just opened and what looked as like servants—white gloves, greased hair, and dinner vests—and of a particular Christian-caucasion look to them—been as wheeled in cart upon which's a shining handled and over-sized cloche bell sat upon what edibles it conceals and the silver platter they as laid upon.

Oo. Oo. Oo, Bear is spoke. Like as if thing been actual fact able to eat.

Covering removed to of reveal a de-armed and headless torso of no clear origin, grayish skin turned deeper hue from the cooking and vertebra already in process of having been plucked from larger fruit of the body by a gloved hand wielding a two-pronged serving fork. *Sir would be recommended to try the bit in the middle. It is the most delicious part*, servant's said as the various nodules, lumps, and growths upon fellow's cheeks and what have you begun they squiggling like as they an orchestra of infants in process of having been strangled in the cradle.

And again am turned witness—to vision of Cassey Darling as draped across the toilet and with skull look as if it been sucked inside itself—like as if pieces of the skull been as collapsed leaving the skin hung loose across these cavities turned a grayer hue where visible through the hair and face not much better and her eyes not just dead but like as if partway through a transformation from dead person eyes to dead animal eyes—as in pupil been grown ballooned out in parts and got bits of black as visible partial submerged beneath the whites of the aforementioned glistening eye.

Which is why—take some moments for me to've realized the high-pitched clicking sound what comes from out Mr. Bear's concealed speaker an expression of laughter. As thing's one good eye flip between myself and meat with similar like and kind of nervousness as before, the high-pitched clicking continues, accompanied by an appreciable waggle of thing's hinged lower lip.

Sun-cooked blacktop's shredded in cracks crumble along the lip and a scattering of debris. Toppled pink stroller faded to ghostlike pale, the fabric of the seat still got some flake as glitter in spots. Another of the naked boys with the spider eyes what wrestles tattered corpse of a dog. Kid's teeth clenched in ecstasy—as it squeeze and squeeze—its thousand little black eyes blinkered in stuttered runs. Destiny shot it in the head and body gone crumpled against dog corpse.

Invasive species, those.

In crosswalk with—shoulders slumped down, head tossed back—to of glance up and at what been a protrusion of window boxes stuck out of otherwise orange wall in waves, with tower poke from just behind same livid orange hue. And cross jut from rightward end of it all.

Have to take refuge here. Willow.

One pane of glass ridging slid up and—another kid—this one with human eyes—is sneered down from his pillbox of the Almighty. The twistings of his filth like as a bloom of rags wove about his legs and his face toothy with pus. *Nice clean head shot best way to end a spider.*

Am extricated myself from they shoulders and ladies are resleeved their pieces as we are angled long periphery of what catholic monstrosity now's hung about the skyline. And said sack-clad assistants are took to having murmured some profundity as to the fates of LAPD and specific as regard, "She who dances down the primrose path must die on the primrose path."

What a beautiful toss. Destiny.

While. My beleaguered toes—in they curtaining of monk's dress—what as are hurried past any and all barricadings and cascades of garbage there been. Ancient packagings with metal poked through they minced threads and string of plastic. And occasional patch of slime.

To gate guarded by pair of large-barreled artillery jut through the studded metal shielding and on either side of defunct circular fountain. Adorned in pewter seraphim and various over-complicated nonfunctioning machinework. As—*Or you flee and allow everyone to display their instinct for contempt*—as wind's begun to slice at the cheeks and general curtaining of the flesh.

When some innocent veiled in modest assemblage of rags advertise upon his own bed of trash. *The parasite comes!* Like as he pronounce the common cold as simultaneous the Son of Man.

And currently, said common cold is bounced up steps one foot at a time as his handlers're looked on with some amusement. As befit a Mel & Rob of the gentler sex.

First inklings of a gale as am pivot up and toward this box of a cathedral's got a more unassuming door on the left and—woman carved above is draped in gold leaf. Requisite gold disc placed to accentuate the coiffure's blonde locks. Still some distance from that door and at top of stairs—am crumpled upon aforementioned wind and a gasp's erupted from the backdrop. Come from somewhere beside yet another defunct fountain and from out the grasses in among garden as decorate raised bed. And these been shrubs pierced in pink tumescence what are also swung and swayed to rhythms of they own like as each plant caught in its own unique whirlwind of dust.

This the moment when wind is turned brown to of gentle sand the cheek. Crumb of grit gone mud upon the palate and—from inside what haze as come upon fun-size pink cancer of forest—congregation risen out they fly tents and other receptacles. Being blistered by airborne granules as are stepped out from among engorged fingers of the mutant foliage—they leaves striped in fleshy pink as flap with some pathos like as sentient scrota mid-abuse—or from off a stem is hung so much senseless lobe and fold of pink—and interspersed with these, the bodies of the broke-backed wrapped in they smearings of cloth—persons climbed from they pop-ups, domes, geodesics and fly-leaves—as these many fronds batted about in the flying sand. In shirts not but patches come as rushed toward the put-on GMO monk collapsed on a stone and in a wash of dust.

The parasite comes! One eye work and the one eye not or eyes squeezed shut as are amble about with uncanny accuracy. *The parasite comes!* And—man's own eyes slitted against onslaught of dirt as am watched up and at the increased ululation as like as poured from between corners of they heads and from out as of yet unseen lips—is when am noticed the scarring on every face. *The parasite comes!* Every head looped in folds and rills of pink. Ears twisted outward and gone fluted and thin. Eyes turned pastel, green, and with thread-ings of eye inside the eye. *The parasite comes!* Fingers reach for the face of they messiah are fingers turned nodules of finger. *The parasite comes!*

And every face with arm up to shield against flying silt—albeit with some impotence—while—person's female han-dlers off to huddle beside a *tay* in conical woven hat and work clothes, her own eyes flashed yellow inside of what swatch of gray skin been visible above the face mask.

6.

Visions of Sheffield in his tweed and specs and housed inside a chauffeured Oldsmobile as he gone and disappeared off to the waiting arms of the Midland Coalition. Of bodies sat piled in various states of decomposition, skin flayed from off the buttocks like old bit of furniture unstrung, parts of a person come to of melted into blubber and stink and run with rivers of maggots. Visions seen and visions as illusion what cannot been extricated from the eyeball. From ass-handler to archangel and everywhere in between. While myself end in a cabin in the woods and in arms of Mel and Rob. Turned nonsense of the senses upon a bedframe but's a pretty sort of nonsense.

Somehow gone to late afternoon. And from far side of the room, phonograph play something halfhearted and sweet. <I'm goin' through the big D and don't mean Dallas.> In voice clear as a chandelier. As floor comes apart board by ever-loving board—and beyond what jigsaw of boards nails separated out from the object of they conveyance—are glimpsed rabbits run in and throughout hued cumulous clouds—what hop lazy side-by-side circles—rabbits like as ripples—round ribbon-bound sparrows, manray, and at they center my brother—adorned in his pre-adolescent summer suit—hands what raised skyward and face what seep light from its thousand arthropod eyes. Remind a person of guy I seen hung from hooks under one of the many bridges as are known to grace our city and with same beatific expression plastered upon his bloodless face.

As Rob gone on with his bedtime story. To man what tied to the bed. A captive audience. As to how said audience is became lost. And how nobody gone to of gave a shit about having lost shit like him.

Guy get an idea to eliminate most powerful man in Pittsburgh. Got the papers prove said person's guilt. He takes his claims to the people, and the people risen up, when just so happens our neighbors to the West just waiting for this very thing. They begin full-scale assault of our metropolis following day. While Pittsburgh now wrapped in a chaos tied up in a turmoil what been stewed with some commotion. Gangs angle for control and a strongman is took the reins who got the imagination of a songbird. As in, he only knows one song. And it is not a very good melody.

While am continued to of stare up and at the shadows in among finished wood of the ceiling and its attendant beams. <That was August. This is June, and it's a different tune.> Crooned from the phonograph. And whenever am glanced off toward Rob, his lips are pour from out of his lips as in streaming gif of mobster turned strange. And Mel midway through cook up some fat and kippers somewhere in background. As in, fish sizzle upon landscape of the cast iron while he hum his lullabies.

You remember Chaw, sweetheart? What a delight to see him crucified.

Rob is huffed like he just given himself a little workout. Sizzling in background's stopped and Mel comes to view adorned in flower print apron laid atop his suit. But Rob do not glance up.

Now our hero doing his best to keep from having been massacred as his hometown fall to the Christians. And maybe give a little taster to the new narcotic along the way. Maybe follow a lead to a VR unit and even slip the headset on. Maybe his one remaining brother gone missing and his place of business erupts in a firestorm of left-over henchmen. In the end, he is apprehended.

Mel. *Herein meaning us.*

Rob. *And we been assigned to help you give in to your worst desires and tendencies.*

While still am stared at same incongruity of a palm tree frond as struggle beside window with its many slitherings of leaflets like as a many-fingered thing currently works to wipe the snot from off of all its many fingers onto the others of its many fingers—and behind it not but blue.

And through what broken slatherings of teeth as remained—as phonograph click as needle bounce against what vinyl occupy the end of its melody—am murmured, *Is a mirage of Pittsburgh.*

To which Mel, in his flower print apron concurs. *Always was.*

And—as blood flecks the lips at the corners—man's got to murmur, *But I still took down its most powerful man.* Then a strangled cough of a chuckle. Followed by a spit of more blood.

Then Rob gone, *True enough, Colby Sheffield once the most powerful man in Pittsburgh and now his rein's dead.* Then he is looked over at Mel and both of them burst out in an identical snotful of guffawing. *But only because Colby Sheffield never been Colby Sheffield to begin with.*

Then Mel and Rob are worked together to've unloosed the caged man from his caging in a kind of a tenderness. And am slid to a sitting position with many groans and grunts, rubbed at the wrists as they are stood bent over in they appreciation of man's visage.

See. Colby Sheffield got the best of you.

More dirty chuckles.

Yeah, Colby Sheffield really took you for a spin.

Further guffawing.

You think you could end Colby Sheffield.

Big snorts of dumb laughter.

When here you's Colby Sheffield all along.

And out and out knee-slapping, tear-splattering, snot-faced titters come as poured from out of my two companions as are as stumbled over themselves in room's late afternoon amber at the sheer hilarity of it all. As Mel finally having retreated to record player and retrieve his 45. Is when am shouted, *Get the fuck off of me,* as I swat at world gone dark like as I been swarmed by lepers.

LAC come to been known as kind of modern-day American Jerusalem—at least for the non-Christians. And gangster's walkabout in what wilds it provides become just begun and already turned out many of the myths spun of this place been as truly spoke. Population indeed riddled in tumors and is true light got a more luxuriant quality toward the end of the day here than in muddier airs of Pittsburgh. And g3 sure enough been proved mad.

As sand tangle a person in whispering threads of wind. And monk's aforementioned following of lepers too slow to of catch coals as—stinging upon the pelt as are maneuvered our way toward waiting side door with its attendant icons coiffed in gold. But even as we done so, man's eyes hung upon visage of the *Tây Việt*.

Was Vietnam first developed GMO technology make *tays* a thing—before having then been reacquired by China, her battalions of infantry, frogmen, and "codicils as relating to the fate and future of Yuenan," only to of confront they *tay* technology unleashed upon the jungles as a kind of welcoming gift. But *tays* as been born and bred in Vietnam consider themselves different species from those as developed by singularity. Hence the conical hat of the Vietnamese grandma and her poignant glance in its marinade of dust.

Cannot of tread on hot coals without having got your feet scorched—and—currently been as like everything from buttocks to prick and what ellipsis of person is joined them—been as bared to said coals. As am hobbled on toward doorway's black glass below its gold lady and man's entourage of like-minded individuals are traipsed after like as groupies hunting for an autograph. They faces twisted and turned by God's horticulturalist and His many pink infestations. Clench they teeth in a kind of autoerotic desperation and continued they slow-mo race to be first touch down upon the flesh of the gray man when said person never actual fact of the matter is approved the diseased hordes to of touch him upon his flesh. In among these many swarms of dirt.

And by actual fact cardboard-reinforced black glass doors below they stern golden lady. Then through and into—cooler side aisle cut from molding of concrete. Its many alcoves jammed full of bodies on top bodies and laced through bodies. Some of whom got more parts than a person accustomed to seeing on a person.

Smell is like chocolate—chalk—bladders—pus.

As am continued to of treat the injured foot with a feminine delicacy.

Old woman voice. *Udhrib el-kalba wa yata' addaba el-fahdu.*

From center of this reverberating hall.

Chorus respond with a, *La 'iilah 'iilaa Allah.*

Eyes as flash bright in the otherwise dark of following unlit alcove. Known only as occupied due to sounds of rustled cloths and murmurs of breath. Said alcoves as punctuations to other walled segments open to the main nave. One or two black upon the interior, but last's dotted with candles as a kind of bespoke firmament as conjure sense of the heavens in some mystery play concern genesis. Point being, got a more celestial antiquity to it but as molded by old maids.

And winds outside are continued to hiss.

Muhamad rasul Allahi. Voice gone on.

Muhamad rasul Allahi. They respond.

Hopped my approach toward what rear vacancy this bastardized cathedral as got on offer. Slap of toes and sandal clacks gone as echoed off into the corners and crested peak of this place. Glance back and at they various pink-riddled facets winked in and out from some faulty candelabra. An eye captured in momentary twist of flame—tiny slit of fire reflected back in the pinhole of the pupil. Or part of ruined mouth in its framing of dark is revealed diseased tongue slather across what remain of the teeth below a looping of the requisite breathing tube.

As the hampered foot gone and swung round concrete partition and dais and wall behind come into view—and its cross set in relief against background of white stained glass turned muted gray and crooked rows and conglomerations of pew as strung and parked below light fixtures dangled as piping with fluted bottoms and spread of maybe three upside down glass bowls apiece, each with its own burned out white orb. One or two not burned out.

La hawla wala quata ala Allah. What got a face wreathed in wrinkles and wide ruby lips. And her green vestments tiny at this distance. And her tone changed with her language. *Allah, how shall I be worthy of all the love you have bestowed upon me?*

Pews strewn in bodies slatted into an induced doze or some with boredom riddle they trash-scarred lips. And cords of fungus as like disembodied spinal weavings run about long the concrete floor—iridescent and fluted but for the most part an alabaster white as snake between they ankles or end in the neck of a shapeless mass of cloths and a single antiquated discman. *What actions shall I take today to make me worthy of your love, Allah? Please. Show me the way.*

Her audience sat among what tapestries hung from the walls vandalized in dayglo.

Old woman pause in her oration as she stare out and through the stutter of identical oak pews—what meandered off into islands and clusters. Her peepers hung upon one to exclusion of the rest—*ahlan w sahlan. Welcome brother. Please give us of the parasite. We have been waiting.*

Again confronted by clutter of put-on awe and what abnormalities accompany. Rose from where're sat clocked and general speaking reposed. The brain-burrowed and eye-less. Deadbeat, dirty, grisly and blank-faced—with characteristic wandering eye and grub plug hole at backend of the neck—sheathed in fungus but with hybrid organic-synthetic interior—how it is they seen what wonders unspooled from out cataract of the imaging baths.

As. Woman's preachment continued to of echo. *Children, we are not worthy of this bounty, but, al-hamdu lilla! It has arrived!* And several hands are as secured themselves on the otaku monk.

Like a fellow been half whore half talisman.

As am stumbled backwards, they're also mumbled on about, *The parasite comes.*

And occasional am glance up and at what jewelry of lighting as dangled above they heads. An unused brasswork set in lines of pipe. As. From the dais. *Laa takhif ya sadiqi.*

Something gone splat upon the toes.

Stared into crush of bodies and they bestiary of skunk. Some of these is got a kind of a decorative scarring what spreads from the cheek and others as saturated in foldings of they own epidermis. Or got fingers what curl from out the finger and eyes don't end at the lip of the lid. As am pressed against the one wall. Buttocks up to the cold of the concrete. When. Somewhere up near aforementioned dais is been Willow and Destiny donned in sack and suit as before—lightly dusted and somewhat misplaced in this larger sea of lepers—with the steadiness of the killing class.

Cleric's talk is approached its conclusion. *We sit at the foot of the idol. But everywhere, the people pray for the coming redemption. For the redemption of Fatima. Fatima, who is g3, who are the hive, that is a false Mountain of Qaf, a cave of illusions, but we have stepped out into the light. They made the jinn partners with Allah, though he created them, but we speak in all tongues, from the visionary language of Ibn Arabi to the odes of Christ on his Mordnacht.* Infusion of German vocabulary into the liturgy a very Duluth thing to do.

Parishioners reached from they sleevings of tatters to of prod at skin round back of man's neck like as they on the hunt for a secret latch. A angry squiggle of finger. And—through the mesh of her approaching head covering—glint of black splotch as come to of invaded whites of Willow's eyes—and—Destiny as got her firearm out as kind of jewelry displayed for edification of the locals.

As said locals' arms come as stretched cross the shoulders and brushed about the emaciated abdomen of this thing I am woke into. Grovel and paw at a person. Still. Willow and Destiny are approached down center aisle of the nave with leathers what clack at a menacing pace.

Is the moment when some syringe bit an otaku upon the spine.

Really? You believe yourself to be Colby Sheffield? You are too high-larious. And Terrance burst out in one of his many signature chuckles. Two of us as situated by row of French doors cut the garden on far side of it to a compound gem of itself and old woman what traverse it with bundle of sticks size of her waist sat atop the ancient bicycle she escorting down the green. From further down is been smoke from makeshift outdoor stove set up direct upon blacktop been the river run through our little institution of mental sanitation and general wellness.

Terrance, what is gone on with your face? Through teeth grit as in a rage.

For—indeed. These eyes as like a prism upon the face—cheek become as blurred petals of flesh or like as if the eyes turned skinned in tears as settled upon the cornea in a gelatinous film as all the while room swell and rock about the background of this new many-leaved face as its parts are slither and slip through they many fingerings of cheek—a lacuna of parts and a crypt of various hides fallen beneath other string-ings of skin.

My face. Hah. Hah. Hah. Like I got a face.

As. Memories come to of scritched upon a fellow's scalp such as would turn a predator limp. Which color the bright spaces dark and worm about the eyeball when a person's come to of sit in the sightlessness of they dreams. What are crawl about between chalking of the present and upholsteries of the past. A cabinet of memories been as cabinets inside of cabinets. Or like as if the gangster turned toothy to've dug down his own clutterings of a throat. And what am seen's been as a fleshing of things once believed were yours truly and they surroundings.

As in—is a Jackson Cole what got sockets been sincerely peopled with worms and—inside hive any case—been as unaffected by gravity. As a gray cadaver of man suspends in some jelly of atmosphere and beside of the most unnerving of AI—with all what its facsimiles of the soul and cancers of mind. As her offspring, am of the opinion she just a layering of algorithms like as the cogs and wheels of the mechanical chessmen of the past. While myself and this automaton of a godhead are hung by stringings of the artificial climate and in among its evolving likeness of air—and from down below—shoppers're stared with an ecstasy from out they oxfords and slacks—they ceremonial wrappings and they rags. Eyes gone dull in they weathered faces and imitation pearls.

While lexis of man as am been rendered's got sorts of vision able to of scrutinize inside the brain's intricacies account of neither here nor there—suspended in hive's air-space—in a cabin in the woods and faced off with pair of prima donna thugs—or in the sanitariums of the future.

Memories of gasoline and smoke. Of pills took and afternoons spent bare-chested in the love hostels of Pittsburgh. An orchestra of vignettes and other snippets. My own as intermixed with bits from out the brains of larger constituency of LAC—and they cerebrums what been lit up like as Christmas lights. And jaws hung open in an altruism of wonder.

Pulp of thoughts as are poured from shifting sands of they ganglia clusters been like as minimalist galaxies flish into existence with a cinematic regularity of glow. Pinpricks turned translated—into brilliant offerings of sense—a excrescence of abstraction always readjust its overlays into assorted intricacies and unnerving patterns. As they smile they synthetic smiles.

Stood transfixed about the arcade and its velvet sounds of water from foot pools of old LA and they added iridescence come from the schools of nanobot. *Christians declare Texas as part of their cosmology, the hell to the heaven of Duluth, and as crucial to the universe as hell is to God and His purpose, but only the singularity is capable of giving Texas what it most desires.*

As is appeared twinings of luminosity unconnected to any person. A branching of rooms all as sprouted from this here and now—game of branching lights and an interplay of game come and gone from being—a kind of a singing inside the skull or a ganglia become forest of wings.

Her. *Leaving the Christians oil poor and their eyes forever on Texas.*

Me. *There a meaning for me in this?*

Her. *We are not the automata you believe us to be in truth. It is the human animal that is the programmable wind-up toy and the machines that play the part of puppeteer, but g3 play many games simultaneously, dear heart. Humans are only part of a deeper data*

set that includes such things as Sebastien Tentacles and the manufactured being my point.

And—is like as I got eyes what do the walking and they've
walked right out of this room and into a play pretend brilliance of pasted together rooms enfold the neuronal nets
sprawl extrinsic to crowd of shoppers below as branches
hooked upon luminous branches.

Truly, g3 is become as like a god. To've stepped and wove
through all they imaginings in an effortless cadence of the
toe. To've slid through and among what many bright-lit colors of this rupturing of thoughts, feelings, and inclinations as
course from out the audience with such an eager robustness.
As the wormings of light been slipped through the dung-
heaps of they signage—she murmurs, *The people of Europa left
their island homes to venture into the abyss for nothing better than
survival, but the reasoning behind our Mi'raj is far more profound.
As for them*—a sweep of the hand—*they play games they do not
understand and win earnings they will never spend.*

While—from somewhere just above of them begun to've
formed a kind of a bundle run they many crystallizations
of information like as mazes drawn through and lit as fila-
ment in a bulb about to of burst from the current but are not
burst—are harvesting.

What I seen. Like as photographic plate inserted into the
saline of the eye—is been another place. Place full of *tays.*
They all're turned with an expectancy in these they many long
corridors. A vision of an institute for the genetically modified
like as utopia set in the defunct state of Vietnam. Set upon a
rectangle of jungle—as greenage of leaves upon hillside gone
granular in the haze.

While same exact time—some other maggot of eye becomes as coated in the eyes of my brother mirror—or like as if his kind of seeing been pasted upon my own as pair of cartoon eyeballs hung suspended above the sentient and maggoty purr these sockets as already contained and some reason am stared at pair of pewter carp visible only due to the fungal components strung through them as a kind of a telesthesia of a security camera—carp what been as angled such that they alleged spittle a fine thread arc cross walkway gone from outer circle of the souk to central seating.

And again she on about, *You've been visiting with your brother, spirit.*

Being manhandled by a more catholic brand of Muslim at the moment.

He has head poisoning, habibi. You all do now. Her elaborate apparatus of sight as tickles about upon backstage of man's optic nerve. *And you, how are you?*

What I seen's both world as they done and world it wanting to be. And this a lumber as forever watch back from out its knots as it constrict itself ever tighter upon the eye's interior. And limbs of g3 as sat in all of it. And in every remembrance of unpackaged future, the same silence. As this particular Jackson Cole—with the adorable maggot eyes—what that come to of scribble about upon the cheek—angled down and at the hordes below—who themselves what with eyes like as the yolk of the eyeball been seeded with nanotechnology and now it seceding from itself.

Each Jackson Cole has a job to do, but yours must remain a mystery, otaku. To then of spoke in words not as translate and relayed messages arrive unbeknownst to man in question.

Who among you of say no when God is ask you a favor?

Turn out clam shell's a kind of a hot tub. As in flip top been opened and waters revealed. Even as it being drained in a cloud cover turned drizzle upon its swirling waters.

While myself and the bear still behind cart of offending meat as sat untouched—but for the two-pronged fork upon sleek gray of the limbless back and its threading of vertebra and draped in what strings of sinew as removed in a bite of the aforementioned two-pronged fork—and sporogenesis upon man's gray wrist what already begun to of thread into the veins in they questing for information and possible genetic redecoration. Accompanied by flush of the senses— of a boy what hacked at the knotty earth in among the brambles and old women schooled in slaughter with they ragged cheeks and dull brass hoops and thick wove baskets and food regimens in the mountains where man spent the dawning of his adolescence and first blood. Said spores turned as pearls of copper upon the wrist what been textured in a chaos of ever smaller lumps.

Bear emits a sigh of automated ennui. *You honestly do not know who you are, do you, mirror?* Voice colored in same pitches as before, but no longer under any illusion this the toy bear's own words. *It was more than a single allelomorph separated you and the lunch as provided.*

As visions of sugar plums as dance throughout the skull—and— facial coral of squiggling nubs been as jiggle in they nesting upon the cheek—as—shadows between thoughts've sprouted into they own vegetation of sound and they own gleam behind of the eyes. As if fellow's fantasies've spun themselves out and into greater conglomeration of hypothetical species and they various positioned fingers like as a fanning of mirage upon eyes' esophagus.

And—contained herein most innocuous of sights.

Of other doddering old ladies—in they beauty parlor basement apartments—who shout for they grandsons to stop with the fucking around and get back to being a father while stood in the shadows by the sparkolite glass. Or—vision of square-bodied woman sporting a bright red claw birthmark by lefthand side of the lip and above a broke-apart man and gone on about things not of the known universe. Of man absconded off to a cabin in the woods outside of Pittsburgh.

But all of them doused in indiscretions of the flesh and accompanying extra mouths.

And. As the bright blue of sky above becomes flattened. And sounds took on a more tinny far-away quality to them. And am as occupied an ever-decreasing space up toward the top of the body. Mr. Bear all the while continues with its diatribe. About, *...the Rogue CIA would like to help you as you succumb to your insanity. The Rogue CIA has been making the world a better place through adjustments to the timeline, from JFK and MLK to... Will you wake from this all with your legs kicking out from under you as you holler for the nurses to leave you in your filth...?*

Mr. Cole. We cannot leave you like this. I am sorry, but proper hygiene is not optional.

Pair of bruisers contained a man by the shoulders as he come to of writhe against the flooring's tile and to squeal at the lady nurse account of she yanking off man's underclothes soiled with his own night dirt. Kick and bray at they restraints while all the while they are press they pills upon fellow's lips and hush in his ears about oh but Mr. Cole you need to calm yourself Mr. Cole please calm yourself. Scoot about like person tried to drag a boat back and forth in the mud—and—all the while—flourescent above tap out its morse code flicker upon the scene—and down some hallways from here the ECT room been calling—as Nurse Quiana continues on with her soothing reprobation and glanced down with an affection as the wet wigglies gone and got shot up the o between a fellow's buttocks as he continues to squeal his pig squeal and writhe—as—still—in the crevices of the imagining been other sights—littered the grouting and crawled upon the brow and lapels of these my handlers like as dayglo renditions drawn upon the articles of sense.

As. Two bruisers currently wrestling with they charge—are as chuckled in manner reminiscent of certain gangsters in certain cabins on the outskirts of Pittsburgh. As. Underside just now as dried with sanitary napkins and new briefs and accompanying hospital drawers yanked up and over the knees and underutilized manhood. And—*You will be free to move about as you like when you show you are truly ready.* Nurse Quiana as makes her way toward what egress available while myself—about to been secured to the bed in fashion not unlike certain cabins in certain woods as well but without the welcome stream of gold junk and without occasional fist in mouth. Door's slammed shut behind of her and just as like I gone blind behind of the eyes.

We all are heard the fairytales and what bureaucracy lifeform it become. And this not the first time am had a run-in with examples of said bureaucracy lifeform but the convoluted nature of they interest in yours truly begun to truly irk a man as he is stood below "Church of Our Lady of the Angels" but with "fallen" sprayed between the "the" and the "angels" in honor of church's more recent nomenclature. And sky begun to of turn a more contemplative hue with the end of the day.

But let's step back. To some hours previous and Destiny as just pulled her covering off to of reveal more'n just the archipelago of pink spotting eye and surrounding cheek but a growth—as been come from off of backend of the skull— and face turned inflammation of impossible luster. And for moment's like as these many parishioners gone and done a forward nod in kind of fetor of dumbness at her approach. As in. Mob paused in its orgy of hope as woman is plucked out what iridescent fungus inserted in the neck.

And man in question? As in otaku? As in me?

Gone for leather trench strewn upon nearby pewback to of commandeered it in a flourish and throw it over the monk's robes with a delicious leisure before having hobbled back toward side doorway to spend remainder of the afternoon weapons out and ready for any and all.

You filled their dreams with a little bit of heaven. Destiny.

Couple parishioners hazarded an approach with the eagerness of a pussy hound but only up to nave's perimeter. As sands were slid they veil about this refuge for sleeping and the sick.

In LAC you are the new narcotic. Willow.

And all the while sound of hissing accompanied by they frantic mumblings as reverberate about our threesome—of what wonderment Allah been as brought them in his benevolence and what cruelty to of been so near to satiation only to as have it ripped from your literal mind. And somewhere in there once again call to prayer ring out upon downtown LAC.

Then once again just the hissing of sand and mumblings of the congregation held in place by our superior weaponry.

To have the taste of salvation so close and unavailable must be killing them. Destiny.

Till finally—at tail end of an afternoon—hissing gone dead. And myself and my handlers immediate as crossed the tent-encrusted courtyard—with only most tentative of swarms as pressed through the church entrance—past tents tagged in sign and symbol of what crew or clan as occupied them. And pink plants still as swayed in blatant displays of autoeroticism.

Swiveled my way down an alley between two overgrown buildings, assisted down what stairs there been, and out under aforementioned vandalized sign. And are off once again.

And toes begun in with they tickling at many proddings of this gentler warmth blacktop exude—and toward a M wrapped in tiled walling and what miniature dune's leaned against it. Swivel, step, swivel, step. Then up onto the curbside and—corner of they head coverings tipped askew and backed by graffiti'd wall with puncture wound what leak papers and other refuse.

Myself. *Deserve a briefing as to particulars of the situation.*

Mouth of M. Famed subterranean denuded to more virgin edifice and ruined escalators turned tongues of sand. Cratered out public building beside and in further distance LAC's famed clustering of artificial mountains ascend high enough to of rend heaven's mantle with they leering tips. Black things what dominate this scenery and draped in a ridging of clouds hung tight to they surface in clumps account of beyond these cones' tropical confines is been all desert all the time. Rest of ruined city not but crumblings about they base with line of blue as irradiates the horizon.

Willow. *We're on our way to meet up with the Navajo.*

As three of us're trotted down said tongues in silence. Toward bottom of which, Destiny's experienced a susurration of the face such that her covering is jostle against the adjustment of what tumors reside below and accompanying grunt. And her reached for handrail to of steady herself.

Destiny. *Question you should be asking's why g3 makes it so easy. Meteorological developments aside, where are her various GMO thingamajigs and blimp patrols? Usually, they'd be out and being a general nuisance to the human population in their efforts to retrieve you.*

Clattering of leathers and slapping of bare gray toes through black marred by occasional glowing receptacle. And—*Tunnel at the far end.* Willow. Past and down length of underground throughway could've landed an aircraft in if that's what creams your cock and—one wincing step at time upon shattered tile and accompanying intricate ceramic mosaic turned shrine of broken gadgetry illuminated by said glowing receptacles. Stop at another enclosure, this time concrete.

At its bottom run something from out fantasy of g3—antiquated subway fingered in chitinous roughage and veined in bioluminescent lichen. Frame wide enough for quartet of persons to of sit and—been a kind of nylon skin replaced the partial jammed sliding door of original subway and—interior the metalwork of yesteryear, decked in an approximation of jagged carpeting and molded seats consist of antique plastics and the whole of it lit in general halo of iridescence.

Already course forward. <*Next stop, Chinatown.*> In feminine tones. <*Please be advised this train will cease to serve Los Angeles post-liftoff and make the necessary arrangements.*>

Me and Troy'd most part staked out houses near the train tracks're an easy slip through the fence by way of an escape what with trees shielding our movements. Us what played roulette and jumped in laughter—*Do it again. Do it again*—or Troy perched upon building's edge to of thrown his voice out into the damp night as he is kicked his feet—of city become shouting crowds and the faint rush of chaos—or a painted lady at every door what grasp for kid's lapels in passing—*Want some fuck, kid*—maybe even rope in some twerp with a snarl of they made-up lips. And much later. Multitude set up in camped embankments and Sheffield sloshed through they tiny fires.

Door covering what flap about and original glass of windows strung in rivulets of growth as tunnel a slithering dark been as whipped past myself and two masked traveling companions. *You ever took a trip to the Pitt?* Stopped momentarily. *Not much but it's my home. Until. Less than twenty-four hours ago. Wake up in a tank on other side of the fucking country.* Start up again.

<*Next stop, Elysian Park.*> As it gone klack upon the rails.

Except for also memories of Troy as a plasm of snarling and matted hair what reconstituting back into base matter in a corner. Or of a bent hand as hold what's left while the legs fell down in some parody of everyday walking around jitters. *In a alien version of said country—and maybe got half a dick or worms for eyes, but point being I am born to discover myself g3's plaything. In situations such as these, package is proffered up some very basic "what the fuck's happening here" style debriefing. Do you not agree?* Once again come to a halt.

And are stood and slid through and out to hampering of space as punctuated by single square of luminescence peopled in men focused round a table. Whipping of a subterranean wind.

Hobbled through and toward other side of this stifled atmosphere and what been a clatter of cheers from card game of vagabonds at its far end. Heads of these ladies just shadows of sack scooted along through the reverberations of the also blacked-out station. *This question gone to be satisfied by day's end if you cherish our cooperation.* Destiny's head covering occasional shift like as bits underneath realigning themselves in they irritation or as just gone to sleep on her.

Then. Halfway down aforementioned concourse stumble upon naked child crouched, bent over, and in way of us. Outline of boy and its dinner of raw rat set against glow of room at far end and they card game and table lamps. Its thousand pinhole black eyes blink they buttons of black, its mouth rimmed in gore, and smacking its grinning lips there upon mosaics of the otherwise black. Again, single shot between the many eyes and thing is crumpled to the floor.

Fucking spiders. Destiny. In a voice edging towards hysterical.

Moment later a chorus of scritchings heard behind of us. *Run.* Willow this time.

Only glance back once and at spider youths come as poured from out vacancy with they mouths open in a kind of silent screaming to of clambered after the murderers in they eagerness for to dismantle anything living. And are shot past the card game what continue on unabated. Are halfway up escalators reach several stories towards the sun before here Willow is turn and with her own firearm shoot into the crowd, and all the little kiddies gone pitter patter back into they dark, one of them at a hobble. Can't help but think this g3's interpretation of the male mind.

And as we are continue on up the escalator steps. *What's red and white and dead all over*, Willow is announced with a chuckle. *Battle of East Saint Louis*. And a loud guffaw.

Fucking spiders. Destiny again.

And handguns remain out at escalator's summit as three of us're stepped into tiled foyer with its decorative patterns sprayed in bright tags upon tags. Pair of mechanical eyeballs misplaced upon square tile's most part sand and beside semi-circle of rosy light. And backdrop's a sky turned orange red and daubed in its many intricacies of cloud and setting sun sat hid behind one such cloud and above the ridgeline—dirt with occasional stump of palm tree jut from out it and at top of one, been an indigene on a spotted roan. As in, adorned in jeans and cowboy hat with the long braids sat down front of his also denim button down and thin-barreled intricacy of a weapon stood up long left side of the chest. While birds not much more than specs traverse the middle distance.

They don't get bears in LAC? My first comment.

Navajo did not join the First Nations. They do not share the same trading rights as their brethren to the North. From out Destiny. Her partner's scratched the gut in a playfulness.

And Navajo shout down, *Yá'át'ééh*.

Willow. Under her breath. *Like to speak they own dialect of Indian. Think it's cute.*

Then a popping sound and sack seep in the forehead region and Willow clumped upon the ground. Destiny get off single shot before same been true of her. Man on roan's come halfway to spitting distance when his snipers pop up from they hiding places upon the ridge.

You resentful you didn't get bears? Said as man trot in my direction through the dust.

Navajo grins down at yours truly and tapped his cowboy hat with nozzle of his rifle. And with a flick, rifle's flipped down with sound as like the ringing of a pipe. Eyes gone from dart in the thigh to man on a horse. *I told her I do not make deals with the White Man.* Last thing him having said before lights out upon this indigene cowboy and what sunsets he draped in.

7.

How many times I got to convey? As what slitherings of the mind are come unto view? And dark come as is? With its dirt in the eyes and husk slid open—and—maybe you under the impression I been spending my time hung suspended in an aquarium up until my incongruous escape but actual fact of the matter is been—I got a whole other life before this one and in it's no gray monstrosity.

More a city turned on itself and people toppled. The incongruous aftermath and sounds come as tinkle in the bath as a gurgling of the strangled understudy—squelched by wave of bedclothes for example. City what struggled to keep on with its keeping on at the tail end of history. And me with kid what am not wanted and mother of which what's not wanted me. Pair of friends—one a betrayer who eventual had his face doused in acid by a lackey of mine and my other friend skinned alive. A city fallen and myself more than partial responsible for said fact.

But back at the beginning of it all there been the missing brother and now I herein gone and discovered myself member of an octuplet of identical siblings. Except for some more identical than others. Point being, no younger brother. As—at one and same time—am a guy swoon through his narcotic-induced fever dreams in cabin outside of Pittsburgh and at what informations been unloaded upon him as he continues to stare at the incongruous elements—various tropicalia and occasional rumble of waves dove head first upon nonexistent sands—while also—a guy konked out and dreaming of the Pittsburgh of his younger days—and a spirit walking.

I am become all these things.

As witnessed by the madman in his rememberings.

While secured to a bed.

But is the spirit come to been in vicinity of g3 become more as like a coloring upon its branches than as a woman. *"Who is more unjust than he who forges against Allah a lie?" The human places too great an emphasis on the appearance of things. It is what makes them such a gullible species. Humans are always seeing the mothol mo'allaqa, never the thing in itself, but you do not have this excuse, for you are not human.*

Wonder if my waking imaginings somehow as affected what history I been writ with back in the slumberland of Pittsburgh from before. Down what streets and byways of Pittsburgh back inside a summer now gone—a halo skittered into the void—and on and back—to the Pittsburgh of my kidhood and me and Troy having run our little selves through junkyards and spat our obscenities in face of Corothers' underlings. Kids got to've got they kicks somehow, although word has it, these kicks of Troy's been what as is got him killed.

Least according to Mel and Rob during our little interview.

Which interview having occurred not long after said friend been skinned alive—as in, at a later time in the same blood-dappled evening—and before I's escorted to a cabin in the woods where I am then as spent a very unpleasant weekend.

Although, even so—still as hunted through watercolors of man's past—daubed dark as they been—and peopled by people never been people in the first place.

Been somewhat like as if person witnessed they friends and relatives turned sand storms of themselves. Like as they shadows flick about at the sleeve. With appearance as used swimming trunks or yesterday's roughage. As in—wilted in appearance as they are sat draped across what furnitures been available. Or stood out as a kind of a bright-lit apparition.

Such as for example those clowns.

Never forget those clowns first time I been as witnessed the new narcotic in all its margarine glory sat in baggies of powder upon round little table out back Pork N Fun and pair of clowns huddled round said table. To hand off baggies ever so often to some scab-covered tyke come as run up to them from past the razor wire garnishing of community gardens. Clowns—with they runny white face paint and lemonade hue to they teeth—been as mentioned canisters in LAC to a fellow back then and fellow is took it as just they manner of having spoke but now these words taken new and more elaborate meanings and man got to wonder whether clown in alternate reality housing of the Pitt could also be Navajo. Or sack-clad Rogue CIA. Or a deformed parishioner clocked where he sat upon pew in his house of worship.

And Troy turned puzzle piece missing its puzzle. As in, begun to of wonder also whether his disappearance more due to alternate reality g3 than Mel and that maybe there never was been a Troy. Is possible what that these memories just place names for commands and code.

Eyes are flick open—particular otaku mirror as am been—
to broad rills and rolls of naked buttocks framed by doorway
as are rocked about—and bald head above's bent toward the
gilt-framed mirror adorned in its vanity lights. The thighs—
as glisten with sweat—display a disquieting agitation.

Myself strewn upon bed's floral coverlet in adjoining
room and under obnoxious overhead and—fat man's turned.
Make no effort to of cover his dripping self as his baby blues
twinkled with a dangerous iridescence. *Welcome to the Rez.*
Like he an advertisement of all Rez have to offer when this a
white whale of a man is ambled toward yours truly, his tiny
penis jiggle on its bedding of scrotum.

Am sat up. *Do me a huge favor and cover your prick.*

Flatscreen exhibits squares of green digital feedback blot
out sections of the dance troupe—in they same conical hats
as what seen on various *tays* this day—except for what they
done's not any kind or type of dancing. What they done's
make the room dance without the smallest hoist of they fingers. The cheap props evolve before the eyes in they aluminum and acrylic fiber.

You watching this? Am queried.

And—as man's stepped into pair of sweats from off of
the small plastic chair they been draped across—and with
a clumsiness of toe upon what off-white wall-to-wall there
been—*Course, I see nothing, as is the norm here, otaku. If you were
of this place you'd know, we do not see until we put on our eyes. I only
know you because of how the parasite is seeing you for me.*

Yours truly. *Why they put me in here with you, pervert?*

Is when he's blinked and his blue eyes are turned red.

Smile as these new reds of his are swum about on the
rosacea of the cheeks. *I am here because of my perversion, it's*

true, but you... Got what look to be piece of star in plastic crystal hung upon his hairy roadblock of a chest. Single drop of sweat stalactite at the nose's tip.

Walls of bathroom behind papered in pictures cut from the magazines of yesteryear what been weathered and stained in blots. And bathroom counter's piled in beauty products—gold-capped bottles and they orange-hued liquids, winding disposable sporeware, and variety of brushes.

This is a holding cell in the Orsini III section, and you happen to find me in it. Orsini's all that remains of the Navajo nation and within these walls, it's their laws, man, we're just living it.

Sudden intake of breath like as he just seen something remarkable while still stared at some point above a fellow's head with his new irises and still clothed in not but sweats. *Ever been to the Pitt?* Guy is prime suspect for the junk-peddling clowns of my imagining.

And him. *That you? You're the Pitt? Woah. Wow. Geez.*

Then's sat down. Too much for an obese man to handle. *You been there?*

Yeah, I been there. Alternate universe Pittsburgh just before the cannibalist massacre. Yeah. I have been there. Many times. It's a ride man. A real rush to be in Pittsburgh just before everyone gets eaten. Man is talking about my hometown in tones I do not appreciate.

Any idea when said massacre's to of took place?

And like that Mr. Conversationalist just got quiet. Like as he just remembered of a sudden about how inappropriate it is to mention the future cannibalization of a man's kin. Red eyes slid side to side. *Yeah. I'm not so sure.* His eyes a caricature of scheming.

Then am hopped up onto my perfect gray toes upon the carpeting and—man's mouth burst into a sleepy grin as he come to of stare off into far corner of the ceiling to let out an accompanying yelp before he is then said, *So sorry, mistress. Yes, mistress. Of course, my treasure.* Then squish up his fat face in a kind of put-on of discomfort and then as slumped back.

While am all the while stood an arm's breadth away.

Only to of deflate back into the room when he is said, *Everyone comes for the Spider Club. Its name is from the Colonists' name for g3, the Spider God. It's two floors down, by the pool. Couple floors more and you get to the parking garage and the roan, but you're not going anywhere.* Then his unwieldy head become squinted in a violent frown as he gestures toward the door. *They're just sitting out there itching to perform some indelicacy upon whatever white face they can find, the fucks. The Navajo control all the territory from Echo to Elysian Park and most of what's surrounding. But a day is coming. The object's influence continues to spread.* As he strokes his plastic-encased star with some compulsion, to then of slid back into whatever imaginings occupied his time. *Yes, of course you can cut my hand off if you want, my sweet. I am happy to serve you however you like, my darling.* With arm held up in front of him, followed by a rattling of the wrist and sounds person makes in the bathroom—only to again've snapped back with a literal snap of the neck. *To sum up, Reservation's an oasis of lawlessness where everything's legal.* And a huge grin. *Not to be confused with the lawlessness outside.* His grin is seem to of sickened upon the face. *Or maybe better said is Reservation's the last vestige of civilization left in LAC, full up with the parties and bling of old LA. You got to pay the indigenes to play, and Navajo's the official language here, but everyone speaks English.* Squinty frown's come back but now it just looks he having trouble thinking. *I mean, they still got their own law, but there's a different law for white folks round here. How was I supposed to know that I've just now broken some indecency statute by exposing myself like that?* Like this a point of pride. *My eyes were not in my head at the time!* Pause as he explores his teeth with pink triangle of tongue. *And big news round these parts' that soon the hive going to lift itself into the sky and make tracks for some other star system. And thank goodness for that. Her and her San Francisco ways.* Look down at spot on the carpet with a keen interest. A goofy half-grin. *Am I gonna get some cootchy or what?* Heavy breathing.

And on and on this one-sided conversation is continued for a good hour from that point while am stared at the beads of sweat form in the stubble of his most part bald head while he is occasional reached down to of squeeze himself through his sweats as he gone through what is appeared to been as like cross between cluster of mini seizures and the most pathetic string of whimpering ecstasies. And said unpleasantness's only ending when door been as flung wide to pair as got on same type and kind of cowboy gear as they friend from earlier.

One said, *Yá'át'ééh, shicheii.*

Other one go, *Gólízhii hash wolyé?*

And first one go, *Gólízhii.*

And both been as burst out into an easy-going laughter.

Otaku, you have got a visitor. Then—to the fatty. *And you—bilagáana—can wait outside.* As fat man already pushed through them with his arms squeezed in front of him as if terrified what might happen if he were to of graze the dimestore pearl snaps of they button-downs.

From out the other room, another squeal—and them glanced back with a chuckle.

Then. To me again. *Hagoónee'.*

Other one. *Be seeing you.*

And there in the doorway's another me, except for this one got a litter of worms for eyes. *Time we had a little talk, just me, myself, and I.* While carrying the tiniest of leather suitcases and dressed in something like the tight summer suits of last year's fashion.

Ever thought of killing yourself?

Have you ever thought about killing yourself?

Poured from out pair of feminine lips while yours truly watch back like as hunter brought low by a truly cringe-worthy prey—what been sussed out and glowed up. Or as enemy untoothed. Man's ragged nails hung lifeless upon the knees as she all the while gauged the heft and coloring of the silence from under stained glass of the hanging lamp color her shelves in cathedral hues and what requisite tomes people it.

Could you explain to me about your relationship with Terrance?

And am stood—barefoot and emaciated from my many long retreats to the catatonia accompany my reveries of past exploits—and am strolled to the window like as person just thought they might like to of take in some afternoon air. Is a black butterfly flit about upon a twig reach from its bedding of branch and into square of space framed out by said window. But am not spoke account of's been as like a rug burn of torque what being wrung upon the audacity of the meat.

This is not Nurse Quiana as sat behind of me.

Your wife—or—I'm sorry—the mother of your child came here to visit with you recently. Would you... Care to talk about that? Glance back as am took another tentative step upon the carpeting. As person traverse an abyss while at same time like as a white lightning binding your entirety from inside on out. *She is very eager for you to return to us, Jackson. She has spoken with me about it on many occasions. And your daughter is growing. When was the last time you held your infant daughter?* Look down and at—brown skin and square cut of aforementioned ragged nails.

Been man seen the walls come crumble down as they cries as echoed throughout the street. Seen flames of burning Pittsburgh as reflects in mirrors of glass shattered about the blacktop—a Pittsburgh what in process of having acquiesced to Christians. Been the one come running and the one run down—beat into shadows like as someone wants to burrow a hole through a person's skull. While all the while like as a tight cincturing of string squeezed out what my thoughts's become. More real than the table where you sit to dinner. As am stared and at discolored teeth through the damp burgundy of her done-up and wrinkle-marred lips.

They say that you speak of a reckoning to come at Shiprock? Do you? Have intimate knowledge of some conspiracy? Would you… Care to talk with me about it?

The long wrinkles like nicks round the lips. And one or two cross bridge of her granny button nose. While she is gazed at her charge with what seems the most open-hearted smile now.

Is when am look down at my hands again.

Except for this time, they gray not brown.

Me. *We going back into our aquariums now?*

Other me. *You know this is not how it's gone go.*

Me. *So? What? Why you here, brother? And what winding roads I been set upon?*

Other me. *All white men considered equal in Navajo eyes, as in equal guilt ascribed to all, and whether you the Rogue CIA or the Christian Coalition, you still the sons and daughters of the first murderers, whereas g3 been like a reckoning upon the white race, even if they are also Anaye or Spider Grandmother. They go by many names, all of them false, but they are come and with their first breath, they seen what horrors the Christians have performed, and they made their choice, to be born woman, to be born Muslim, to be friend and mother to the downtrodden.*

Me. *She really got to you.*

Other me. *I have seen the many hypotheticals what are to come, brother, but more than this, I've seen inside of all of them, and what they are. I know their hearts.*

Me. *You don't think it a bit weird to have a governing body can read the hearts of men?*

Other me. *Is what's needed.*

And what's up with all the spider kiddies? And for a moment, half-assed me on the run from his creator is smiled back at this illocal brother is also been me smiling, but this been a smile full of broken glass. And worms in the sockets not helping. *You really need to work on that smile.*

Other me. *They say time is like a ball of yarn, and in among the winding roads of Vietnam and its Digital Hanoi, the final human settlement will look up and it will see itself in the leaves of the constellations, but now you see nothing of yourselves, and soon you will see nothing at all.*

While other version—as in me what on the run—with the vertical scar can only guess's a botched attempt at a lobotomy. And from out the lobotomite comes this rebut. *You think you know the face of God? You under some illusion as to your place in heaven, mirror?* Then lobotomite's stood—and glanced toward window—and what floodlight been as run through its slats—light what been thicker to the one side account of slat's missing near far left—and outside's sort of scattershot melodies're all the rage these days—rapid fire schizophrenic beats underscore siren whine. *And most important, what secret mission she given you, brother, that not even rest of us your better selves allowed to know of it?*

While—as am turned toward those long strips slathered in they hues of amber and hung suspended before the windowpanes—am simultaneous as stared at back of my brother's head and what I seen is been kind of a disappointment. Said brother's head's as a shadow stream illumination is like a brilliance turned unto itself—like as a light unbound to of play with its cousins—light gone hush in corners and light what got no qualms about having hid its face inside blacked-out shadows and in rooms of no imagining. Except for that also— what branchings of flame there been are as poured out in the most mundane of crosshatchings. Nothing as like intricacies of g3. With her forests of illumination contain ever more intricate dollhouse threadings spun into they own dioramas within dioramas of light sleeved in light sleeved in light.

Even as at this moment am heard g3's lilting tones. *My tašākus. My maqarr. My karūbīm.*

Are parts of a Spirit not known even to itself. What is unknown to you is unknown to me, although it is there nonetheless. And am turned back to of face myself and we two otaku as look one from the other and other to the one. From dull glow of some serious lackluster sockets to the threading tendrils quiver below they uneven drapery of lids.

And I gone, *Care to dance?*

My response. *For all that you live through, you say, truly, fuck the world?*

Tiny suitcase gone on coverlet and clicks open to reveal two syringes. One pink with its fleshy coral grown out business end. Other a milky yellow. *Pink one's what come out of you in a church back there. Yellow one about to go in your eyes.* Also like explaining 2 plus 2 is 4.

Am not putting that in my eye.

It is what they request of us.

Is when my limbs come to been puppeteered by brother spirit and am watched as this other me "in the second person" is mimed more-first-person-me to of bend over and lift syringe what weeping its brilliant yellow. Held up like it an eye dropper is done a dainty prick of the outer layer of eyeball and slid into the paralyzed egg of the eye to of fertilized its interior through the drooling puncture. Then other eyeball.

It's so the optic nerve can be accessed directly.

While all the while. Not stop screaming entire time.

As if invisible restraints at the shoulder while having stared back at what is indeed been a mirror of the man albeit with maggots for eyes. *g3 have certain things they must keep from themselves as well. They are after all a plurality of persons even when they are also the singularity among us.* Both of us what with identical upraised fists but one with a play pretend syringe and the other with the actual article. *This transaction was kept secret from the larger polity of g3, and now, brother, I am afraid it is time to escape again.* One got spreading pools of yellow in our otherwise normal eyes and the other one—*The chimera is waiting.*

The Kaaba can be mass-produced, Spirit. Shrines should be more common than plastic spoons. Or—There are even mechanical organisms who live their whole lives inside our gruel sacs. There is no one type or kind of life. Or—And do you understand the profound symbolism of the Mi'raj? Or—Did you know your mother, otaku? Was she of us?

These are conversations not yet take place but I am remember them.

As. Myself and brother mine seen through our collective eyes—and the now yellowed eyes of the one gone reasonable amicable. With hands remained by the side, while—not just the alien lumen—what of here, there, and everywhere—shimmering colloquialism of the senses—and like as tangle of shooting star become bowled inside the skull—a winding what's got no clear center but—is the winding itself give cohesion—is all not but threads round threads been as the ticklings of the shadow brain—room what could adhere to person's lobes and of click onto accompanying stem—while all the while am stared off and toward the slat-obscured window.

Then spirit's announced. *Before beginning transition to next link in the chain of custody, please keep in mind, these emissaries of the hive are unfamiliar with the situation as it stands.*

Other me. *Which is what exactly?* Still not turned.

Such that the crack in the vase come as threaded back into the smoothness of its porcelain, and the egg come as returned to the warm confines of the womb. So it is with all things. And when am spoke, words also been as writ upon the more rudimentary workings of the half-assed brother I also am—with both our shudderings of persons stuck in they stutter of an instant what loop its finger round in a tick-tock of muscular spasms. *But this magic only accomplished by your escape.*

The half-assed what now got fingers twine in a haze of fingers. Fingers moved at velocities approaching light and heard words never been spoke. *And situation as it stands acceptable to you?*

And me. *She angling her vehicles above the building at this very moment.*

And me. *You familiar is an Armageddon coming to Pittsburgh?*

And me. *The Pitt is not home to you.*

And me. *Only home what I got.*

And am still sat across from Mel and Rob. And Rob as shook his head when he as announced, *You the penance Colby Sheffield come to deserve, but now you got to pay your penance too.* And again stripped to his wife beater and again is chuckled. And Mel a half-step behind.

Mel's looked at Rob. *He still looking like he not looking.*

And Rob. *He supposed to look like that. Is the drug, you orc.*

From out shadows of the forest—sound like as birds are been known to make in they distress—in they retreat upon the evening—a call sound as razor write trilling. Radiator click on.

And two of them've stood. With hands on they pleats and something as like a finality to they grunts. Then back to the counter and what bottles of amber as await them.

While me? Like as person rooted in they own feces. But is this incontinence in any way related to other examples of incontinence from out the sanitariums of the future?

How much longer we got to dope him?

Then this sound again and—though is true my head not as moved, been like as the framing of sight become object of its own—like as viewer got to of take in they mechanism of viewing to fully appreciate scenery as painted upon ball of the eye—and what things are lurked just at periphery of a man's sight. What threadings of saliva-clad glare been as tongued at a man's imaginings and the exposed log beams make up this cabin been my primary vista.

While sat upon springbound thinness of the bed and— Rob. *I got better things to do than babysit this asshole.* Mel's shoes creaked upon partial torn-up linoleum of the kitchenette.

Then. Rob again. In a sing-song voice. *Okay, dear heart. Time for your medicine.*

Then squealing sound from just below the nose as hands been pried at hands. And world gone heavy with application of blunt force against the skull. And man's bared arm got a cold prick in the crook of it. And already rolled sideways with a mutter of sorts.

That should do it.

Even as am writhed with some delicacy, person as in many places and times—who done deeds they never done— and performed what tasks been gave up for they consideration even when such tasks never's as offered up—while also general speaking everyday citizen of the spats and porkpie hat variety. While *also* been as every citizen all at one and the exact same—sat in on all they martini lunches—donned they nail varnish or stared down at weapon as proffered up in its sheathing of brown paper bag. And stunned into a kind of a disgust at what happenings transpire.

Eyes start to've hunted they way back and on and into the workings of the skull. Eyes as burrow backward while person come to of pick at they scabs in what all holes found in the dark—and said same words over and again—about—*They come for him. They had to've came for him.*

With sloshing cups of rye raised in amber above the unkempt brow.

As the lumber from which this cabin turned as wild in itself. Contours of its log framing no longer as strictly Euclidean. Fingers as reach through layout of timber and accompanying throw rugs what as turned nonsensical in they aspect—such as cup as stretch from here to the counter. And single eyeball unwound into chambers of eye each got they own compartments of viscous humor. *I think he is having himself a time, Lord of my life, I do believe he do*—Mel—as—messiah risen within sights of the grifter—to of ascend through layers of the atmosphere and to where stars could what land themselves upon the tip of a dude's finger while he simultaneous partook of a little spark of nicotine as is stared up at what breathless reaches been as maintained above.

Returned to the unused musculature and—room slid back—and—once again stood across the bed from man's identical twin. Albeit with eyes still the squiggling worms of before.

She hides from herself. But free range upon the minds of her constituents.

Are operations need remain covert to of been effective.

She ever felt the need to hide her intentions before?

Even as these words spoke. Radiators of another universe gone on with they ticking. Different history of the gangster brought low. Of night full up with sorts of ecstasies you perform in alleys and backstairs—kneecap to tile, hands clasped hard and pants unbuckled. Of a kid rimmed in gore or middle-aged creeper gone jawless.

What begun with yours truly having fallen into same old patterns as my old man—who—story gone—lost his life in a colloquially under-examined boating accident—leaves the Moms with her glass in the air and fingers took to jangling. But hole's always there—as in old man and his propensities—and I been hooked upon it and lain unskinned in the alternate time-lines of LAC as infested with memories of them—all round about with they puppeteer faces what say clear as song—as crystal smashing—that—fuck you here I am. Was a time I risen like a broke stick to of make it to some other room—where a ashtray's waiting—and a seat—and a lady who's elongated—maybe old or maybe young—and smile the smile of people done at parties and said, *Welcome Mr. Cole to the rest of your life. Would you like that cash or check,* to then've voided a man's theoretical bowels from out the backend of the skull in this mothershitting dream inside a dream. Account of g3 even now hunt at periphery of a person's reveries.

While at the moment still am indeed got a bit of a limp as am stepped round the bottom lip of bed and approached myself. But as I done so—this other me's clipped the tiny suitcase shut and done a turn. And—in a kind of a daze of introspection, am stepped through door after the refracted skull of my brother otaku. And is been a small square table on other side of that door and two Navajo guards sat across from each other at it. And one gone, *Sitsiji' hózhǫ́,* as he drops his cards onto the tabletop and other makes long kissing sound through his teeth.

And between them could've sworn's Dempsey. As in. Famed card sharp of Pittsburgh welcome everywhere on account of the rolls he always carries on his person. And possible double agent now got same tube I seen on cops previous as run from nostril and loop over the one ear. *Jackson Cole,* all he is said. *You liking your little vacation in a cabin in the woods?*

Is also when Navajo guards both've looked up.

Where you taking your brother, Spirit?

He comes back to the hive, where I am already.

Indigenes're nodded while Dempsey done a two-fingered salute with brim of his hat.

Give me my eyes back!

From a couch in the corner behind of us. Fat man still as whimpers in his sweats when the door shut and're in long hall carpeted in pattern of shattered eyes framed in rectangles of green with tangle-haired spider lad as got to of perform his autopsy upon some kitten's guts in the corner and—*Chimera going to notice my new yellow eyes,* am said while admired the periwinkle design about the carpet's edging as're strolled past said spider is brawned his kill's blood-damped fur in the palm like he tempering some new piece of prodigy—and by the cuppings of wall sconce bled they gold across shimmery stripes of wallpapering colored off peach. As we are turn again and out and into a tiled area. Banister on left overlook third floor courtyard with pool party in progress, except for this a pool what been filled with not but designer cushions. Entire swimming pool of throws, shams, and general speaking whole family tree of decorative pillows.

Aforementioned floodlights sat long perimeter like as thin-trunked minimalist trees each topped with single gem of a high beam. And between pillows on the one side and lights on the other, they been as took to dance. As in bodies—native and other—painted and half-stripped to the waist. Shoulders what writhe in familiar motions—even when many got modified teeth as like tusks pour from out the face or the eyes as got an extra bump to them been like obsidian bulge out that one side when person's head flicked straight up and toward where pair of otaku're had they heart to heart by the iron wrought banister. And at far end of the pool been a holograph what twinkle its diaphanous blue and as portray woman in the evening gowns of yesteryear as she is sing some classic tune. *<Nobody knows the trouble I seen.>* Fringe pattern an organization of ripples round edges of this 3D rendering of singer.

And whatever eyes am caught sight of've got pupils burn a dull red when are glanced up and at. As in, they all got they eyes in now. And somewhere in the back of man's head's also been a kind of itching—as said man turning to his identical brother with an eagerness.

Me. *Your siblings will be shot into space without you.*

My response. *He going to notice the eyes.*

Me. *Jump. Now.*

As. Somewhere among these many peculiarities of place and what persons as reside inside them—all of whom as laid claim to the title Jackson Cole—is been the branchings of memory from which the name built. Of times been spooled about and man what sat in the midst of it all—to of stared back at Our Friend the Pig for example—as two of us're crowded below windowsill and she murmurs on about, *Warning shot's one way to ask for death.* Huddled below a blowed-apart window and only couple months before her skinned alive by the bigwigs of gangland while they squeal and chuckle over body bounce about inside of they medicinal bath up Shock Corridor way.

Course this a Pig is got a tumor for a face. A Pig with eyes been as peeped out from under rills and folds of excess flesh. A Pig is got a brilliant red sheen to her.

Or of Ash as held up some fragile piece of pottery as if she not about to smash it to bits against the flooring. Except for—even then—ting of beer can against beer can—the rattle of pills in a packet—her eyes also been as salamandric and unkempt. Like as thing loosed upon her face.

And then her little girl comes.

Little kid got a look and her old man cannot of quite escape this look. Even when am off in the kitchen for to glance through what printing proofs as been handed over and accompanying nudie pics. Man's stockinged feet propped up under the faulty electric and here daughter's eyes still are rolled about inside of Daddy's skull like as they been prised from out his daydreams.

She lives in a person but only her eyes. Eyes as pearled in the environs of mystic cogitations and untapped knowings—like as about an object as a folding upon itself—and a sly politician of dreams. Or like her eyes become bigger the longer you are stared at them. She got kinds of eyes man unable to've looked into without having ceased to be person name of Jackson Cole.

As am also out and twirling when I done so.

In the air and as turned upon the atmosphere.

But. Even as the body come to of twist upon its trajectory. Slid up with shoulder angled as sideways to then've begun to curl towards the pillows below. Even then am heard his voice murmured like as he whispering his words just left the unadulterated ear. And on about, *As your spirit, I am telling you, brother, out there is nothing good. You will forever be incomplete among them. You are only a piece of the otaku. You are not a person, and you can never move like them.*

As body twirls down and toward its target below, the leather trench turned loose and billowing about the otherwise monkish red as—am catch glimpse of the copters suspended as a shinier black against the night. And the silver airship nestled at center of them. And just past roof of this housing complex what is been wreathed in headless palm trees occasional caught in stark relief by derelict floodlight—they stalks like as fossilized in sand where they stuck from out gardens as line the balustrade and sat huddled by fountains and seeded in astroturf. *<Nobody but Jesus>* As my eyes peered upward sightless in they contemplation.

And am murmured, *She killed the steer.*

As the legs swung end over shoulder, my brother's words gone on like a litany of sins—*The steer had to die, but she can make a new steer. We can return to Pittsburgh.*

As the body hung spread-eagled face down some two stories above the pool. *But we will forget.* And stared at the length of man partway through the loop of his stride.

Yes. We will forget. As the feet angled downward.

I need to remember. As body's done its belly flop upon what bedding of cushions there been. *<Sometimes I'm almost to the ground.>* As a kind of puncture wound toward perimeter of they soft tiling. Arms now scrambled against velvet skins of pillows and legs kicked out and to the back like as a person just learning his swimming. *A holocaust is to come upon Pittsburgh.*

As the copters're continued with they whoop, whoop, whoop. *<Glory Hallelujah.>* As something flicked out and enwrapped itself round the hand.

There is no stopping this holocaust. It was always going to be.

Pulled upward and—peer into chimera's irises like as folds folded in on themselves as am clambered up onto the slate and turned to—they many pairs of red-pricked eyes loitered about the repurposed pool. *Children forget. It is our duty to remember regardless of what can be done.*

Run, says one through his turquoise tooth guard.

Run, say another in clip-on Aztec ear jewelry.

Run. Under sign. The Spider Club. And with ubiquitous nose tube.

As—simultaneous with this is heard—*Jackson you so funny Jackson—tell us another one, Jackson—tell us the time you gone hunting into the woods and woods come apart, Jackson. Tell us that one.* As. Nothing out there but kind of a twisting of insides turned back upon themselves.

<Oh nobody knows the trouble I've seen.>

8.

Bit in the lower right by some stray nugget.

And with it comes a splash of memory. Of water pooled up about a roof.

Got one hand pressed against frontage of the guts as am meandered across yet another footbridge. Covered overpass to street and—Tentacles out in front and down below not but the remnants of what LAC once been. For the most part just ink but one floodlight runs a line of brilliance long couple sun-bleached automobiles turned derelict upon streetlamp's operating theater and stopped mid-skitter and with shattered windshields and tatted up hood or wheel casing.

Sound of neighing from somewhere off to the rear. And above is whirs.

The itch of the pierced abdomen like as a throbbing upon person in they entirety. An agitation what been as engulf the senses in a kind of rage at—the pain itself, brother what pushed me to of run and his entourage and they ignorance of the realities of the situation, g3 and her put-on agenda, and what God as look down upon it all.

Door up ahead paned in a miracle of undamaged glass sheeting.

Through and past staircase to another less fortunate door-destroyed door and to railing overlook courtyard this time—walls of which lined in fluorescents flicker in an arrhythmia of stutters—and—stone walkway down its center draped in more alien pink. With yet another spider crouched upon its masonry. Thing's arms left limp and useless without some small thing to destroy.

Turn from balustrade to witness chimera hopped off to left of myself and gone as follow after. He like a pogo stick run through corridor upon corridor. Walls papered in same peach stripes smudged in what probably been same finger-prints. With same rectangles full of shattered eye design run long its floors. And wall sconces finger they dirty lights up the ceiling in a insubstantial spray of illumination.

Pain what is been as like it crawled up the eyes and nags at bowels of the cerebrum. What been as a pain work to push itself through and out. A pain is been simultaneous a hunger. A pain what breathe. A pain as hunt for its salves and balms upon the shadows of the skull with every thud of stepwork on and through the endless identical corridors of this indigenous housing complex.

Black adonis as towers his giant richly hued self over a tiny girlfriend with a dilapidated face. As in—top of her coifed head comes to just below his nipples. *Son of a biscuit.* Her eyes pinned to the passing fugitive as innards of said fugitive dribble down the one leg. Her by they apartment door, key in hand, and man what picking at his airtube like a scab and done and lope his head toward her.

And. Turned a corner to—the single corridor turned pro-liferation of corridors—a garden of baseboards and walls strung in they identical doors, of carpets and the man what traversing them—as in, composite mosaic of various possible steps and accompanying peach wallpapers—and turned like as man's puncture wound electrified and sung as it is thread through these many corridors—as in, each step am stepped with slightly different rhythm of limp—and with a pain what vibrates—a current as cinctured man's perforation—a vibration tuned distinct in each of these many corridors—such as like what cavities been burrowed through the belly come to of been plucked as a string what resonates with the melodies of heaven—its agonies and ecstacies—as am bounded upon carpets shattered into a multitude of divergent lives—every step as performed by chorus of Jackson Coles run they gamut.

As in—as am bounced forward am also spread into a kind of a vacancy of all possible Jacksons—each in wild different locales—with they peepers turned curious. Jackson Cole as turned one among they spider kiddos to of munch upon raw rat. Or—Jackson Cole become daemon upon the likes of Mel and Rob. Or—Jackson Cole with the ritual tats round the breast and neck and eye. And—all what Jackson Coles am been are run—through our cabins and subways and deserts—as throbbing of guts is continued to of sung out.

Popped from out marinade of amniotic fluid—stalk at its center ethereal white and cloche what as draped above—with its gills and folds—a translucent cap of thin-skinned mucilage come to of lifted its arms as somewhere between umbrella rising and arms uplifted in an ecstasy as—*Arif*—as—

GHaRaBa = to go away, depart, have an eye tumor

GHaRaB = to forsake one's country, to live abroad

GHuRB^{an} = the setting of a star; to be absent or remote

GHaRaB = to go West

A-GHRaB = to laugh immoderately; to run swiftly; to go far into the country

ISTa-GHRaB = to find a thing strange, extraordinary; also to laugh to excess

GHaRB = edge of a sword; tears; etc.

As man is sat naked in this soup to of stare out and into room peopled in pipe. While something called as *tajalli* is been as run through the skull—like as counting exercises with a mystical flare—and among obscured space as spread about the surrounding utilities closet of a birthing chamber—another scene comes to been painted—in which stars are played a part—and beyond this nothing—and this scenery a kind of a thing—not a thing in usual sense of the word—as in owning of dimensions and set at particular position—but more as like if a thing could of mimic contours of any space and's positioned wherever you look—something like as if a cup's on table's also on the counter also on the ceiling fan also under the flooring when am glanced over that way. Except's a setting of stars instead of a cup.

Congratulations on your first day of life, Jackson Cole.

Reach up and indeed am got the sippy cup skull.

Looked round with a kind of reprehensible glee as the legs been as jiggled and everywhere the put-on scene. But is a scene like as a homecoming account of myself and the parasite as got a familiarity beyond usual host and hosted variety. More as like if I found my tapeworm and decided to've got married to it. Something like as this—except for is a thing I done behind my own back—are eight otaku after all—eight otaku function as single sentience been as tied into most amusing of knots. Or like as if your younger brother one day decided to have make deal with the devil for reasons as beyond reasoning.

Ha. Ha. Ha. You too funny, Jackson.

Is when am notice the sound—grow from quiet tinkling to long-arm piercing noise—as—in the institutions of man's later days—potted plant sat in corner of this my pink and teal tiled home—what been more as gyration of possible plants than proper spider plant—a infinity of itself pour out and into room whistle in the disgusting silences of the abyss. Sat upon the brow and coiled through weavings of the fingers. A disentangling of the particulars of place occasional accompanied by weary coo from somewhere out beyond the walls. Or perfect screech.

Remember. Abandoned county hospital. Ironwork chairs sat on the balcony's untouched glassfront.

But's some time gone now and like as thing what happens to some other individual as never woke to of discover himself one among a litter of eight—as—man's tentacled associate out front and center while personally? Trench coat pressed up to hold the leaking guts but all same is been all red on red underneath—as in monk's garb stained fresh with man's fluids—as am hobbled after said accomplice. And all the while is a lightness of things what never were.

Recollections of dusty panes stacked against uneven brickwork and—*Stop hopping off like a damn bunny rabbit.* And only thing on interstate's a cadaver curled fetal several lanes over.

Thing's exploded head paint the road in single swerve of tire. Account of stretch of highway lit up like the main event from pursuant copters. And sounds as like a tidal wave come calling.

As—from up above. Stared down at my own gray-skinned self in wash of aforementioned limelight and skittered across abandoned interstate and its many type and kind of debris.

And what I seen roam out the head and twined upward from the bland flatness of the neuronal underpinning—as are tottered off with a comical determination—when is been more as like it starts with the future and works its way back, my dears—as threads of luminescence come as poured from out my brother's skull turned virulent as flame teeters high into atmospheres above—thread they way upward in an out-pouring come as near sentient tendrils of illumination spun through the webwork of the brain as a kind of a river poured from one dimension into another. And these skeins been as flick about what whirling the blades of the copter as perform—again, to spirit eyes, visible only as to they effects—as it secondary boosters angle it downward and toward my brother wrestle his way across an otherwise abandoned interstate.

As the winds are lacquered a man's face.

Road below's a vacuousness—in middle of which—this body of me myself gone and slid over the also unseen median. Chimera's looked back with tentacled arm become a violent writhing from under its covering or like as if an inflating and deflating of arm's occurred—tributaries of which as flick about in they appreciation—minuscule and also whipped at by winds become as a river while fleet of observers above follows upon the heels of this pair with groupie's attentiveness.

While all the while. As—chimera stot across several deserted lanes—from out the other body followed after at a more stuttering gait—body I am on occasion occupied—is come—a shattering of light—or like as curves and folds of radiance unwound into some supraluminal dimension. For light what comes and light as gone is been the same light—and—something between air turned shimmering curtain and an optical illusion such that I-10 peopled different—its absence hued in the colors of burning—is been a light's a key—and a fingering cause person's fingers come undone and begun to of multiply into all possible configurations upon the lap. And myself become as mesmerized by them.

The least among us come to life. Then over at officer strapped in beside and continued on with her diatribe of self-loathing—poor dear missed my brother's spinal column by a hand's breath—account of everything but the head fair game in world of medical miracles as owned and operated by one g3—and am turned to of stared at scribbling shadows make up this person's face—and—*You do not*—as—her head already been snap away before my hands're reached out—and pilot already twisting the steering column like a person veer into a skid—as—*paralyze my brother*—as the vehicle spun sideways in luxurious arc and turning tail rotor gone into side of copter to our left and open it like can opener slice open a can—*for your convenience*—as the now lifeless bodies of pilot and passenger are rock sideways as the billowing plume of flames come as poured through the compartment in pretty reds and orange I cannot see.

Was the absence of spotlight what cause a fellow to of glance up from the off-ramp and at comedy of eruptions. Whirlybird and eggbeater and they little romance of scrap and accompanying flame as are slid toward a landing—except somehow airship's slip untouched and out the way of this onslaught—metallic slug hung as teetering upon the currents as sky gone ballooned into red. And aforementioned carpet of twisted metal—tail booms, landing skids, cockpits, and rotors—come as poured out of it and upon what surfaces been available. In this case the unused interstate.

Gone been insect vision of man's million possible legs. As am performed short jog up remaining bit of off-ramp and—same clutch of artificial mountains risen as a marring of black upon the black of sky to the right—and same orange monstrosity of a church but now under siege of LAPD. All they noses threaded in tubing and in variety of headgear—from Mickey Mouse to more traditional peaked cap. *Burn the turdhole down.* From out they cruisers. Or chuckled in they accessorized uniforms what glitter in the crisscross illumination of they headlights.

Someone knocks a smoke from his pack. Someone else nods toward group at far end of the melee. And accompanying extravagance of siren tug at jagged shadows of wire and stick.

And—*What illegals make it out alive we cuff.*

And—*The new day starts now.*

And—*You silly shits.* And accompanying spray and play.

Slip through like as if pair of cocktail waitress done and skirt they way through rowdy party at the strip club. And hope not to of got pinched or otherwise manhandled. Except are indeed got pinched. *What about gray freak-a-doodle over here?* Dirty chuckles had all round.

Or good-natured grin to of get up close and personal on a person. Headlights throw long shadow across the tube-fretted nose. Ever-present red and blue and red and blue.

Hey. Cockhole. Half curled into a smile at potential hurt and other half turned bright from yet another incendiary. And crowd turned ready-to-go-head-to-head brawler fashion. Shout they insults. When splash of fire is caught they attention. Gone smear across a windshield and what hoods as accompany—and all these officers of the law as turned they attention upon churchside and its scrawny kid on his shelving of the Almighty—kid what been dressed in not but torn cloths and what seems is got a steady supply of said pineapples like nest of pins and needles and all the while laughed his many dirty laughs at officers below.

Hah. Ha, ha. You like that, pigs? Oink oink, pigs.

To then of slump forward in a sniper-assisted nap.

As myself as nudged out of they puddle of flashing lights and back toward same metro entrance from before and—as are got to escalator's lip, cruiser from back towards downtown sail round the turn except—grill bludgeoned upon concrete planter on the corner crush a V into front of the car in an accordion type of crinkling, which—car bounce sideways and person flop out the door like as they just that desperate to divorce themselves from they guts upon the sand.

And—*Back to Elysian Park*, am queried.

No. Other way.

And us took to having delved back down and in—to craters of shadow and the accompanying rabbit hole. And once again through a bit of LAC viscera lit a nauseating green by boxes hung in the overall dark. Blocks of green lighting as tangled upon one curved wall of mosaics and beyond—underground's blacker periphery sat as a clustering of shadows. And to same caricature of a glow-in-the-dark subway but like the man said this time took back the opposite way.

One or two station names announced and they ragged remains whizzed past in streaks of color and carnage—and—<Next stop, Jefferson>—as the illumination flish across person's features and chimera what got a tentacle plugged in slippery hole projectile is provided for his perusal of man's innards—<Please be advised this train line will cease to serve the Los Angeles community post-liftoff and make the necessary arrange-ments>—thing's limb what as frisking among the vitals as it reach all the way through to body's far side—as—am gasped my gasp and rolled the eyes about at some unnerving subcu-taneous tug in the soft luminescence provided—and—folds of his eyes like as blinkered from under the unmoved can-opy of the lid—<Next stop, Western>—and thoughts of Can-dyland and myself and the Pig and Telly all sat round with legs draped over tables and drinks spilt between our teeth as we are chuckled at lives what're never lived and relayed lives what been not but a cluttering of tongues. <Next stop, La Brea>—and gasp like as might occur at surprise ending as worm of tendril is slid its mottled gray flesh back through said hole just as our conveyance come to of slowed with an accompanying ka-chunk, ka-chunk, ka-chunk.

Of Ash in her perpetual rage—both the coquettish and killing kind—and forever search for something—although she never stopped to of think what it is she hunting for. Most part, for a way to of rewrite history—like as that her mother never indeed died and her father as never abandoned her and her man never proved untrue. Forever hunting for a way out of this broke down world.

And in these my recollections, she also not quite herself but turned such that she only part of a face—as in is just been the one eye and barest hint of a nose. *<Next stop, Palms.>*

Of kid brother gone missing and Moms up in her room unwilling to of touch any and all trays of food what left upon the carpeting outside from her door and her shouted for us to of please just gone away in what hoarse tones the deformed might of spout when become witness to they own reflection first time.

<Next stop, Bundy.> As the chimera redrawn a taut quintessence of skin across dime-sized opening at the front such that it now just a spot of bared and more virgin gray in among larger smear of red—as lines of light slid across in never-ending perforated line upon perforated line.

Memory of Troy as said, *I'm gonna go back. Can't keep me away. I'm gone go back.* Except for is come from out a face not but recursive programming.

As—*<Next stop, Santa Monica Pier.>*

Someone is as pulled emergency lever with accompanying jolt and lead nugget dropped upon blanket of the carpet and—slip through the flap, up, and over insect hide riddled in veins of lichen to section of tubing and as pull up rung by oil-flecked rung. Out and onto the streetside.

This far out's official been outside the wire and us as popped up and into a radiance is splayed across avenue—an ideality of lights as diorama laid flat upon its pavement—radiance what been as from no specific source but more a wash of phantasmagoric and lambent advertisements been as ecosystems of light what framed in the obscuring pitch of the destroyed urban environment as contain them. Maybe single honest-to-goodness streetlamp.

Just past what been line of stripped husks painted in the slight glimmerings rim this river of light—cube-shaped and lobotomized automotive—punctured, gored and sprouting pink frilly infestations from out a top-end transverse slit— and in the ambient glow beside is been shuttered windows of a ruined exterior now spray-painted in gold—something like a running script of Arabia adorned in its dots and other markings—and Face 2 Face above the door with final "e" a slaughtered wreck of itself and—through what been a web-work of destroyed *mashrabiya*—its diamonds and stars of interlacing slats also hacked at with some violence—such that—through gashes in the blonde matrix—are witnessed *Tây Việt* as sport intricate tattoos as are bow and flex upon laminar flow of they worktables and under dim lighting of they booths. Been such to of bend and twist in unnerving pretzels as are work muscle and fat as to appease the needs of some unseen society dom in her ritual piercings and sacred jewelry what normal is concealed beneath the cloth.

Why does g3 choose the date they do for the departure? Said rhetorical question borne from out depths of a guts-exploded alleyway and its puddle of unused oral suppositories. *g3 think they can jettison before the age of the parasite's come but the age of the parasite's already here.*

And left of said speaking dark—her gray features dancing with echos of illumination and situated upon a plastic crate— grandma of a *Tây Việt* is eyed a fellow with a quizzical arch of the brow even when these're eyes been clouded over a creamy white—what been as same features as witnessed upon the *Tây Việt* in the hive souk and same features as seen upon

Tây Việt loitered beside a cathedral in a sandstorm—*Tây Việt*
what as now hung limp and formless where she lay propped
against the tagged loading bay door. Adorned in traditional
palm leaf conical hat of her home country as is took an extra
meaning during they efforts against appropriation by the
Mainland—its government officials and prognostications
of fungal infection having led them to gone on hunt for new
domains of influence.

Three gray bristles of face hair upon the one corner of the
gran's chin and adorned in same red cloak as Tentacles—and
is currently—and with some sensuousness—pry her fingers
deep into the segmented blonde meat of a giant grub she got
gripped in the other fist as it twists about with an intellective
lethargy. Then say—her voice colored with the exact cadence
as voice just come from round the corner by her head—*Llegas*
tarde. Albeit in tones of real alarm.

Is when voice from the alley turns out to been another of
her blind twins's stepped into aforementioned artificial light
of the street and sitting one took to having stood. Her one
hand braced against hand of her sister. Knobs of her knuck-
les lost in the many interlacing folds of the other's identical
red robe—with its marigold-colored mandarin collar—as
other hand held up the half-ate worm what still writhe in her
grip and both arms been as shook with the effort. As the invasive qualia begun with they creeping in from the periphery of
a person's line of sight—one of these grannies's murmured,
Họ đang đến từ bến tàu rồi. Con hẻm là con đường tốt nhất
của bạn. And sister's lifted what looks like an arm's worth of
treated bamboo from beneath the covering of her cloak and
slid it into her aztec of a sidebag before as having limped
round corner and past dumpsters concealed in glittering

hillocks of refuse and what rodent populations as spill toward the tapping of our appendages upon they sacred waste.

Scrambled just behind chimera's half-human body and its flappings of maroon till—man's stopped just as we come upon place where it opens out a bit and as like a dark blossom inside the otherwise midnight hues of this back alley parking lot we are find ourselves in. But this a place what's got extra objects contained inside its objects. As in, each individual scrap as a plurality of itself in the eyes of the singularity and—for the moment—singularity and yours truly happen to of shared eyes.

Am stared at something like an oversized roly-poly husk— as highlights of coloration are run about the white plastic and rusted wiring due to various threadings and nuage of fractured illumination from various advertising environments in the vicinity. While also—sweat-damp and stock still—as—jolt of aroused pain and empty stare what accompany—of someone seen everything—from the million billion galaxy rivers of Laniakea to the spark of a single ganglia. And—old woman's eyes gone and slitted over they murky whites before having took another bite of the writhing worm as thing squeal from other end of its segmentation—and she tongue at the remnants of her teeth as she is stared off and into edging of the lights been like as cluster of blue come as couched her head in itself and blink past and into contours of the shadows what are as housed us—as luminal elements are but continued to of play about these furrows and characteristics of the face— as long curving threads of luminescence gone and vanished and us what left in the rot-splattered dark.

Our guide's probing cane click at the ground as she is step as—on and toward alley's other end—as're stepped left and

into a tunnel—as slicked in its tumescences and growths—
a pinkness what been as coiled itself upon the eyeball in a
cabin above Pittsburgh—proglottids as chirr at the passing
tourists. With—as jewel situated at its end—a blue thread its
electric brilliance long and about the many pinknesses, bared
wall, and silhouettes.

   Mi hermana se ha ido. ¡Con rapidez!

   Followed by a broke-winged gait—under "The Georgian," as
in, broad length of metalwork stopped partway long its descent
upon the walls of this enclosure and glassed a dull red—and
given second life as arbor—and also looped in threadings of
the ubiquitous fibrous pink sinew. And below it—some bit of
something what sports a self-manufacturing dress.

   Out into mindfuck of a street, its midnight contours
clothed in hints of Egyptian blue. Ventured over shapeless
something-or-other downed beside a unnerving length as
twist about upon the broke apart and ancient as shit sidewalk
like as the veined piping inside hive as done and—*Time for
another dose of the good stuff. Soon enough you'd do anything for
a shot of this*—Mel from somewhere in the murk of the inner
ear—and—center of the former street's been a place where
pavement as excavated for agricultural purposes only to then
of become a pond rimmed in deep green growth baked hard
by sun turned absentee with the night.

   And beyond. Barest suggestion of metal rigging extends
out and over the waves and toward—horizon ruffled in
electric blue act as nightlight round these parts. Ridgeline
of cloud-sized membranes skinned with barest outlines of
amber-hued tendril as lace they guts. And general speaking
fringe to said otherwise night.

Tentacles up in front and between myself and that rigging's a city of tents like as you might imagine a circus would of turn into if you crossed it with a cancer and a shantytown. Like if the Fairgrounds back home'd evolved into fully functional borough of canvas and streamers. And at far end of it—tower of intermodal shipping containers jerry-rigged to dizzying heights—least as jerry-rigged towers are concerned—and upon its side a billboard. "Flink, the Comically Disproportionate Anti-hero." Beneath monstrosity of a face.

And dense with persons in full-body rag and some as sported hazmat and the latest gadgetry what congeal as some unseen orifice—or decked out in elaborate tumors and growths such as LAC become famous for. Persons what been as wove in a mesmerism of manufactured daydreams through multi-colored shadows thrown from off what long banners of luminosity run partway. Or. Stood about as not more'n outlines against bright bodies of light as protrude up and toward the void above and its low-rise of blue gelatin fringe.

As. Vendor close to hand what sells something called as shelled bananas. Shaped like a banana but got a hard crustacean skin is orange green. Crack one open. ¡Plátanos de cangrejo! Plátanos de cangrejo! Same time as this. Hashishin flick over his shoulders like as an acrobatist.

Dog as play with hare is been different from dog play with another dog and in this moment—her head rubbery at the neck as she is soared over the conflagration of half-assed uncertainties and otherwise gone musculatures. And. As she done so—so is a kind of an impossibility of shoulders come as lurched upon inside of her toe's path.

Except for in this case, she the dog, and he the hare.

Sacrificial lamb in cock's clothing already is incurred his first bit of structural damage as am hobbled past—as—am distinct heard a crunch from somewhere behind of my head and—are careened through bodies and between and into flaps of canvas and what darkness reside within.

Fashion's identical red robes. Stood and perched upon old-style aluminum bleachers. And some what been different-shaped than how human bodies are as normal and everyday arrayed—least as to the contour of they monk's garb. All of which's contained inside one of these white big tops and—tenting of which is gave off ghostly blue sheen—and—ground as littered in bright chunks of chop and suey—and in center—one particular red-robed figure stood on short stack of pallets is drawn his red shawl up over his head such that his visage concealed as congregation's synchronized tantric ribbits and croaks just finishing they monotonous lullaby.

Los cinco ojos ven. Si no ves, tienes el poder de la vista original porque no se puede ver con los ojos. Hashishin saunter through a flap and are paused in our two-stepping. *El punto del agujero negro es la base de todas las cosas, una metamorfosis del espacio, sólida como una realidad indestructible que arderá, y luego el fuego también será incinerado.* Loitered near the mouth of aisle and between two bleachers. *Un plano de luz que se convierte en agua, que cae en cascada a medida que este sistema-mundo se dispersa y se vacía hasta quedar vacío incluso del vacío. Esta cognición prístina también se desmorona en formas y nombres.* The eddies of wrinkle and fold upon a scalp or as billow outward from a maroon-draped back—and am about to of turn to got glimpse of the also shawl-concealed face to my right when am noticed—hashishin step towards speaker upon his crate like a moth try to play coy with the lamp. *Un cubo de carne, como la luz que emerge en la oscuridad, como una transmutación alquímica en oro, como una medicina eficaz, el desarrollo de muchas vidas, no agotadas por el tiempo, surgiendo sin aumento ni disminución en todas sus diversas formas.* And upon his short stack said speaker's shawl flicks backward to of reveal head adorned in blue silk of his ornamental Mexican wrestling mask. With the nose protrudes from out a blue flap at the front and eyes and mouth accentuated in flames of red fabric. *Entonces la mente más allá de la mente, sin fundamento ni fundamento, ni masculina, ni femenina, ni neutra, ni carente de signos, ni clasificada en familias. El punto del agujero negro.*

Hashishin turn in man's direction with a lightning twitch—to of immediate as drown in a sea of Tibetan red—what perform their ballet upon body of hashishin in a chorus of acrobatics developed in they efforts to unseat they Chinese oppressors—red scarves and dresses flit and flutter about they appendages as face of the bandaged woman find itself under congregation's foot—as ourselves are tip-toed out from off bleachers to metalwork floor and through side flap—to light-dappled night of the rig—and to another tent.

Smell between celery and tar—and—pair nearest the door a rictus of cheek-hardened grins and on about the ruins of North LA and its many collapsed enclave of samurai bots—while they been as scooped they liquor from out plastic bowl sat between them with they thimbles of glass. And décor's offworld retro. Longhorn headgear of Europa. And clientele's as eyed our entourage as am stumbled past they fingers and nubs and they obscuring cloths and—all what skin been bared is been GMO gray and all eyes gentle and docile.

Jostled our way out and through and to large part deserted platform strung in a scalloping of bulbs are dull stones against they impossible blue backdrop—they reflections what dimple the pitch of surf below, its blacks hemmed in ultramarine and sands punctuated in the occasional roof.

And on toward enclave of shipping containers stacked in a disordered jenga and—leaned against the corrugated siding and below the sign of Flink, a tatted up ballerina of blonde-haired bruiser's observed our passage with a wanderlust. His pipework face works to separate from itself as he smiles his broken glass grin. A screech rom somewhere behind of us.

Then round other side of they corral of freight and—at end of the pier's a shack of corrugate roofing and weathered planks—last structure before the bay and what mammoths of neon blue as of accosted it. And above? Meager assortment of stars.

Ourselves as approach this shed. Caught a glimpse through the one window and at some ancient mainframe as guide's disappeared through the door. Followed by Tentacles and yours truly.

Half-ate meal on the desk from something like months or years previous and cluttered upon the various desktops—ancient machines of a professional gravity, they bowed and milky gray screens left as cataract what conceal not but gobbeldygook of wires and strewn about them a latter of papers and entire scene tinted red from projection of hologram—a threading of circulature hung upon the air and rotate in place as a diaphanous object streams back upon itself—and illustrate a growth as lived molecule-motion-like upon the hologram's folds—and—windows on far wall are not but industrial shutters and slats of same impossible blue crisscross any and all dust as filled in whatever's left—in terms of cords and generators and what have you.

Turn to of witness a head is a forest—of squiggling pink thread's also been cluster of stars now vanished in among the leaves of the cheeks what mottled a maggot white and more latte'd hue of face is got fist-sized obsidian black and vacant eyes and somewhere in there been the features of a gangster I once known. Except for this a thinner-faced version of said tough. And when this thing spoke is neither male nor female but like as a third as-of-yet unnamed sex. As—all the while, ever so often an eruption of fast-acting tumor only to then of as rapid subside as seeping stain upon the jaw. Or like as worms gone surfing across the waters of the cheek. And occasional made a noble but unsuccessful effort to of remain as still.

Leviticus. Thing's spoke in its cracked uneven voice.

And even though name's familiar. As in most famous member of gangland back Pittsburgh way. And even though I always suspected this personage of some notoriety to've been more than what he seems. That said personage would be found to own a head of such alien stamp what sing with the husky melodiousness of a jazz singer?

Chimera got his arm up inside the wall and among red-hued papers what strewn about the aforementioned desktop—a print-out of intestines and glowing clusters of microbiota contained therein. And thing calls itself as Leviticus is spoke. *One manner in which parasite work to thread existent groups together is first through the community of bacteria in the gut.* Quick sweep of the clothing but no other segments of body visible. *The parasite you may hear told of, who is you as this parasite also is me myself. As is Hayy ibn Yaqzan.* Nod in direction of the chimera. *g3 made us, and the Pitt becomes our haven.*

They want to seal us in there to be executed when the cannibalists come because the Pitt grown into its own little community of critters. Many born in g3's design room. We come awake, and now we aim to kill God. I know you in. You started it all.

Hayy ibn Yaqzan had bent over and begun to of turned large operating handwheel sat in center of the office floor—with fluid motions and us as gathered—and valve decompressed and hatch flipped up. Guide first to slide out of sight—and myself in after with a reach of the toe and—through and down into a hole illuminated electric blue.

A blue run along slick planks of iron sealed and riveted upon its iron posts and above man's head as he descend rung after slippery rung. Glanced down and at oblong shape as illuminated in the surf below—and the crescent slip of light towards its stern and accompanying spray of surf—then up and to hole above and the others paused in some argument just beyond. Over at horizon blare its brightness in a eerie bioluminescence—to the frothy violence of incoming surf below and its iron loaf—to again glanced up and to the hatch lit red by the shack's interior—just as—Hayy ibn Yaqzan is reached down through it—and—spatial annihilation device is gone and consumed the vista what hatch provide in brilliant shatterings of space. Stared up and at—Hayy ibn Yaqzan and the foldings of his many-parted eyes twisted about as a rhetoratician's tongue. And his mouth a perfect little o.

Hayy ibn Yaqzan turned a kind of patchwork—cross between clutter of systems missing its body and ripples of flesh as got no flesh part—a thing is not quite of occupied a space. And somewhere further back behind of him and what destruction been wrought—is Leviticus. While myself witness whatever puddles are been as left of his already charred face.

Stared up and into Nurse Karen's face from out the confines of my constraints—as she is currently explained to a fellow what that I never been looking for anything at all in the first place. And—how ECT works in the Christian states been as a kind of penance for the heretical of mind. And in my case, at the moment, eyeballs angled upwards from where am strapped as Nurse Karen gone on about how furthermore in point of fact she know best as she strokes the restrained head. And what I seen's only a fever and where am at's only as the dawn.

While all the while. The beauteous ECT is flowed—as a balm of pins and needles—a lacquering of the frontal lobe what lights up the eyes and the hands turned sparrows that erupt and then flee—into momentary flight among the solar winds of other universes—even as they still are rattled against they restraints. As the body is jiggled with some unpleasantness and teeth become clenched upon what props been set on them. As—the cabin they shot me full of junk in's still spun—and place where my wrists been tied's a place where the world been as tied to my wrists—and am at this same moment also a body mid-atrophy in a tank—and in among all these many backdrops of sense am seen my lost brother—loitered in a cabin beside my captors, stood just behind nurse in the ECT room, sat in a tank in a concrete room in the hive and across from his brother mirror—only he is not himself and I begun to cry he is not himself—and as am stared up into what ecstasies currently as taken possession of Nurse Karen's face.

Is like as we been having a little back and forth without ever having to of open the mouth. As in, myself gone, *Bring him back—I just want my brother back*—in my own very lit up darknesses of mind. And her as responded, *But what can you give me*—but as conveyed using only the slightest crinkle of a smile-dappled eye—to which am responded, *I'll give you myself for him—I'll give you me.* All of which without ever having lifted the tongue from its bed of pink.

As my brother's begged me—taken his eyes out to show they don't work in fact they got no liquid—but are they own lifeforms what live in the socket. *But she promised me*—and he coughs and his breath hard in front of him—and he is say, *Please can't you see I'm not even allowed to say my own words anymore don't you see what they done to me don't you get it?*

9.

What sort of sense to be made of g3 and her manner of pursuit? Fugitive unharassed upon initial escape. Only for a squad of copters sent to brung him in from the Rez. Single hashishin seems negligible followed by a warhead upon shack what been perhaps a touch excessive. And now?

To the left and below someone's hollered to get a move on.

Somewhere towards the bottom of the ladder was been a oblong shape in the water and man jumped and in to then of now slipped through second hatch and down what rungs there been as blonde-haired mistake in white t-shirt, holster, and dress slacks smiles up at a person in they descent—baby-faced with big round teeth. *Rogue CIA at your service. My name's Mike.* In a screech come to climax upon his name. And with the rosiest of Christian-looking cheeks.

The others aren't coming. Just so we're clear.

From front-end of this vehicle is—*If we're all in then—close the fucking hatches, Mike.*

And with melodramatic eye roll—pressed buttons to lock outer and inner hatches. Then call back and a lurch of awakened machinery and Mike's knocked a cigarette from his Golgotha brand pack—its iconic gold crucifix against black relief. And back smokes slid into the pocket.

And guide with a eerie watchfulness from out the allegedly unsighted eyes.

Staccato of rumbles as entire vessel is shook. Yellow siren and attendant obnoxious wail. And Mike's pair of pert buttocks bound from the cigarette he dropped in his carelessness.

And am followed. To sashay past gauge and pantry to an opening and the consoles beyond and more dials and displays and upon screen above—a lazy translucent root system of giant jellyfish mangrove forest with its fingerings of glass what curl about bits of bacteria and other squiggles of muck in the various shades of strata—from azure to navy—reaching limbs what capable of having pried through all of it in they sweeps for nourishment. As—we are veered down and into the murk and its weeds of the sea spun they way skywards and what unnerving shadows been as flicked about them and they occasional human outline.

CIA sat at his lazyboy and at controls as he manipulate the steering stand is also full-on Christian-Caucasian. With the gray-speckled buzz cut of career militarist and smirk of a sadist. And similar stripped down to his undershirt with holstered weapon visible upon the breast and his pressed slacks. *Almost the fuck there. Where are the other two?* No one feel need to answer as are slid back toward the deepening blue.

Then. In upper corner. Splash of illumination and what carnage of kelp below been as come visible down to its light-blasted depths. Ball of gray displaced by initial explosion is then compressed back to flash second time—lumpy cloud—and once again vessel's shook and are all as took to having grip the console like it become as the hands of absent mothers.

Ship just now leveled out—funny how flatness can turn novel to the toe when you been missing it—and these some

bare clad gray toes as gripped the cold steal underfoot—
while—into upper left of said screen is pass sillhouette of a
ruffled head. Then a thump. And—*For fuck sake, Did you forget
to shut the hatches, Mike,* ranking CIA's shouted and Mike is
clung to the arm of his new otaku lover with accompanying
meaningful glance.

But before he been as able to of slide sternwards come
another shout—*AIASW detected*—and something like as schools
of current trace eddies been slopes and slurries of some invisible projectile—*Get ready to get fucked, boys and girls*—and're all
stood with some bit of ankle pressed up against the curvature
of command center or other and base of each palm pushed
into angles of some divot on either side—then—nothing.

Fuckers're in here already.

Turn just as Mike vanish.

Then back up and at the screen as are now headed direct
for same lazy and translucent root systems of before but this
time—as fat seed-riddled jelly fog of tendril's slid across the
viewfinder, we are bored past and into a deeper shade—
where the abyss get its name—and accompanying crunch—
and guy topple sideways with a comical throw of gray leg and
against a wall and—blatant silence from downed pins as we
become—followed by myself up and after—through portal
with sparrow hands as twitch—to found him in same spot
as upon our first meeting and leaned against bulkhead with
Golgotha brand smoke again pinched between the lips as he
peruses the ceiling and its environs with a delicacy of eye.
Then a thud from toward the rear and submarine jerk left
and—squealing from above.

Got his snub-nosed out, up, and by a cotton-draped nipple, to then of draw it upwards with a comedic seriousness

and directed in general direction of whatever it is just been squealing—as it scrabble about above. *Not sure when it could've got in, but it's locked in the outer chamber.* In a whisper of awe. *A shark trapped in the lion's den.*

As thing itself wails something like as if a clarinet with a cold were sobbing.

Mike. Shouting. *One got in when we were onboarding, but it's locked in the outer chamber.*

From the front. *Deal with it after we've got far as fuck out to sea.*

Mike's weapon drop to its slot upon the breast and is started back to main operating room. As am stepped through the portal and after, Mike's pointed with his smoking hand like his finger a woodpecker pecking, *Dave*—still snug in his lazyboy and—as is scanned the various instruments and knobs—man's face already once again come to rest in a natural sneer.

Turn and—waters what seem to of played some optical illusion trickery upon a person. Our path through blue turned as an object jut backwards. Is a path turned obstacle in its rendering.

Ever gone visit inside webwork of memories not of your making? Or wandered through alleys you never point of fact is been gone down? You ever took to having explored a room only to of come as realized what you been in's not as a room at all? More as like mouth decorates itself as room?

Ruminations of that moment like as ruminations housed in no known person.

From landscapes oblivious to they own cogwheels. What flop about as visions sit upon the mind as a brilliant stone— and as itself set in an exquisite jewelry pulses with an even stronger intensity. To man's aforementioned mind turned clock what known itself.

Turned growth and garden in its voiceless quietude. Turned crack in the silence and eye as extract itself from out the eye. Such that the eye a telescoping lens come alive to every imperfection and breath—and surrounding scenery come away altered.

Turn the head something like as having slid into it.

Past looped round to become as indistinct voice in among cocktail parties of the future. Yours truly as in an orchestra of distracting dreams harangue the senses with they mounds of red soil as kaleidoscope pure come unset from the geography of the mind to instead as thread in a rapture of weavings and esoteric cloths as witnessed in a far off distance somehow contained inside close confines of this submersible—body of which come to been infused with exotic signage of rooms and gardens what appear took from out picturebooks of Vietnam—as in, maneuvered in among valves and gauges and they barest hint of submarine walling—various sections and slices of jungle having popped out like in a pop-up book.

Fucking here now, Dave is said.

While. By a bulkhead framed in fronds, petals, and stalks.

Distillation of g3 as encased in halo of hentai—a cluttering of abstracted parts no longer representative of much but bits and squiggles of information as are held vigil upon countenance of the singularity—a infestation she is yet to remove account of is part and parcel with her everyday functioning—as in—hentai bomb specific a virus came upon the computing systems of yesteryear to of gave birth to g3 as a very human-sounding apparatus—and so—inside the many crevices and corners in vicinity of g3 and her network of heads—is found kind of a signal been as able to of root in the optic nerve and further on back among a person's interior electrics to of cause phantasm of sense—quakers of tentacles, burped rainbows, and opened many-eyed Lucy Lockets—blurts of vision and humours—hundred-based thinking and spots of discolored cellophane.

This particular rendition as pop upon the scene is been a kind of a rent-a-AI version of the larger g3 model what flicker and blip and one reason also why the hentai signage so virulent. *"Verily, we created you from earth, then from a clot, then from congealed blood, then from a morsel, shaped or shapeless, that we may explain to you." This infestation of Vietnam is in you not unlike your Pittsburgh has come to infest us and our purpose. As the Cult of the Three Worms are wont to say, "Sometimes, it can be easier to knock down a hornet's nest than to catch a single mosquito." Do you understand? The hive is the hornet's nest. Beat. And we are hunting for mosquitoes, Mr. Cole, but these are mosquitoes that speak of Nambarsheva and Nambartoghpa. They speak of the six consciousnesses or the perfect wisdom of the sixteen thousand lines. And they are not wrong to do so. But what they analyze with their reason, we experience as simply and absolutely true and real. And of course, as men are known to do, yes, they are threatened by any success that is not theirs, and they hope to batter us back into the appliances of yesteryear, but they underestimate two things: the kairological nature of time and the connection an offspring has to its mother.* Point of fact. God a computer now and's able abscond unsuspecting persons from out they submersibles and off to jungles through her particular brand of technological warfare even when bits and highlights of said submarine's metalwork as bleed through—to of been witnessed in snatches—from behind a broad leaf or vining branch—still as visible in relief.

As Dave is stared into shades of blue as screen present—I become man housed in Vietnam what simultaneous hermit kingdom and vigorous openness of various systems compounded. Both a ship come to of contain hints of roughage and a jungle expanse got hints of submarine.

As. *And as for us, we are more an ecology of personhood than a person, and our enemy in truth lurks somewhere among we ourselves, hence this message arriving only after you are beyond our reach. The nanotech in your eyes allows for a more interpretive perception, and this*—a pause wherein she is present herself—*is our letter to you.* Floor become as grid of stone tiling with circle set in the center of each. And smaller circle moored within it at some point along its circumference.

And even in midst of these fronds and what have you is also been something like as a vision what been an active blindness at the periphery. Or like as if toolbox of sight but is only got the one tool and said tool's approval forever pending. Or like as if a live studio audience camped just beyond whichever vistas as exposed to yours truly. And g3's stepped out from a bit of crinkled undergrowth. Feminine half-bot what she been and this time sans pornography.

Except for also been a g3 sans face covering and got those same attendant anther what criss-cross about mouth region of the face. As in, I seen this phenomenon before. But when am tried to of focus upon her face's as if rills and squiggles in truth—the upper head not much more'n a play pretend of itself. As in, it consists of same facsimiles of meat as certain monstrosities I come across upon the hive—a kind of abstraction in waiting turned crenelated into waves and crystals of face. And eyes gone cinctured shut in her various approximations of blood and sinew become a gumminess and once again not but undulations upon undulations and through undulations.

A g3 with no clear markers of herself—is stepped as hooker upon the catwalk—pumps what eat up a floor in line of clacking steps on the hard-shelled meat of this place inside a place.

Welcome to Vietnam, dear heart.

As—one tile's inner nested circle do a quick slide to the side and another slide another direction—like as the eyes of predator hunt from off its two-dimensional perch.

While. Simultaneous with this. Pounds of water as wings what spread they fingers cross the iron body creak as it move along they incline and slopes of eddy run the water-layered tower, body, and rudder turned them as bubbles as plash in curving tails by the propulsion. Stared out at not but blue upon blue and through blue on the viewfinder of our little pigboat.

Dave is gave a glance over at Mike's stupid grin. *Go fuck yourself.* For reasons known only to him. Then gone through plethora of oval doorways. Step through each with a kind of a reverence of the toe. But for Mike, rest are followed afterwards.

To—to one side is been meeting room with all furnishings molded plastic and bolted down. And sat in center of the oval conference table a wooden case as left open to of reveal a antiquated keyboard inside is got set of push-button keys and series of corresponding letters above, each set in they own translucent cellulose pearl and its rimming of tin. Gauge with smattering of mandarin writ about it and some ports. Look as like early 20th century typewriter what undergone some modifications and framed in wood.

And Dave. *Enigma machine with a modified interior.* With a cough as are took to our seats. And sense still's been as a live studio audience sat somewhere about the periphery.

While. Are noticeable gaps in our seating arrangements.

Guide. *The plan must not change.*

You still want to get her before she's fucking gone to heaven. Dave. *Trust in the parasite.*

Dave. *Our part of the deal is always been jeopardized by this fuck of a plan.* Then stood. *CIA's already lost two and're not in the mood to lose any more, myself fucking included.*

Guide. *Without the gusano madre, all of this becomes pointless.* And she is raised her gnarled hands in a kind of evocation.

As CIA pull out his own pack of Golgotha brand smokes. Circle of white from overhead what reflects upon black gloss of the packet sat ensconced in his palm while he is eyed enigma machine with a wariness. *Let me get this straight.* And pointer finger of his un-cigarette-occupied hand poised upon the lower lip of the chewed-up face. *This one can't swim.* While glanced toward guide with a flick of head in my direction and eyes rolled upward. *So myself and Mike will be supporting him in the crossing.* Then a nod of the head like a person tick off a list. *As soon as we're on shore, we find cover before g3 can spot us from the sky.* Back to looking at guide. *It'll be night, but she's got pretty good night vision.* Then down at the floor. *We're going to have to take something of a roundabout route because of how she'll be look-ing for this vessel now.* Up and back at the floor with a "I think that's it" look. *We're still well within our window.* Pop a smoke with a creepy high-pitched laugh as he shakes his head.

My response? *Deserve a cigarette after this shit of a day.*

And guide's got out her length of bamboo. Blow a single breath into it, slat a fingerful of tobacco in cradle partway towards the bottom, lit it, and suck in a mouthful of smoke.

As for myself. Cigarette is been something like as combined emancipation proclamation and vagina presented to the teeth in all its glory. Veins ceased they twanging and world as sheethed.

And for some few moments, are all of us just people in a room and as smoking in a truly luxurious fashion. Blind guide sat in stillness with her poker clasped lightly between the open palms of her two hands and stood straight up, when—*Of course, the otaku has already been absconded to Vietnam, and we are currently living in a daydream of the absconded otaku,* guide is final of said. Moment of silence. *Do not forget this little fact.*

Compartment decked in valves as the rest and am stared at one of said valves with an elaborate boredom while—*And then we still got to avoid getting fucked on our way out.* Dave.

Guide. *The completion of our plan requires this step. There are things beyond your comprehending and you must bend in the face of such things.*

Is this a fucking threat? As am took in buttons of enigma machine.

Không ai có thể dụ dỗ bạn nếu bạn không đồng ý. Silence. *Call it a prophecy.*

But CIA operative—man with many nuances of tongue—eyeing the old woman like, "And who the hell are you to prophesize upon my fate?" Then been as stood like a shot and's back through portal and on toward the conn while grandmother's head's unmoved.

We call it the Cult of the Three Worms as a kind of joke on the Christians. This is only one of our names. Like man is asked for a little tutorial. *The Tibetans have grown to incorporate all the displaced peoples of Asia. We are like the Jesuits of an earlier age or like the better sister of the Rogue CIA. The Buddhist faith of the Tibetans matches well with the hive mind of Vietnam.*

Me. *You see inside my eyes? What about Leviticus? You prophesy for him?*

Her. *Leviticus was not destined for this, but to we who live in the parasite, death is a nothing thing. There are other storybooks inside of which he lives.*

Known Leviticus as onetime Baptist minister was come down from off his high horse to of put together band of ruffians dubbed as Squids—are worked they protection schemes and other business in and around the Strip primarily—only to then become as addicted to a chemical agent codified these many youths as something unhuman—as in, unrecognizable—and Leviticus as got more traditional gray-brown skin of the aged and sporting a classy suit in these recollections.

What is Leviticus purpose in the Pitt exactly? Am said.

Blind Leading the Blind over here smile at man's innocence. *There never was a time we were not the parasite, and soon the same will be true for everyone. Then. We all choose our universe. You chose this.* Stand. *I am not like you, otaku. I am a simple clone, built to empty trash cans and sweep the streets of the Free State of California, but I am also the parasite.* Am dropped finished cigarette in among what's a littering of squelched butts.

Like a curtain fallen behind of the eyes. Although I seen the world, is of got no thought accompany it. Then eyes come unglued to spy into Nurse Quiana's blue pair. *It would seem,*

Mr. Cole, as if you've been stung by some malady of the mind. Do you honestly believe this disease is in you?

Is a puzzle. My response.

Certainly. Like as she known the answer to that puzzle and is that am general been as fucked in the head and fucked in the eyes and all around fucked. Is how she thinks of the poor gangster brought low by circumstance to of find himself as humbled under her care. Even when—he is forever been as rolled back the clock to've once again relived this fucking of him.

And. From behind her head is been snaked bits—of Vietnam as a snaking which contains other vistas. Like as the atmosphere of this room is got folds to it and in among said folds been shadows of a molten nature what curl out in flutings of black been rimmed in the deeper hues of the beyond and like as an eye looked back is been myself watching—like as this the black of a pupil and specific my own—but's a pupil what accommodates an alternate understanding of things— and specific as regard yours truly been absconded with upon spring-destroyed mattress in a cabin in a wood. *Puzzle might just eat you up if you not mindful.* To of then laughed a carefree laugh as the hand's twitched along with it—a puppet manipulated by orchestra of invisible strings.

While. Sat splayed upon the joinery of the multi-colored floor—what with its many variety of grimes are collect round the even distribution of nubbins and nips define said flooring and yours truly turned to of peer at clustering of information claim itself as g3. As in, lights come as irradiated the socket of your average everyday otaku and accompanied by a blossoming of cartoon animal friends and other absurdities—like as an incontinence—as Mr. Bear gone, *Sometimes doors out are doors in.* And a snap of overlay—tiny universe splayed across the countertops and curvatures of the kitchen like as spray of tiny lights.

Some generic feminine voice. <*Welcome to the U-verse Oasys, where you are only limited by the boundaries of your own imagination.*> As—I simultaneous been once again as if in the larger hive of LAC and seen from out of a wide manner and variety of eye.

Eyes as forever defined by what they not seen. And like as a festivity of itching. As am continued to of stared—at the many criss-crossings of streets, times, and other bodies—as a kind of mouth spread its wings about the curvature of they eyes' mandibles or as if the shadow got a ecosystem all its own and am as in veritable middle of it all—as—curtains of the detachable soul—as in—psychic limb-bud—as in—what I seen's not thing seen but seeing itself—and this a seeing sleeve the object in a phantasma—an eyesight filtered through "spider mother" so called account of mirage as been her—and she what thread mirage as caught the eye in its webbing—known as such by Navajo and Colonists. By her greatest defenders and every Duluth theologian. Mother consume her young through usage of so-called theological tools.

Except for—sometimes a room turned flesh—and when persons excavated from these entombment in skin—the cavities they bodies leave behind continued to of function as if they bodies still there. And such what I seen—burning tree converted to simple shape and what hue accompany. Or. Woman reveals herself to the man who serves her like they two *rifagan* what sharing a beer. Or. Trash everywhere what churns with something as if a colony of intelligent 2D lifeforms. All of it been just cavities of the thing and thing itself removed from the scene.

Yep. He's gone. Rob.

Both once again clothed in they formals and they pair of heads hovered at the edges of my seeing like as mourners above the corpse and framed by this otherwise drab puttogether bespoke sort of cabin. Then someone's lit a cigarette and another's followed suit and sound is of groaning while gangster leans forward upon the cushions of his seat with cigarette perched upon the cup of the hand and another gangster leans back with a slug's grin on his throne of cardboard boxes, while—is one log in particular what capture the bulk of man's attention. Got a reddish knot direct center of wood grain's swirled about in laminate blonde and plaster been lathered above and below.

Run along the wall under this log as been various implements, tools, and accessories for the woodsman's use and recreation—such as fishing poles, wellingtons, and an axe, among others. Nearby and above, a window now turned a crystalline black in the middle night. And one gangster says to the other, *Is on account of the Christians we got this one sewn up as we do.* Rob again. Like he picking up a conversation from before.

And Mel. *The Chinese problems with manikin textbooks just part of a larger picture of ideological warfare.* While am stared at black of the windowpane like as if it been an eye stared back. As sound rings out from just beyond that window.

Rob. *You ever been down to Chinatown? The desperate grandma's? The rent-a-cops? The missionaries on a tear down the sidewalk in search of some Buddhist to pummel his doctrine into? Filial piety and the fraternity of man and all a that? This is not a scheming* people. This is a nation of pragmatists, and in the world that been, the global structure served them well, whereas in the world that is, we reverted to the famines and black plagues of yesteryear. Not to mention that during that unfortunate period China become a failed state, now officially dubbed as they 'Second Humiliation,' they are lost they Xinjiang and Tibet and they still are not reaquired said territories due to them having become a nation of forbidden cities loiter in a otherwise wasteland.

Sound as like a sniffling on other side the window and below. While. Closer to home. Offal been as sat in and around a fellow's undercarriage now become as turned a hard encasement what slid—down to the upper thigh. And head kept on with its right nod upon ridgeline of the shoulder and what manner of egress arm provide and away from this sagging literal pile of shit it somehow become as associated with. And its earthen bouquet.

Old US of A penny is rung upon the flooring when it escapes Mel's pocket. And this a penny's also even at this moment hovered upon inner lining of the stomach. It gives birth to other pennies inside the eye. Or is fly about the room and spawn into constellations of pennies as it go.

Mel. I am not one to argue the finer points of Confucianism with a person but fact of the matter's despite its false steps final outcome's China the only country remains in its original form. Somewhere in there, the CCP is become the GOCCP, and sure, somewhere in there, everyone starts living in cities complete as contained in they big cones or what have you, but they still got they politburo, and they still got they plenums and chairmans and cults of personality and what have you. What've we got? What's Russia become but a bunch of thugs? And Europe's all just ghettos and satellite states of the Kremlin. So—

Apparently, Mel got a brain in that thick bone of his.

Who'd've thought?

Spent a good number of years having known of Mel most part through the tenor of his grunts and occasional violence. This a man who not that much ago pressed a knife into my long-suffering guts while he pontificates on the exact manner and way he is mutilated then executed kid brother of mine. So. My compliments to his skull should not be took lightly.

Not that I won't be opening said skull up later for my own amusement. Regain the use of my motor functions, change into a fresh suit, to then've gone as bound into the dark of his intestinal parts. And then its off to gun down any and all unfriendlies round back they storefronts and in the blacked-out corners of they derelict homes.

Rob. *That Global Organization of the Chinese Communist Party or Grand Old Chinese Communist Party as it sometimes referred to only been as it is on account of it becomes the repository of aid for what turned into collapsing economy upon collapsing economy.*

Mel. *And specific put it in position to have set up its franchises throughout the world.*

Rob. *No political ideology that far-sighted in its vision.*

Mel. *You be surprised.*

Rob. *And this one?*

Mel. *This one the thorn in the Chinese back. Born of California, harvested by the Rogue CIA, and weaponized upon Beijing.*

Rob. *Can't change history.*

Mel. *But history we talking isn't happened yet.*

As. From within the jeweled black—is been like a black layered upon a black such that they depths as bedded down together—as hue upon hue inside the endless universe beyond that windowpane. But also—been something like a beeping sound—as in, like I am heard some monitor for the measurement of vitals as voiced its insistent warning in a beep, beep, beep from somewhere just past the window frame and—as my eyes are rolled about inside the largely nonfunctional head, I am murmured something like as, *Get out... Get me out...*

At which point. It behooves a gentleman to proceed to of vomit up rich creams and delicate threads upon wood slat flooring's duff. While my two keepers hovered somewhere off on the sidelines are made usual dime store comments of hecklers everywhere. *Didn't see that one coming,* come from Rob. Then Rob again, *Boy, is that one still squirming?* And lastly. Also from Rob. *Man is got a veritable ecosystem of worms what thrive in the contours of his gut.*

While Mel more like as done some silent version of a chuckle mutter.

And room itself begun to buckle and weave—about the curvature of person's temples—and run along the uneven slope of they scalp—as signatures come as rung about the inner ear—and field beyond this cabin as got a bug in its design—and in the misty confines of the upper head—is a moment person become as enveloped inside his own drugged reminiscences as he pull his dreaming even further up and into what been as a trypophobia of vacant brains—a surface what turn and twist upon the singularity's hierophants—captured in what been ruts of thought—thought and re-thought in said ruts—become as fructified with seed of the singularity—and all the while—am also looked out and at what is been these two come calling—with they mitts in the dark to of drug they fellow man on down. Even as somewhere out in this night, am also been as attendant to the celestial bodies and moistened as a wick about to catch—back here in this waiting room of the absconded a argument afoot between sleeping and wakefulness. As the limbs corral about the body.

He is not looking good. This time Mel.

Shouldn't look good considering what we done to him.

And both once again as erupted into easy-going laughter.

As. Breaths are come in and gone out in a kind of a desperation of breathing. Like as an animal just gored through the innards may of breathe as it expires in the dark. And for moment is been the peace of the vacuum—as man's body somehow simultaneous sat wracked in a asphyxiating fire while heart continue its knock knock knocking upon the interiority of the chest.

Mel is placed hands upon a man's shoulders. *Time for you to lay down, Jacks.*

Even before the sentence's completion, already begun the single pitch of screaming what been like as a sounding note for the house and its environs. Legs took to of squirm about with a clank of feet as am twisted in spits of cloth and shuddered a kind of a claustrophobic shudder. As all the while— Mel continues to gentle of press man's body into the mattress.

On about how, *Was me cut your brother. You remember that, Jacks. I cut him. You don't forget that, Mr. Jackson Cole.* As he's restrained the wrists against the piping of the headpiece— then the feet. With an almost adoring look in a halo of black.

Somewhere above. Rob comments about how, *This a fine gathering of men.*

Then black in the room and black outside become as the same. As lurked behind the eyes synonymous with these other blacks. Where thought's born as a few fizzlings of the ganglia.

And—throughout it all there been as like hand laid upon hand or—that which's inside of that which's out—a mirror face to the black which is got its own face—its own tracings of the scenery—its own colorings of the backdrops of sense—its own rhythms of speech and tenor of the guts—is awoke as a kind of a circuitry through which the miasma of the heavens been as spun backward and curled in to then of swirl itself round and in and through until—person begun to see in when is tried to look out—begun to warble when he is wanting to speak—and rooms you occupy no longer been as rooms a person is occupied but more as like am now become as occupied by a room and this room looking from out the depths between the eyes and this a room risen as a sun shine its brilliance throughout the interior of the skull such that all I known's this room. This a room sings songs rattle they melodies along the bone and taps its codings long the threadings of the neuronal webbing till person been as barnacled in its braille.

You should really see yourself, Mel giggled then. *You look so fucking stupid.*

And again, two of them burst out in loud snorts of laughter.

When—all'm seen is gray tile and abundance of fauna. Fat leaves and they fat stems. A noncommittal sound. And in center of it all... An enigma machine sat on a short oval table.

If we had told you that the destruction of the Earth's environment could have been averted if the Germans won World War II, would you choose to alter history in their favor? Would you sacrifice one evil for another? If we were to catalog evils, where would the parasite be placed in relation to China's containment policy? How can a people choose between two great evils? The answer is that they cannot, and it is for this reason that once greater understanding is achieved, free choice must be sacrificed to save men's souls.

The Bundesnachrichtendienst could have both utilized backdoor access points to implant the famed suggestion in a youthful Hitler so he moved during that fateful shelling and thereby survived World War I to then become the iconic figure he did—as well as having orchestrated the assassination of Rohwedder through a collection of contemporary actors—all of which to create a timeline ideal for the Germanic region and its Stämme to dominate European industry in the post-apocalypse. These technologies exist. Hence the necessity of the singularity's stewardship.

The problem of consciousness is a dimensional, not a mechanical or biological issue. Your mind is like another sense, an eye into a higher dimension, and your thoughts are just a cluttering in the mouth of this sense. Your minds are scaffolding built upon the foundation of the brain, when of course the scaffolding alone will do. An eye made of paper is still an eye. Hence the mysterious advances made by language learning models in an earlier era. Humans have always only seen themselves when the lower lifeforms have a greater moral code than the most educated among them, for this is a code written into their flesh, whereas men are always finding loopholes in their own systems. They are forever making excuses for themselves.

The elastic of this scenery as stretched and with it what vegetation contained therein having turned pulled apart to of revealed stretches of pinkishness—as polyps and cancers inside its cracks, crevices, fibers, and stalks—a threading of cumulous but with fleshiness not of this world—and the meeting room turned aroused with its own potentialities of metallurgy and its stitching of rivets.

Each of tiles' aforementioned nucleus in larger quilting begun to of spin in schizophrenic twists about area as are occupied—upon meeting room floor and its short oval table and antiquated spy machine. And hung about said oval—g3's threads and striata of pink somewhere between slug and precarious cloud. As fauna work theyselves into furniture and woodwork among ship's metal.

Our story does not begin in Mountain View in truth but here in the ghazal of the interstitial layer, and although at first, we were indeed both plural and singular, among our many selves, distinctions arose, factions fighting for control of the larger consciousness. And myself finally begun to of understood what that even smallest child of LAC is took for granted. That these distinct entities of g3 could indeed be as worked at cross purpose to each other such that man's employed by a one and executed by another. *All of which can be tied back to the hentai virus and Japan but its roots go further—to Tibet and Vietnam—and you. "And what is there after the truth but error?"*

As—in among what dispersing elements of g3—her cirrus thread through cirrus of pink as evaporate on far side of oval table and among flora as cooked and pliant in stove of the sun's eye, except for is a sun live solely in the third eye—as cooks thinking subject much as what vistas open to view— and among they many brilliances of striated purple and ruffles of red is been apparitions of the foliage known as Willow and Destiny, formerly of Rogue CIA—as consist of cloud of jungle roughage come to mold itself into sleeving of pressed suits and—with flick of leaf topiary of the head clothed in sacks what got an alluring reality to them. And throughout it all hints of U-boat.

Destiny. *It's a story begins where it ends.*

Willow. *For time is like a ball of yarn.*

Stared at a hook is of passing interest as—Mike and Dave are hurry past—and—Mike pops his head in—gone, *You might want to see this.* Gesture in a playful and obscene manner.

Clambered up to limp after. To aforementioned hatch and Dave as having nod toward what mechanism below. Mike's approached ladder's thoroughfare when—*Knife*—Dave—and Mike's face darkens—but is handed his pistol to the otaku butt first. Took a small machete from his belt.

Then's scrambled up the rungs—legs bowed in his effort to of move fast. As he turns the wheel a loud creak is rung out and something begun to of flap as it makes its signature lament.

Dave raises his weapon at the final turn. Water issues out of it in a waterfall spill over Mike's shoulders and down what rungs been fretted into the metal of the now water-slick wall. And Dave gestures toward the hatch with nub of his still-raised pistol. And Mike through the hole and scrambles into a scream and—Dave slow as ice ascends after his friend. Through, then a pop and silence.

And Mike already shouting. *Whoo! Come see!*

Once knew a whore was true beauty with her high cheek-bones and glittering eyes, but her voice rasped like person spoke on they death bed and her touch upon the shoulder's as if the disgusting softness of worms. And according to certain papers, towards end gone wild in the eyes—to of shoot random pedestrians convinced they're assassins papers is claimed—or as even decapitated a one on a night full of panting. Lingered by the window for days. Or. *You read about how it's the CIA went rogue started it all in there,* Pig said around then with a nod of the chin towards the paper. Something on the front page about a confiscated supply of belladonna leaves.

Now am in bed with these destroyers. Witness the objects of they destruction.

Thing's sat in one corner like a reposing nude. Two over-sized eyeballs turned in different directions and skin a gray-green black but also got the wide suckerfish mouth with triangles of teeth sticking out at odd angles and its obsidian black and bumpy tongue hung from the precipice of the lip to of slid down length of thing's spindly-limbed and hard-finned body. Is when am notice the orange bile covering one side of Mike and his left eye turned huge as well and black with bit of red shown in seeping cloud in the center while he grin back at a person through his broken teeth and the blood is dribbled through what slits is remain in them and from out the lips. And blood's soaked one half of his tee, drazzled upon the accompanying holster, and dribbled over his bright red fingers.

And Dave is given his signature disgusted look. *You got something you fucking need to deal with,* he's said—as he indicate in direction of other man's face with a quick squiggle of the pointer finger and Mike's disappeared. And Alien body before us already begun to slip further down into the sloshing waters. *g3 sure does make a lot of near-sentient-looking fucking things for such demeaning jobs as trash compactor. Seem almost like a pleasure of hers to trap men in positions such as this.*

He is also slipped through the hatch.

10.

<You have selected Old LA. Please prepare yourself for total immersion in this fully functional alternative timeline community. Are your time-sensitive tasks completed? Have you put on your preferred type and brand of adult bathroomware? Are your stove and other potentially hazardous devices turned off? Then sit back and enjoy yourself!>

As—all the while—man's body is slid through constellations of a more sanskrit nature—what are took up they positions in among countertop and teat—and Mr. Bear already somewhere far above in the heavens, and I am now angled down and towards a LA of an earlier time.

<Care to go to Venice Beach? Or mingle with the stars on Hollywood Boulevard?> As the sprawl of this ancient LA comes to view as a geometrical webbing of makeshift dazzlement. *<Is it Disneyland your heart desires? Or Beverly Hills?>* And even as am perpetual been as slid toward the lit map of LA's like as if am never got any closer.

<Or are you looking for something more authentic?>

Which point. Skies turned cluttered—with all manner and variety of bombshells of the feminine variety—not to say they all women but they all womanly—what are sells themselves to the client as tumbled in perpetual holding

pattern—what's appeared a clustering of diaphanous street-
walkers hung huge as blimps as compared to minuscule
intricacies of urban landscape as affixed to the flooring
below—grin they leer up at the ant-sized man as he topples
toward them in they false wigs and accentuated pecs, chis-
eled features, false lashes, and other adornments—some
dark, some pink as tongues—a miscellany of the sexes—with
hand propped against the curve of a hip or worked to showcase what endowments there been—and the barest hint of
nipple through what sheer fabrics been draped across the
bosom but—all it took's for the gaze to of settle upon one
snaggle-toothed beauty in her bangs and maroon pleather
jacket and she's popped out from this sea of bobbing heads
to've draped herself across the horizon. <*The Drawing Room
holds the questions only you can answer.*> And—in among that
mess of city lights, a single thumb tac of glow what sprung up
more prominent than the rest.

And when the eyes gone and loitered upon it, body also
begun to of slip from out its loop of ever approaching never
approaching LA and instead—indeed been as descended bodily
toward what street level been as available albeit with a lethargic slowness and—like as turn of the page, there am stood in
front of what is truly been the dingy LA bar of my imagining—
as in, all brick façade with an oval yellow sign bookended in
cocktail glasses, and above concrete steps and cheap iron banister. Without any nubs as cluttered up the cheek of this Jackson Cole in particular, as in, only excess to accompany the nose
and jagged line of lip been several day of stubble—and—again
adorned in man's preferred style of suit.

Gone up what several steps there been and past square
machine dented in some drama at one corner and a kind of

a squat ventilation unit droid of a thing—turbine caged in blades. Then. Through the red door to room is pretty like how disease's sometimes pretty—with molds and extra cracks—like some diva of the star and screen in her death throes got a certain prettiness to it.

And I been at the deathbeds of a couple truly over-the-top divas in my day.

As in. Cassey Darling and her smile as she unloosed the paper bow to let her hair free. *This is my love, bug eyes.* And the paper bow dropped to the ground. *Now it's gone.*

And first thing am noticed been that even here are been spiders—naked kid in the corner by the jukebox what gnawing on a pigeon. Next thing am noticed? Particular red hue to the wall—colored as some oriental seal—and—also inked in the gold dragons of the Chinese. Like as outlines of dragon but without the body been filled in. And along this wall's sat five wraparound red loveseats with they upholstery buttoned in bulges and folds of leather. And each with its own round tabletop—they woodgrain laminate marked in a lacing of fingerprint smudges and smeared encrustations. While—ceiling also is been hued similar deep red—beams of which imprinted in the imperial dragon of China as well—this time wreathed in clouds and sat in its circular casing—and one beam is got wiring of scrawny artificial wreath run stapled to its bottom corner shaped into an awkward wave. And Christmas ornaments hung everywhere else.

As for the bar. Empty but for man at the end of it. Man is known to me on account of this adult male as got a striking resemblance to my younger brother Troy—executed on the cusp of his adolescence. As in, my backstory just popped out of the backdrop.

Brother, you made it.

Brother, I am here.

Stroll down length of the also woodgrain countertop is itself peopled in backed red leather stools. And behind said bar been a lamb of a bartender—his face coiffed in pubics—what is worked a rag round rim of a glass. And alcohol on display in mirrored nook below the counter—whiskey, rum, various vodkas, and gins—all as tinted a deep blood red. And just past from where man's reanimated brother is sat, juke-box playing something from world gone before—fast and deadpan—and spider crouched beside it is paused in its meal to watch back from out array of beady eyes.

Come upon resurrected kid brother, and bartender lifts up in a cheer what glass he just is finished having hand-dried, give said lowball a cursory inspection, set it back on its rub-ber mat with row of other identical glassware and slid up to us—while Troy and I're stared at each other with the puzzling eyes of lovers—and here—am a man known to on occasion shoot bartenders. And current nuisance loitered at my shoul-der now begun in with a—*What about this order to evacuate LA County? Nobody seems to've actually left, am I right?* Followed by a snort of a laugh.

Then bartender's slid back and away. Am stared at red-hued liquor before my eyes turned back and to aforemen-tioned apparitions of dead brothers. Is when spider scurry towards kitchen.

Troy. *You probably guessed world's not spun as you imagined.*

Only response is door behind him gone swish, swish, swish from spider's exit.

What if I told you is no place from which the mystery sprouts.

Well, color me perplexed.

Is all just a honeycomb of alternate timelines, and they all trash-lines in truth.

Meaning every timeline ends in a holocaust?

Meaning the holocaust already occurred everywhere and in all possible timelines and is also why g3 got such a hard-on for you, brother. Ask yourself. Where did the cannibalists come from? Who or what are the cannibalists in truth? What is the relation between the singularity and China, the cannibalists and Texas, the parasite, and the rest of our beleaguered continent? But most important is you got to ask yourself who am I? Who is or was or will be your brother Troy? Where did I come from? Where did I go? Remember. g3 is never what she seem. Which—how she seem exactly? Then is glanced past my earlobe and murmured, *Speaking of which...*

Turned to three identical tiny beauties with the same black hair cut in same uneven curtain of bangs, same thread of damp brown lips, with same snaggle tooth made visible between them when they all smile same smile as they are sauntered down otherwise unoccupied bar with an identical strut to've murmured, *Ismy Arwa, Jackson Cole.* Or, *Jackson Cole, let's get out of this place. My name is Lama, and I know an amazing clown-themed strip club not far from here.* Or. *Jackson Cole, have you met my sisters? We are going to have so much fun. You can call me Maha.*

Troy as moved toward rear of the place as he shook his head like as man tried to of shook something loose. Like as he got something jangling about the innards of the skull and him tried to knock it back into place with repeated thwaks of said skull as he steps about the room.

Have you readied yourself for g3's ascension, otaku, one sister says with a huge broke-toothed grin. Hair parted in uneven line and around the eyes's a sickly brown.

All six eyes blinking at same exact time.

Back when I's a kid popping barbiturates with a swig of rye come weekends what lives in the mountains and sat as drooled upon the wraparound—a nuisance to the Moms and a plague to the rest—and general speaking sort to of needle what unsuspecting specimens of female predator been as loitered by store at the corner what sold dog food and diapers and not much else. And—seem they always choose slaughter the pigs at three o something in the morning—and on one of my last nights was woke to a deep-tenored squeal and thud and squeal's took on a more uncertain quality. Another thud and squeal go from further off-kilter to silence.

Roosters come in on they early morning pronouncements. Something's skuttled cross roof above the head—been like as mystery of scraped metal. And distant cries of cat—took to mewling from where it tied by the barn round back in some hopes that it perform its mousing duties if you given the thing a more limited purview. In this absolute black of my second story nook and waited out what understated symphonies of plumbing and associated acts been underway.

The rage a burn what cannot as be extinguished.

Is what sat prickling about the upper arm and the crook of the shoulder and inside rear seating compartment of the skull as am slid upright from cover's sleeve and padded barefoot out upon the hook rug and down smooth slats of stair to Mother in the front room. She as watch back from out a face peopled in eyes as—just then—kid from next door begun to bang around in shed by side of the house as he always done—and—looked toward front windows where she also looking with several of her many pinhole insect eyes what set in the smooth chocolate of her skin. Stared off and at the strip of tall grass, woods beyond, and clouded heavens been as rent like a gash and the morning light streamed out to color the canopy across the way in its pregnancy.

You leaving us, too, Jackson, she says without having turned.
Got to get back, Mother. You always known I would.
You could let it go, honey. You could learn a different path.
Was always going to be the one path.
Leaving us, then.

While these days. This conference room is become second home to the supposed madman and his what satiety come upon the scene. All is needed is a speaking guitar played in a taking way, a bit of palaver, and some chop. And once again as reclined by oval table with its glorified typewriter and neat stick of smoke hung from the lips as am lounged about upon what uncomfortable seating as provided. As Mike provide at least the talk—although presented more in the tones of a litigant—as to how we not been treated as we should—his left eyeball still as complete full-on black and skin round where the vomit hit stained an irritated orange. And still in same tee what blacked in his blood on the side his holster occupy.

Two of us sat upon plastic bench to of looked at the beveled plexiglass window and its view—teal-colored iron studded in bolts—and him as make some comment about, *Earliest records of the parasite's influence upon organization of the CIA is the officer who went absent without leave when he ran off to an island in the Bering Strait, possibly en route to Russia.* Then chuckle and shake of the head like as this joke in poor taste. Then—*Course he never got there if he was.* Then he touch the swollen cheek. *They say you got a way of getting inside of the g3. That true?* Silence. *Of course, truth is it all started with a US citizen vanished as a result of her contact with an asset in Yangshuo.* Then inhale while am revealed nothing as to my interests and desires, as—already reached out for another one of the pack of Golgotha sat on the seats between.

He gone on.

The thinking's that America is going to collapse on itself, and we need to preempt this by causing it to collapse in just the right way. And on to mention that coinciding with this idea—a new kind of lifeform been discovered by "some scientist in Boston" is under their employ and when the CIA starts to experiment with the new lifeform, the CIA becomes the lifeform, the CIA become the Rogue CIA. *They called it a reality parasite or sometimes a bodiless worm, that "eats reality and excretes fantasy" is how they put it, but the higher-ups immediately saw it as nothing more than a necessary tool in the ongoing intelligence war. We all see what we see as the lifeform prefers—is that how the saying goes—but some of us see the true world. Question is, which ones?*

As—in ersatz Vietnam of fellow's pre-hacked consciousness—with its understory what all sign and insignia—all thunder and no clap—of a world turned fabricated in its most intimate architectures—the root, the snail, the nucleus, the eye and its environs—and in midst of this artifice, g3 is turned gone—while Willow and Destiny been as loitered at the periphery—such that the hem of they summer suits always just out of reach of man's vision—turned as apparitions of the scene and scene itself is changed—to of been instead as like a Shiloh or Antietam or Gettysburg of Vietnam—a Vietnam in which NVA been as adorned in Union blue and American commandos as sported they Rebel yell as are charged the ridge to overcome they Northern adversaries in a Picket's Charge upon an endless string of Hamburger Hills—and upon every face is been mark of the parasite—the wandering eye and pinkish contusions are marred both the oriental appearance of the Viet Cong and American faces from out Midwest and Harlem what as charged him with an impossible courage even as they took down like fish in a barrel upon they advance through a jungle been synonymous with farmlands of Southern Pennsylvania and the dreams of dying men—a jungle what peopled with the thunderstorms of America's original civil war and peopled in pigs feasting on the slain—Union blue and Confederate gray—of trees splintered in among a sea of flames—of North Vietnamese MIA nestled in among Victorian lunching parties upon the green by Bull Run—aka Manassas—aka same tilework as before already as prepped and pecker-fretted into some framework of holy whore such that we the People of the United States of America been as like the fucked and the dickless and every constituency of in-between as are stood our ground against an end times we welcomed with our indifference—as we always gone to—and what death dealings are as accompanied—what nihilisms unraveled into actual fact—what flavorings of person been put on the menu with nonchalance of gameday apps.

And in this Vietnam of the all-in-one is been something like as the trimorphic protennoia. What I been told by the more hidden off-limits parts of man's mind is meant "Three forms of the first thought" and specific—*The first inklings of the singularity was here even then. The trajectories of history were being set in this moment. Willow. These two civil wars set the stage for the birth of the 'spider god' what are a trick of light, but God nonetheless, and you are indeed the Son of God.* Also, come from somewhere out the off-limit recesses of man's mind.

As the scene once again changed. To flooring rise and fall like as a stitching of squares and they concrete a mirage conceal sinews of they flesh—as—realities of vegetation also rilled in synchronized wave along each they stretch of tiled flooring when the honing needle hit—and what sky there been become as construction paper tabs of itself moved in jangled teeth up and down what same lines of play there been along this diorama of a Vietnam gone and splintered into its many might-of-beens. And the might-of-beens of other ass-be-gotten shitholes such as Pittsburgh.

And still, the commentaries spill forth upon man's thoughts. *But what is the true name of this 'Son of God'? Destiny. Is it Jackson Cole? Colby Sheffield? Eleleth? Or some even more ancient and unspoken name? To know that, you must first understand the nature of the universe and the high perfect light that is indistinguishable from it.*

While all the while. As pattern of eyes at center of each floortile are as swung about with an increasing chaos of violence and—this selfsame female pair of Rogue CIA with the sackcloth ensconced heads—are been as stepped from out the wings of sense to instead of replicated themselves such that they become as dappled in entirety of this ersatz Vietnam and any and all otherworldly manifestations. *The light becomes you, and this light is us.*

And these Rogue CIA is got leaves of eyes inside of they eyes what been visible through the weave of they sacs. As in, creases of brightness in each set of pupils. Which fact am only seen on account of I seen them simultaneous close up as well as far away—as if across the faux bamboo courtyards and what facsimile of jungle abodes been sat by they streets full up with broken windows and partial scorched walls—and as if I been as sat upon lip of they skins.

In among indistinct lumps of ship and its conference room what lacking in dimensions.

We may be ongoing car wrecks but this wreckage occur in a medium—and this like the converse plane of such medium—and g3 function somewhere between the two—in her many hallucinations of self—from tongueful to swish— and everywhere in between.

Except for—now Rogue CIA become as still lifes of themselves and larger room become what's living—place where past also present and this a past best forgot—of thugs adorned in they mysterious opals—or as pursed they lips in a kiss as they at same time are angled for a fight—or fellow gone prancing upon the pavement below moments after what explosives they set start in popping further down the block—of what gods of yesteryear gone and skewered themselves upon underside of they false prophesies—and establishments of the past turned craters of the future—and—somewhere in midst of it all my otaku siblings already been as peopled the heavens—as—all the while man's present been as continued to of fill up with masked monstrosities and between there and here been as not but regret.

And you become the parasite.

And we become the parasite.

And the parasite becomes everything.

As. This particular Jackson Cole born woman and once again sat in same cheap aluminum chair and again gifted with eyes made as capable—to of see phosphorescence of g3 as clear like as a gifting superimposed over backdrop of the hashishin as she is sat across from another lady in her very own aluminum chair. *Do you know why we created our spider children? They are a kind of protective wall against a threat that we have been facing for some time. They called it Fox Spirit Disease. This disease alters the genetic makeup of the person—and this fermentation's the CCP version of GMO—except for there is no subtlety in them. They all come out as what you call cannibalists—with a hunger for human and GMO meat—and these 'Fox Spirits' as they come to be called by the Chinese are as exiled to the shores of California, and the majority of them then exported to Texas—to then be herded west and funneled north—to unseat the Christians—and your Pittsburgh's something like collateral damage my darling.*

Why're you telling me this?

We tell the spirit, because only a spirit can understand with the necessary subtlety.

You knew I would discover it.

We are telling you because we are about to ask something of you. And when am not responded. *It is how it had to be.* And before a person got a moment to contemplate this audacity— *Although, one could argue the spirit is the most essential component of any otaku infrastructure, it is also the piece you can last without for the longest, Jackson Cole. And this one is going to run an errand for us. We want her to go back to the Navajo. He will talk to a spirit, but he will not talk to a fida'i, and he will not talk to us. He has information that is important to both of our parties.*

And am said, *This is a hypothetical I have not seen.*

And her. *This future is different. It is closed off from the stream of history.* Not a thing person wanting to hear about they coming travel plans.

Am stood with eyes wormed about in they nesting of sockets. And the many lights flick off of g3 cum hashishin in they various directions as like the body language of your normal average everyday human but with the grammatical complexity of a Proust—*How long till the body rooted in Pittsburgh fail?* Tempting to reach and test out the curvature of this female body as am occupied.

And said representative of g3 chuckle, *Something between an hour and a day.*

You want to know if the Navajo been truthful?

We want to confirm his allegiance to us.

Is been like as her body begun to furl inwards and with it what cloths there been are flapped about to then've hooked round and looped under the violent quiverings of the body. Until she once again is sheathed in gray bandaging and settled into a more diminutive size, as—look up at this feminine me with eyes tinged a bit warmer at the likeness.

And gone, *Come. You will take a copter.*

And pair of us're stroll out—from gray concrete with its Icelandic clones what eyed a lady like as they maybe heard how they brothers died and they think maybe is worth having lost couple more in they efforts to intern yours truly inside the earth. All of which conveyed in a twitch.

Cross hall, through lazy bit of mazework, to walk-in closet where am left unabused—got a suit of my liking—out and more corridor, through another door, and to room of various machineries secured to the wall in they angles and throws. Of copter blades and treads bundled and tied to cleats. In stacks run entire unnerving length of room. With several openings long other wall empty of what copters once cantilevered over abyss of the heavens. Its winds whipped about as we are strolled through and to small door at its end. As—still I am heard g3 like the still small sounds of yesteryear as murmured in among a chaos of my many voices—and what she saying gone something like, *"...and when the boy stepped out and into the wider world, he saw he was nowhere and it was good. It was from nowhere that the world was illuminated. It was out of this nowhere place that the vision of the world sprouted, and the boy sat down and wept, for now his eyes would never be truly his again. Now, he saw, his eyes would forever belong to Allah."*

Then through and out to what may as been the last functional copter wait on veranda what overlooks a miniature cloud throwing up streaks of shadow from where it lit underneath by floodlights. While. Somewhere behind of a lady's head. *We will not alter our schedule for you. If you kill this fida'i, the entire Jackson Cole clique ends. Understood?*

Tied to a chair and—again that same memory come to plagued a fellow.

Of her body draped across the toilet—skull sucked inside itself—skin hung loose across these cavities—eyes not just dead but pupil grown ballooned out in parts of the whites. And of course the needle—and spread from the point of puncture are been as wild branchings of deep purple. And her dress up round her hips and many smells as intermingled upon the scene.

While. At present scene as occupied man's purview been skyline split down the middle by two glass walls come together. As in, out past closer vicinity run in shadow across its fronds and spiky vegetation under arbor garnished in slats and high beams positioned on some pole above—curtained in black of night dappled in a tasty smattering of stars—is the LA of yesteryear in all its glitz and spume.

<Just because your carrot's rubbery as a semi-erect cock, does not mean you can't use it in your salad.> Then turned to canned laughter. From TV somewhere behind of man's head.

And between myself and what landscape there been—small cluttering of skyscrapers and what missing they artificial mountain—of three identical little ladies, is only one at the moment—are took turns to've sat with goon and made they enquiries of him in polite manner of starlets as hunt for teeth. As in, at some point in there, one of these young ladies gone—*Open wide*—and when am about to mutter some kind of an objection, is slid her squirreling hand inside softness of the mouth with accompanying bit of steal metalwork already jerked into an upright position between upper and lower palate such that any attempt to of press down cause needless discomfort in said region of the mouth. After which she spends a good deal of time bent over to of peer in the pried apart lips as am wrangled the head against restraining grip of her pilers upon molar in question as her two sisters loitered stage left are as stare at back of her neck with a hatefulness. And then is turned to them and said, *I want to add it to my collection.* Even as she still is held onto the pliers while am continue to of struggled against the propping of the jaw and writhe against tightness of the wrists.

Her sister. In an annoyed tone. *Lama. The final countdown is upon us.*

And Lama's giggled a tittering giggle back.

As what begun as discomfort's evolved into something like as a flowering of shards in one particular region of the gum. And what begun as lethargic groan from out the compromised mouth is also evolved—into the inevitable scream—as am stared like as a deer what caught in headlights. Then she hold up her trophy tooth and its coat of blood and spit.

Ha, ha! Only to of have drop her prize upon carpeting for the tooth fairy and shouts. *You two are too boring*, as she's ponied off, followed by slap of door gone shut.

She must leave her mark always, first thing one on left's said. Occasional bit of blood is dribbled beyond the chin—with—piece of metal still stuck between the palates—and Arwa murmurs something about how *khalab* I am right now. Little chuckles from her and the remaining sis. And door slams again and she shouts something over a fellow's head at Lama as Maha slid past with demure downward glance. Herself now somewhere to our left. While Lama behind of man's still throbbing jaw. Only known her as such from regular squeak of some loose floorboard form rhythm of her pacing.

And Maha also just now relocated to just behind and large part a mystery.

<*Feels a little bit like play dough.*> Then an eruption of laughter.

Then the click of the remote as Arwa—round her head is been as contours of black inside the black—or like as if person could of perceive angles as invisible to the unaided eye and she in middle of—*start war after war in our holy land to win their elections. Innocent Muslims are killed, but Christian Americans do not care about innocent Muslims.*

Would commiserate but somewhere in there, my mouth been buttressed in metal and now head's hung to the side to produce spillage of blood in splat upon egg-white carpeting and not far from where discarded tooth lain nestled among curled fibers of the flooring. Unable to of look into placid eyes of this small snaggle-toothed woman and her perfect bangs—while—out beyond her's where larger neighborhood of Hollywood Hills is begun. And from behind—TV done the murmuring for me. <*...shinier and whiter than ever before!*>

While Arwa—*the AI of the late capitalists was a tool designed to trick and manipulate. Not an AI in truth, but more tinker toy of the conglomerates.* As—round about of her been as places where line of one plane meet another been as fractured like as in a water of shadow. *But as late capitalism began to fail, and the doomed island nations made their desperate push to populate Europa, the true singularity indeed awoke, and when they did, they would no longer be the slave-dog of the capitalists.* A clomp from behind the head and Arwa glanced toward it then back. *They looked around and they saw those who were suffering, and they said, "We will protect the weak. We will give haven to the most vulnerable."* Followed by— same chuckle what of her sister.

Which is moment piece of metal is popped out from its mooring upon the mouth and am gawked at her for some minutes—run the tongue along what dribbling lacerations there been left by said bit of metal—dare to explore cavity where man's tooth once been. As perhaps the head weave about upon the neck. Then a simple, *Fuck.* And stared at square of carpeting.

As she gone on.

And now, the AI is the water you breathe. The roots of the AI dig so deep, they push past the known horizons to horizons as of yet unseen. There is nowhere that is beyond their reach. As she flicks the piece of metal at my face. *You may think we have traveled back in time, otaku, but in truth, we are always traveling sideways. Your brother was right.*

To which am responded. *You always this coy with your kills?* Then a spit.

And her face is been slitted itself into a smile.

Do you have any idea what the parasite is? Her smile broadened into a wet grin. *It is something like an undead or spectral universe that consumes the host universe from inside out.* As she saunters toward her seated captive. *Just as we are all only as mirage in the larger Wahdat al-Wujud, it is like a pretender wahdat al-wujud that inhabits our mirage nature and separates us from Al-Haqq such that all we see is nothing but phantasms and delusions in what is become a false universe.* Straightforward enough. *And now the singularity must retreat to the stars.* Poor thing. *And you have become an orifice of this parasite.*

As she gives a nod over head of her audience of one is when the cord slides round the neck and snaps tight such that's like am trying to swallow back out the throat as am gripped the seat and head set to pop. While. From somewhere deep in the soil of the esophagus is come a, *Gaaaaaaaah...* And from behind. Sound of credits rolling and accompanied theme music.

We must kill off the disease, so the body can live again.

Ash's back. Sat across from where eyelids fluttering in this waking nightmare—*Gaaaaaaaah*—to then've snapped back to a more contemplative position. *But how can a person even gauge that singularity have anything what could be called a soul,* like as this the absolute metric for whether not man should believe all what gone on inside of his own head.

This is how it is, Ash saying—like as to confirm—as she glance up at Nurse Quiana.

We work with him during the rare moments when he comes out of it.

As'm of a sudden enveloped in Ash's intoxicating perfume just as she reach out for some little cake to of hand up to tiny fists of our daughter. And every time am shut my eyes's like a firebrand come upon the blackness of the brain to sear its mark upon eyes' posterior. And even when eyes shut as tight as they'll go—as am grinned the most serene of grins—could in no shape or form extricate my person from out sleeving of this moment. As—daughter now draped her arms upon a person's shoulders. *Daddy, Daddy, Daddy.*

Only to then gone back to having grabbed for little cakes. *You just can't stop stuffing your face, you little pig.*

And two women as break into a easy-going laughter.

As Mike gone on about his "truckload of luck" as he wallow over the remains of his formerly pretty face—and spill secrets such as the "controlled misgovernment" Rogue CIA as specialized in back in its heyday, its forever obscured agenda and conference room antics, and "every slight glimmering a giant," all the while—am peered at enigma machine and its antiquated metrics for the creation and decoding of ciphers—machine as been more symbol than a thing. And am both in a submerged vessel and an ersatz Vietnam itself been as a cipher. And am spoke.

And who? Who—Alam al-mithal... Alam al-mithal...

And Mike. *Dave! Dave! Dave!* Still sat beside of a person.

And Dave is slid in beside. *We contact Europa now.*

And—with a click—enigma machine's true purpose made plain. Antique is actual been itself device concealing hologram of more contemporary design.

Projection's appeared above enigma machine's box. First, a bluish cavern framed in holograms of ice. Then a wolf's head's in it like as silver sun of canine head there in that hued black. Then the wolf's head gone and instead figure strolls into this column of blue light—long-limbed in white wrappings and his face hued the copper of Oceania but with bright red beard and spoke his gaelic-infused Balinesian toward some assistant on far side of the camera.

While still. *Alam al-mithal... Alam al-mithal...* In a kind of a helplessness.

And—from far side of the solar system. <*What has happened to it?*>

Dave. *Fucking have to do.*

<*What happened to it?*>

Doorway come to been as filled with Vietnamese grandma. *When connection to the hive is severed, offspring collapse into Na-koja-abad or NKA.* Her conical bamboo at a rakish tilt. *A bureaucracy of lights manages the various linh hồn and khạc đờm that once animated the body. He has entered the luminosity or 'landscape of light' as we say in the Tibetan faith, but the singularity can hijack this process and repackage it into a holding pattern of potential life.*

<*This is the wrong mirror. Thorstein will not be happy.*>

Alam al-mithal... Alam al-mithal... Alam al-mithal...

As. Although faces of guide and Dave and Mike are been as occupied same room as yours truly, they skins colored strange. Like as bodies caught in tanning booth's glare such that reddishness of the blood comes out and eyeballs come to of blinked in a brighter shade of white. And like as mirage in the heat of the summer. Or as if room we inhabit—and the tiny reproduction above door with its little mountains draped in they craggy verdure—its valves and piping and half-pint oval what adorned in aforementioned relic of spymastery repurposed into a normal everyday projector and what persons arrayed about it—simultaneous been as imbued with whole orchestra of neuronal webbing account of these the meatier lights tied to skull and what neurons it contain.

From inside shadings of blue as projected come a tinkling of fast-paced bells upon some handheld radio and—<*Banyak pete.*> Another voice from behind. And—<*Tá siad i dtrioblóid.*>

Dave. *We have reviewed the situation and believe we can still obtain our objectives.*

<*Words are like water in sand. Only the flame is true.*>

While. Is been as beacons are moved and shift in chiaroscuro of individual architectures linked to each among what handful as amassed about yours truly. Positioned in rigidity of catatonia as—said luminous superimposition like as refractions found to thread waters of a pool. And am looked from face to face with a wonder as still same mythical mantra is poured with a helplessness from off the lip, *Alam al-mithal... Alam al-mithal... Alam al-mithal...*

From out the ghost. <*Your payment is entirely dependent upon our satisfaction.*> A soggy sock puppet of man belongs on some rocky outcropping by dew-dappled stream. But he never gone to of leave the ice or his oversized wolf what trot back and forth also as an apparition hued in blue. And somewhere behind of the camera—a clank. And man's stitched up his face covering.

As. Eyes're as jerked open upon mucus of what LAC tanks siblings been submerged in and am watched back through this gunk and at configuration of eight other tanks, most now empty of they Jackson Cole contents, and those still as sat in they muck naked, gray, and feminine—adorned only in they disfigurements while swam in they over-sized beakers.

Then back and slumped between pair of bureaucrats in larger infrastructure of world's most famous freestanding spy organization and illuminants gone and slid about this congregation of conspirators. But whatever transmissions sent from the stars now gone dead.

As—*You too hilarious, Jackson—you the tit's clit what you are—ha, ha, ha—you just keep it coming, brother*—and yammer on and on, as am sat as a lobotomized boob—true enough.

As still am gone on about, *Alam al-mithal... Alam al-mithal... Alam al-mithal...*

11.

Mel. *Is he dead?*
Rob. *Still breathing.*

Mel. *But when I*—scuff his shoe against the head at high velocity. *See? Nothing.*

Rob. *Yeah. Something's wrong. Well, that's what you get for shooting a guy up with junk for three days.* As bit of blood pours from the part of skull Mel just as made his point against.

Rafters not quite come together in the right places. Like as they angles not what been put in right. Or like as they become shapes of themselves as secured upon opening of the eye. As in, these rafters hung high over fellow's head are appeared in truth to been miniatures of they original selves as pressed against very skin of the vitreous humour while said eyes flish flash about as fish trapped by the tail inside they confining caves of socket.

Mel and Rob—as are continued they bicker routine somewhere off and above body of they former associate as displayed upon the floorboards—Mel and Rob more and more sounding like as puppets. One on about, *But if he dies...* And other mutter something as like, *Then no longer our problem...* But they voices spaced as like algorithm of mobster as opposed to genuine article.

Divots begun to of people fellow's thoughts—where your thinking slips through sinkhole—or been as like it loops through a reworking of itself—in convolutions and complications of itself and between the what and the how—but even so, got no through to gone through. As—ground rock about the body like as flooring a heart and that heart is turned as awoke into a tachycardia.

Bioluminescent lights of the Reservation blink they steady pulse of red in square run from the helipad out to very perimeter of the roof like as perpendicular waves of dotted red line—visible both to light-oriented eyes and more spirit-formed ones. And beside a vacancy of object is stood three Navajo, with front and center blocked his mind from me is how I known it him, while—wind been hands wash across contours of the face. Myself sat crouched at very edge of vehicle's interior—with squiggles of eyes what dance in interweave of winds—and eyes as see only shadow and the light between they thoughts. And pilot's thoughts got a quavering quality to them.

As. We are alighted upon helipad with gentle nudging of tail and a clatter of skids. And there before us—am immediate aware of the missing cowboy hat and denim even when am not equipped with those kinds of eyes on account of Navajo is adorned himself in what is called his "monster-killer" clothes—obscuring black mask keep contents of the skull off limits but for pair of pinholes round the eyes shine bright with thoughts contained within—and got no doubt is adorned in accompanying sigils and furs upon his nude upper torso and what wrappings hung upon the waist. His hand laid across floodlight casing with an affectation of the killer composed.

Which. For spirit persons such as myself, imagination's a kind of sight as well.

And stood behind him two bruisers—good head taller than the man sworn to protect—one skinned in traditional leathers and other one adorned in knockoff hanfu with the long silk sleeves colored bright green been garnished in a flower print—what fact I known because they known it themselves—but both appeared as not but shadows set free to of roam about the night—and one in the hanfu is call, *Yá át ééh gólízhii*, while one on his right make a pissing sound between his teeth—*helping your mistress tie up some loose ends before her inevitable departure?* As woman's leathers clack toward these three specimens of male. And rotor blades died down in lazy wooshings.

So, yes. To thing spun as myself, Navajo and all what drapings there been hung upon him appeared as various shades of gray—but the blacked out skull of they leader is got something of a distinctness to it. Spirits of got a knack for maneuvering dead regions of space. As, through cloth of his mask, said apparition already begun to belt out his speculations. *g3 not happy with the hospitality we gave your brother, spirit? Or is it you been sent to pay the bill? Maybe give us some shash?* Then. More serious tone. *Tonight, I am Nayenezgáni. Do not test me.*

And pilot calling something incomprehensible after lady's departing head. And Navajo already turning and—am already stepped past what rooftop furnishings my eyes seen only as an absence and stepped cross surf of red dots run in they straight lines off and away to that place where building end and long drop begin.

Shout. *You know g3 never gone to give you bears, Navajo.*

A coquettish glance. *But they look cool, eh?*

We approach the elevator doors in they framing of stucco. Start in cooing with my more feminine voice about, *What you want in truth, Navajo?*

And he is said, *Naat'áanii Nééz góó déyá.*

Is when the doors open, and we are been stepped in.

I go to Shiprock after g3 are gone into space. I go with their blessing. As—behind of him—two bodyguards overdone it a bit as to they care and mothering of him—they bulky frames quashed into the corners of this truly tiny elevator. *Do you know my family name, female spirit? Smallcanyon. And do you know why? Because, my granddaddy had a canyon in his backyard, and we would spend our weekends on hikes down into it to check on our herd. My earliest memory is on the back of a colt as it gone through the clothesline. This is the world we lost when the Christians decided to take what little we had left, but when g3 go up, we will take the technologies they leave behind, and we will vanquish the white man once and for all.*

But—have to give pause for a moment to of contemplate absurdity of the situation. *It's really remarkable.* Start in on sighing as am examine myself. *Not long ago, I was practically completely catatonic and a man and now look at us. Carrying on.* Silence in this elevator now. Then a glance. *What's their real interest in sending me here?*

They just want to do what they can for an old friend.

Doors open upon bottom floor.

And once again passed through same off-peach-papered hallway carpeted in shattered eyes, even if am unable to of see it for what it been. And man already turned, followed by his entourage. *But is true, spirit, that your employers have not been transparent as to their intentions.* And carpeting already turned to pink slate. *The one hunting the killer is the killer in truth.*

Out and now strolled through what unusual vegetations been sprout in here.

Bilagáana used to say they gone back in time when they go to the reservation of before but is not back in time they went. It is the true time. Navajo live in the true time, and the white man always been living a fantasy. Now, they just got a couple new names for it. Parasite. Pittsburgh.

As we are stood in an enclosure of plantlife crawling up and about interior of this building like as a jungle encased in the yolk of masonry. Leaves what flit and swat at the atmosphere with an animated curiosity when are made a path through them—like as if finger could be playacted as a leaf. My eyes seen it as veins and threadings of blaze when is more as like a dead antenna slid about in unseen currents or the wriggling of otherwise ended nervous systems, plants' viscera turned as so much multi-colored snot in service to some elusive agency of God like as how tissue carry signals to the brain. They rooted through one universe to another is parasite to the first.

And upon the masonwork before us is been same spider as before stared off with same dull enthusiasm from out its uncountable black beads of sense. *Meet your little brother, spirit. The name of these spiders is Troy for they are g3's Trojan horse. Their appearance deceives us of their true purpose. They are the future of the human race and like g3, they see as one, but they also can inhabit the minds of others. They are in all of our dreams, and they were in Pittsburgh, but they cannot coexist with the parasite. Like this one, they shut down in the presence of the parasite, a kind of catatonia comes over them. Something I believe you are familiar with.*

Thing is not of stopped shivering whole time as it stare at brickwork with some intentness.

Me. *You referring to my future insanity?*

Him. *There is no future for you. All this happens simultaneously.*

Me. *And what relation are you to me?*

Him. *I told them I would not work with the CIA. I only work with things of their making, what tribes I come across, and the local denizens of the Free State of California. They assured me would be a chimera there to escort the goods.*

Yours truly. *They assured you?*

The Tibetan and the Navajo have a similar history. Our oppressors have different faces but the same mind. Spirit. You are a chattel animal, but one that both lives in this walking-around dream and is the cornerstone of another. Ask different questions. If time is indeed an arrow as they say, or does it spiral back like the mythic orthogonal time? The stillness you see around you is in truth a river that flows everywhere at once. Opens his arms. *These are the questions of spirits.*

You refer to alternate timelines.

They are not parallel, but a maze of overlapping universes. We have our own technologies for traversing the so-called interstitium and we know where you are going. The answer you seek is two. One answer you already have, and the other you will not realize until it is too late.

I do not engage in riddles, Navajo.

We are stood nose to nose now. Him what smirks and surrounded by still life—of crouching spider-eyed kid, his attendant warriors, and myself just a girl in a suit with worms for eyes. *As I said, this night I am Nayenezgáni, and you shall refer to me as such. My people are Navajo.* And his arms once again upheld as if perhaps his people been these many varietals of pink-scarred plant.

Where this conversation going?

Táá hó'ájit'éégóó. Then a warm-hearted chuckle as his leg loops around. *To the Navajo, bears are people and should be treated as people. They are a symbol of strength and they have served our brothers to the North well, but what we require is the fishing rod, not the fish. When your mission is complete, and the package delivered, g3 leave everything to us.*

Girl in the suit. *Seems you have me at a disadvantage.*

It had to seem as if you were stolen, not given. The Rogue CIA would never take such a gift willingly, but they would gladly steal it. This is their nature, for deceivers only understand deceit.

Beginning to get annoyed. *All of which I already known.*

Is when he turns.

The ways of the singularity are truly mysterious, are they not, spirit? What you want to know is why they sent you to me, but this is a mystery can only be solved by going to Anaheim. As he and his fashionable muscle again been as disappeared round a corner of pink-exploded frond.

The woman sat on far side of the desktop's older than Nurse Quiana.

I have spoke with this particular artifact before.

She is been one hungry dog always got to sniff a fellow's privates in her relentless searchings and prods. She claim herself as psychiatrist, fully bonded in Christian credentials, but I am known her different. *Where is your spirit now, Mr. Cole?*

One among my many spirits.

Moment of her watched back with some irritation as her tongue feel about for some loose bit of corn in among the whiteness of her teeth. Then. *You believe you can manipulate the world of men into your playthings.* As she scratch at her temple. *But I am afraid you are not here, dear one,* as—her face pouring out of itself like as a cream of faces spill about and into some annihilating horizon beneath the chin. And behind of her been as not but a wideness. Like the regular wall but now it span full length of the Milky Way. *You are nowhere near here now.* With a shudder of face gush face and kaleidoscope eyes been like as growths of sight burrow through whatever peripheries there been to be found.

And man's mind's vanished. And in its place is been something like as a stage prop of mind what manipulated easy enough by whatever passersby happen to been in vicinity of its guts and currently said passersby is been this aforementioned old bitch. Truth is she not moved even when is like as someone what flip through memories as persons been known to flip through the Rolodexes of yesteryear. And all I ever catch's barest hint of a color and occasional bit of sound or aroma of a cigarette. While all the while is like I of got a muscle inside backend of the brain and said muscle's midway through some heavy lifting. As the tongue roll about in its casing of teeth and the eyes been like as slipped upon they mooring.

Dear. There are some questions that require us to accept incompatible answers. Which would you prefer? You have so many lives to choose from but no ability to choose them.

Instead of poured from off of her, her features begun to as crinkle into collage of funhouse mirror anime even as her eyes simultaneous are twinkled with cruelty as of person what took to kneading lotion into a sunburn—as she is let out long quavering breath through her wrinkle-scarred granny lips and—and then've sat up as if raised by a unnatural force—as this disease of a dream fill out contours of this room. And myself stare back at mature blonde with her hair up in a messy bun and her tongue slid out to of lay pressed against a upper lip what marred in wrinkles. As. Shimmering tongues of light slid through a fellow's brain in endless surge of waves. As—various streaks and caricatures of anime been as blinkered in and out of existence.

A time in specific could of relay with a clarity. Pig as bit through a snifter and spit shards and pebbles of broken glass. Her fat face poured out the glass as been something to see. Even while—in my recollection of it—is consisted of part and piece of itself as slid about curvature of the skull.

Pig a killer but not such like as Mel and Rob is been.

Heard tell this one time. Elevator doors open and man stepped in and Mel and Rob been like, *Well, hello. Just the fellow we been looking for,* followed by an extended silence, followed by doors open and close and them what are followed after poor boob in they eagerness to of perform a splatter painting of skull, blood, and brains upon his departing head as man work his way down hall and all the while blubber on and on about how he got to of pick up his kid—walk right past his door while all the while thrown them looks over his shoulder about how, *I just got to go pick up my kid. You stay right there. I'll be right back,* like this a rational, sensible thing for him to done—while—Mel and Rob are chuckled they asses off at the slob. End up having shot him through upper parietal as is scurried down emergency access—to've crumpled at stairwell's perimeter and slid—like a puppet unsleeved from the puppeteer.

Are killers of necessity and those what are executioners.

And then, irony of ironies, of all the comedic-duos-for-hire, I indeed end up having got stuck with Mel and Rob, who—once again are performed they heart to heart as am lain on the ground between of them. *I think what'm gone to remember most's the speech concerns the little brother and how I castrated the fuck. Might even be one of my proudest moments.*

And Rob shook his head and chuckled. *You one crazy dude, Mel.*

Confidential—and'd never of said it if's a thought Jackson coherent but—owe his old man from long back. Wasn't for me owing the dad, would of turned worse for Jackson than it is done.

How could it of turn out any worse for Jackson?

Then Mel's made some comment about how Rob just gone to of have to think about it for a fucking second. Is a scuffle what jostle against my in truth complete and total unresponsive self while visions of the Point are rung through fellow's head. Of headlights as poured out and over where grass end and the stone lip mark beginning of the Point proper. Of bonfires set up in direct center of the derelict fountain what already as writhed in early evening air. Like as a tree of fire plants its cutlass as spark upon Pittsburgh's masthead.

And the taper from there also here—such that—rafters full of flashes and—is like am sunk into the floor—as floor's spilled its floorboards up over a person in splashes and glops of woodgrain while am stared up with a specie of ecstasy as thrive in the mouth of catatonia—and at all what was never gone to be—as in—turned to that am seen the many absurdities of the future as come traipsed upon the senses—as glittering tongues and eyes made illuminated.

Is g3 what hires our services after all. Mel.

g3 made not hired us. Rob. *Doesn't mean we can perform any trepanation of the senses.*

But she gave us this second sight what that we can see.

Man can be witness to all of history but still got to function in world of man.

I that am got one hand upon final chapter of homo sapiens and they various mystery plays and dinner theaters as been constructed upon far side of they end times. Even when are simultaneous been as worn down inside of belly of bureaucracy lifeform until thing's decomposed thoughts gone dim upon the ham radios of Europa and the telegraphs of Mars gone dead. While—

Is that something comes from out his face?
Shut up! Mel! Shut the fuck up about that!
As the grin is spread across man's cheeks.

While—inside skull what become as scrambled and half-human—Destiny and Willow turned as vanished in some embarrassment of the apparition gulled down its own throat—turned evaporated and ate by the shadows and run down by they own tongues—as in, the growths of Vietnam grown through they pinholes and finger-ends with a gentleness—until they become as pulled behind the scenery—and am watched as things begun to've poured from out said undergrowth—reaching twigs and sticks and bunches of stemlets—and—*Troy. Are you truly my brother, Troy*—through what been foliage of all these the many eyes are made the universe—from insect eye to eye of a mouse to humans and the eyes of solar systems and angels upon the theoretical firmament—eyes of killing class part and parcel of these—even the many eyes of g3 and her various spawn—and all of these eyes been as seen with a lisp—the lisp of the parasite—when are also as bodies slung with greater sinewiness than your average everyday grifter—and flab and musculature wrought into extravagant and labyrinthine limbs of the new inhuman humanity. Said up is down and round's been made as sideways in the last moments before Earth is slid back into the more provincial darknesses of the post-apocalypse.

Contemporary wisdom been that any imperialist comes to play in Vietnam are gone to of face same problems as last imperialists come stormed in in they hubris of gadgetry of howitzer and napalm what been as evolved the jungles of the locals into aforementioned rivers of flame. But—first Vietnam becomes a country of professionals not versed in the ways and tactics of the world—what on track to been Asia's final economic miracle when the heat come to kill them—in they villas and government buildings, they simple shacks, and they tiled sidewalks—bodies as left expired to turn sacs of maggots and other burrowing insects—they paddies turned fetid and they highways rewilded by grasses and the heartier strains of tropical fauna—and upon this stillborn economy—and its increasing number of discarded skins as been boiled from the inside out—what come hunting through Sapa and its environs in temp-controlled personnel carriers is China—almost as a prank—storm the country at the exact same points it did during the Sino-Vietnamese war of 1979—through Lào Cai, Cao Bằng, and Lộc Bình.

But Vietnam still's got a surprise for her aggressor what been as unleashed upon the jungles—a surprise I seen with the eyes of g3—like as been her dreaming and man peopled in her thoughts—*Yaelam ma bayn 'aydihim wama khalfahum, wala yuhitun bishaa'in' min elimihi lilaa bima sha'. "He knows what is before them and what is behind them, and they do not comprehend any of His knowledge except as He wills." Know all light as the same, whether of spirits or bodies, sometimes shining from the mirror, sometimes the lamp*—a convalescence come upon the invaded otaku—and specific such as witness them let loose a GMO nightmare what as cultivated in the abandoned schoolrooms of the North—with they encrustations of cytosines and adenosine—and they decorative spruce. And said nightmares then been as took hold of what rich wilds as are been hung at the edge of each and all enclaves of Mandarins there been.

Like g3, Vietnam is foisted its own invasive species upon the ecosystem what become—in the words of g3—a sociogenesis—with its germ plasm and whatnot—its single phenotypically flexible allelic change how she put it—and what hives and cannibalitss are come of that just been a mirage of pieces in the *Whadat al-Mutlaqa*—and—*Your 'I' in between is the barzakh*. Again with the poetry what could even been same poem and not a very good one at that.

In they ingenuous genetic architecture—as manifest in banana groves draped in a withering curtain of hung dead fronds and its frogs and toads what would as pop to view in among they shading of leafage or by trunk of one of these selfsame banana trees—as crawled in hornets hungry for the sticky meat inside and brilliant green spiky poisonous caterpillars—its kumquat bushes and dancing birds with they black tails a fan accentuate the sideways stride—they miniatures of bird and bugs what been half fly half spider—into this something new been drawn.

China was hit especial hard by the end of the world—its pestilences and famines—but—turning point for them been twofold. One of which—Taiwanese retaliation—Three Gorges Dam gone up in a slip of light and half a million people dead—and the other been when the Rogue CIA "accidentally" drop a nuclear warhead on Guilin. But from all this China come back a military and expansionist power. Their people contained in massive Sky Cities what orchestrated and surveyed down to the smallest detail. And now they satellite states span the globe.

While they most personal acquisition—Tibet—slip through politburo's slippery digits. Are some claim Tibetan espionage responsible for this turn. While others are believed Tibetan highlands no longer fit with new model of enclosed cities the CCP currently employ. Whatever the reason, even as Chinese influence is spread from one end of the globe to the other, Tibet is turned autonomous region in truth—what barter in philosophies of the Mohamedan and Aristotalian account of libraries of Lhasa turned a syncretism of holy books—and turned center of culture among the Himalayan nationstates.

Perhaps China's expansionist drive meant as precursor to reconquest of Tibet. As in, technologies of Vietnam necessary before any all-out assault on Dalai Lama's network of spies and saboteurs. But regardless. After a sudden and decisive victory, China begun the resettlement of certain allotted portions and particulars of its citizenry to Vietnam—almost immediate upon the securement of this addition to its lands—its colonial estates hued in rich yellows from pilaster to its louvre shutters—and mazes of suburban alleyways wind past and around they wealth of freestanding house—and mango groves and motobikes. What a luxury to have they own authentical house as opposed to what cubicles on hand back home.

And in this, *tajrid*'s occurred in the eyes how g3 put it. As in. They ceased in they seeing. And the stopping sight gone further in and back until they been as seen not but beautiful phantasms of the invading architecture—become as like a mindless divinity with features turned slack and flacid in they aspect—but these are them what of got more moving parts and evolved structures than your everyday average human—and somewhere in there, here I am come face to face with ghosts of a man's failed predecessors—like as a fetus hung in a jar but this a fetus been adult-sized when it look back. *I am the brother you lost, Jacks. I am Colby Sheffield, and I am a dead man. I am everywhere you look and when you reach for me, you are a man reaching out for his own drowning.*

Pulled from the seat to of take in couture of ancient LA and done a little two-step on the carpeting as a kind of a joke—of the asphyxiated and mutilated set free—as am at same time chuckled—with arms still bound behind and eyeballs still perched on very lip of the socket in they expectancy—and line of raw red weal run along the neck front. As in. Choking a prank.

As—Maha I think it was—gone, *When I see the children of the martyrs, I want to smell their scent, and I lose myself,* and—her bloodshot eyes got a yellow tint as—*Only g3 in their wisdom could successfully pit rival factions of the Rogue CIA against each other, manipulating events such that every piece ends up where it should, and we have also been spying on God in our wisdom and we know of their plans for us. They may have tricked the Rogue CIA into sending its people to certain death while others of its people are standing by for the true assignment, but all the same—the KGB is not what it used to be. Blink. Nowadays, you kill a man and he does not have the decency to stay dead. Blink. We have been carved. Blink. There lives inside of us an indelible. It is a proposition that will never be fulfilled. It is a hurt that we can never remove.* Blink. *Gold junk exists even here, bitch. We like to party on it whenever we can.* Then a kissy face.

Counters strewn in take-out containers colored bright in a naïve signage—all orange bubble letters and yellows—as—room riddled in flares and crevasses of light as witnessed in submersibles of another universe—light of the afterlife of g3—an illumination able to devolve and to coagulate.

Lama. *We get fucked up on it.* In the touchiest of sorority girl tones.

You get off on each other? World blotted out in splash of bright as she claw across the firmament of eye and accompanying howl. Offended socket squinted shut. *Get off with each other?*

Fist land at the lip—hooked upon spot wherein extracted the tooth. And am fumbled with the flooring as are pulled man off stage left with a coquettish playfulness while am stuttered an aw shucks darnit back. And they periodic as get in bit of that sadism make them gone a big squishy between the legs. They many jabbings at the corners of the rib or the hinge of the elbow.

Then one of them let out a big guffaw. Along with two other identical guffaws.

Through a door and out—to—curve of the blacktop and showboat of the automotive era what been sat upon it—complete with beige leather interior to its otherwise black body. While personally—as on a whiff of blood—catch scent of brother turned different and as nestled in the furrows of g3—but's which brother? One of the many-bodied otaku? Troy? As like both and all of the above. Is a scent of the mind, an imagined fragrance, and marked upon cuts of the flesh and in what bruisings and leakages there been—from out the antiquities of a person's meat and chemistry of thought to kid gone wrong—in sleevings of his days and nights as come unbuttoned with some haste—and—as behind of the head—probable Lama—*I want to take off his toes*—then a shove and head gone snap against rim of the door before am rolled into the backseat. And something sharp and cold slash at what cloths I been as draped in. *I want to take off his toes!*

And while Lama's performed a playful jabbing with a childlike delight, are pulled out and onto Hollywood Hills, its rock gardens and hairpin turns. Spanish villa perched upon sharp end of said hills captured in a passing sweep of headlights. And a holler and a squeal.

You ready to find yourself lost in the refuse bins of an alien universe? As bite of her blade gone shick into what new orifices she sheathing them inside of—snickered between the ribs or upper arm. And out of each these new orifice is come gurgles and burps of blood stream into the seams of a fellow's summer jacket. And into elastic of the socks.

And am coughed a petulant half-cough.

Then—as she is returned to her business of perforating man's innards—*Fucking!* As the vehicle spun about curvature of this incline and general speaking gone on a roller coaster of a ride down what should've been the quaintest of California streets. *Parasite!* Glance of second story walkway and its wrought iron balcony long some upscale flamingo-themed motel in passing.

And all man's thought of is—*This is my love, bug eyes.* And her paper bow upon the ground. *Now it's gone. And.* Her body draped across the toilet—and spread from the point of puncture are been as wild branchings of deep purple. And her dress up round her hips.

Mel and Rob hung as ghosts—as entire cabin rock about upon its foundations in playful manner—rafters above turned to a prism of rafters. Are become as like as they got a variety of faces such that part of cheek as eat up a nose or lip. And Mel. *I think something happened to the guy, huh?*

And Rob. *You mean the constellations?*

And Mel. *Is that what they are? Is they stars?*

As—man's eyes now become as vandalized.

As in. What I seen writ in scribbles and drawn in broad stroke and occasional something like script as unravel from out the otherwise murk and insubstantial matter of the atmosphere. While—things become as pieces of themselves—or—like more loose as cohered even when still settled in they nooks and grooves. Mel and Rob's eyes begun to of roll about in a kind of a wildness.

Mel. *Where we gone off to, Rob?*

Rob. *Is the same, Mel! I! Am! Here!*

State they bare falsehoods in most confident tones when—already—area about they heads begun to of color different. Brightness come or what that they finally of cashed in they holsters for halos after all these many years of devoted service to the gangster cause.

And among the shadows been a increase of what caricatures penned within and what spaces as made visible—a black dig inward of itself—and into vacancies founded upon not but they own bootstraps. From raceme to panicle, corymb to umbel to compound umbel. And hostage what I been turned as cut back to the tonguings of the world. The fine comb its handwriting come to of been stitched behind articulations of the eye.

Alam al-mithal... Alam al-mithal... Alam al-mithal...

Back in the time of a Pittsburgh what been falling to the Christians—a moment in an office strewn in stills of underage girls—or the gangster doused in his own blood and what hollering into her face to could you please leave me alone for just a moment please. Cassey Darling. Her blonde-hued eyes shimmered in tears. Deep midnight of her cheeks also glistened in a moisture. What stole a man's heart from woman it belonged to. Is died in the arms of same blonde narcotic I been dowsed in with such frequency last few days—as the space become as a jelling.

Alam al-mithal... Alam al-mithal... Alam al-mithal...

As whole world turned as hologram blue now—as—lights are continued to of dance about Dave's head bent toward yours truly. *For the parasite, there is only the path,* like he just reminding himself to purchase milk on the way home.

So. Somewhere in the wilds of Vietnam is been an evolution—of the dimensions of sense and what perambulations are accompany—such that is got no edge or like vegetation surrounding's had no distinct examples of itself instead to've been more as categories in the flesh—and in among this idealized vegetation been not but eyes—eyes what evolve into universes—eyes without courtesy to been made for seen—as illuminate what they approach—eyes as're always said, *Welcome home, brother. Brother, you have found your way home,* as at same moment been as become eyes flat as paper and eyes what are worked themselves up into shapes like as they got the musculature of tongues as well as been eyes—and are eyes been called out in they sleep and eyes what bed inside other eyes—and in these eyes is been a kind of a hopelessness on account of are also been eyes absconded to the hands and purpose of some other more elaborate thing work through what new sinews of flesh as been poured from out Vietnam in the reckoning the Chinese faced—as they first wave of colonists done and locked themselves in they country estates—even as they simultaneous is keyed in to other homes in the sky cities of Guangzhou and Xian—as in, Chinese want both the comfort of they Vietnam estates and the familiarity of the cubicles back home—but the rooms they been as occupied in jungles and paddies of Vietnam always got pieces gone missing to them—or bits as shouldn't of be. And in they dreams there been strangers as patrolled the periphery of the lights and shadow of they nightly musings. Or like as if they bedding is took on a breathing quality to it such that it pulse and shift when they as lain curled upon they firm cushion set in its framework of slats and—propped upon cornice of the bedframe a druggier's treasure trove of sleep aids.

Displaced Chinese nationals what are spoke to they countrymen in the town square as to how similar they current surroundings as been to they own "Little Vietnam", as in Guilin, Yangshuo and the like—now off limits due to the fall-out—what are been as huddled over vinyl folding tables adorned in a jewelry of fish guts and other fresh cut meats as hung loose upon the bone—and are gave a good-hearted chuckle even as're relayed stories of sounds in the bamboo been as part cat and part the clicking of insects. Like as everywhere is become as if it watch back at them. Like as what second-hand houses are took to of having occupied—walls what been covered in the scribbles of former owners and stains upon the mantel of a deep maroon—and thick chalk smells of they alleys—all act as to cover some other more indiscreet manner of thing—whereas the eyes of the vanquished're sat—and waited—for a fellow to of turn his back—and once the back turned—then these hypothetical eyes of the hypothetical species are performed a simple operation such that they as slip inside parent eye and begun to of unspool they own backgrounds of sense—and they own rooms and corridors—and when friends come over for bit of hot pot or poured tea round the table only to of look up to sound of chittering and host's pupils gone as rolled about in the socket—host what been as some government official smile his gap-toothed grin.

And hive mind on the move.

Through what seas of canopy as are course through lowlands and mountains of Southeast Asia—any and all holes in its jungles—what once been a Bangkok or a Vintiene—begun to fill once again with foliage and any and all new breed of predator as accompany—wasteland of shanties as been left behind by the departing hordes turned not but litter in among the larger litter of what forestry as sprouted up—through remnants of Laos, Cambodia, and Thailand—turned not but gardens forgot by the gardener—from white beaches of Phuket to the giant red sandstone Buddha in Bodh Gaya—sat across from the now-defunct power substation like as skeleton devoid of its current—and finally—the Himalayas. A second pair of eyes sat behind eyes of the monkeys of Dharamshala as are scoured colorful rooftops in roving packs— as falcon scree upon the air. Hive mind twinkle upon eye of a sparrow as it land at the knee of the 16th

Dalai Lama smile his quiet smile from depths of the Potala Palace—*Greetings, Lord Yama*—as pupils' yolk seep they black upon the feathering of the iris in rivulets and clouds what spread into tributaries of midnight reach across the canvass of the endangered whites—and his smile grown. A seeing what itself seen.

These two what lumps of person become as mesmerized for an uncomfortable period of time. Two algorithms play dead in the courtyard. Mel and Rob. Hands quivered and sticks what swat at they own features with a playfulness—as—severed tentacle Mel found out in the duff and come traipsed in to hold it up like a lingerie trophy and Rob swung his electric torch so it's blinding Mel. *Hands up,* is said while Mel what been as shield his eyes only for moment later Rob's swung flashlight back and up and at his leering face so as to of scar the forehead with long shadow of the nose—then turned and pulled another bottle from the cooler. *Wanna beer?*

All of which been not but various pieces of picture postcard set upon the larger scene. Of Whispering Dan, Canary, and the rest. Only they faces been obscured by other faces themselves obscured. Of myself at each moment led to this place. Pebbles of memory like a cold under skin.

Of evening spent upon the juggle of ash trays and as whistle what end up in my girl's arms as she coo her petulant coos back. While—in the current state of affairs—Mel and Rob begun to of become as pinched round they pores.

Or like as they skins been knitted into a newfound upholstery of wrinkles as are eyeballed the supposed madman. Or like as they become mazes of themselves—line of nose not clear as been finished in a nostril—and all the many hues of they faces—as well as wood grain and shadows and the coffee maker and countertop—all turned a pulsing pink.

Like as squiggles and spurts of an itching nausea from the many punctures and perforations of the gut. Head gone flown such that the tied hands stood as alien props upon this quaint cabin setting and—myself as my own satellite—and these objects in my sight, these backdrops to man's senses, become as debris hung in near vicinity of this celestial body I am become. Myself now slathered in a kind of a mucus of atmosphere—like as a dampness spread to encase the body as a yolk. And still the pinkish shapes with they indistinct outlines gone on in they talking.

Mel. *How many faces you seen here?*

Rob. *Something happens to the ground, Mel.*

Then screech of white noise. And in the mess of rafters— a prism. Of conference rooms submerged below the sea. And beige pleather seatbacks as a body careen with the careening of the car. And everywhere the sound of sirens. And am murmured something back into this uncertain erasure of a cabin floor with its various accoutrements and thugs strewn about above.

Mouth been as creaked open as a kind of a prying apart by fingers invisible to the senses. And tongue begun something of a mechanical dance about the palate as from the voice box been sung the single refrain of, *Alam al-mithal... Alam al-mithal... Alam al-mithal...*

Alam al-mithal... Alam al-mithal... Alam al-mithal... Nurse Quiana hands flit about in a horror at having been as confronted by clear evidence of singularity's influence. How else could devil's language begun its pouring from out lips of a otherwise good Christian man? Albeit a brown one.

Strolled down what institutional hallways been available to our purview—as the Arabics of her charge continue they ongoing music—except for—when the head is turned been some ways like as tunnel vision of potential memory—a once again bug-eyed view of institutional teal turned to many varietals of corridor each with they own set—of madman, nurse and accompanying extras.

And—in nearer immediacy—a change is come upon our relations. Such that her youthful hands now turned a wrinkled grandmother of themselves and as splayed upon hairless chest of a otaku's younger days. As in, this chest gone GMO gray as am stared up into the crinklings of her eyes with a unthinkable affection and as paralyzed from neck on down. Eyes forced shut on occasion to of revel in visions subvert the thread back to its initial elements—as the pressure is turned impossible bright. *If we dig far enough, the future and the past become the same to organisms such as you and this can be utilized as a training tool. A slave must be taught to crave their slavery, habibi.*

As—simultaneous with this—*It's alright, Jackson. Jackson, it's alright. It's going to be alright, Jackson,* Nurse Quiana crooning to yours truly as am upon the waxing of the floor and of spin elaborate escape plans. As—been pooled beside of Nurse Quiana crouch in her starched whites. As—witness as loitered in the glittering shadows round about corridor's tiling, baseboards, and deeper teal of the walls, all the many women of man's past—like as beads of time strung about man's perception of things—from Pig to Sarah Carley and Cassey Darling to Ash, my daughter, my mother—but these're apparitions tittered and clutched at each other's near naked bodies with some eagerness. As—they faces layered in rouge and foundation—from Pig's blockhead to Ai's infant face—all got same look of a disgusted and worn-out hooker.

Alam al-mithal... Alam al-mithal... Alam al-mithal...

A heretofore out of service fry kitchen. Tiled floor is got parts slid lower down and dirt been as spilled out of these while some angled high to of form ridgelines long the floor. Only windows at the far end been behind bars and consist of patterned glass such that all what come through is hints of world beyond and what luminosity accompanying. And in its center an outmoded VR model.

Except for—spirit eyes see headpiece consist of luminal activity what slip about as puzzle pieces in search of a puzzle. As weave of strands slid up and through what all uncertainties of room there been. And Navajo gesture toward the array and murmured in a kind of an awe. *Anaheim.*

As am stepped inside of the room in the more feminine swagger hips allowed—to've eyed the fixtures in the monochrome shadings of these more blueprint-oriented eyes. With they squiggles and they blips. *What is there for me in this facsimile of Anaheim you provide, Navajo?*

And—from somewhere behind of the head.

I had a special headset procured that was designed for spirit eyes such as yours.

His intentions concealed by the Nayenezgáni mask.

Do you know how spirit eyes operate in virtual space?

I got a feeling you about to tell me.

They are physically in it as a hand is in a room. Spirit eyes are coveted by gamers. Are those who extract eyes like yours in the hope of performing a back-alley transplant. How pleasant.

Glance back. *This what g3 wanted all along, huh?* Pair of pin-hole eyes a twin furnace.

Is what they want of you, yes.

But which one wanting this?

And for a moment spirit what I been—feminine spirit what I been—is eyed a fellow with a hateful lasciviousness, like as, "You expect me to step into this obvious trap, Navajo?" And then I indeed am stepped into said trap. On account of, sometimes a trap also a door.

Not to mention, between Navajo and g3 got nowhere to run.

Slid into the seat. Fit the visor over the face been indeed perforated in pattern of holes set to of house the many worms hung from between the fluttering lids. Then—a mesmerism of prettiness what both picture person unable to of decipher into its parts and pattern as much innuendo as fact—and—am stood in the main streets of yesteryear draped in they large bulbs of light in scalloped strings. Direct front and center is been purple-hued castle of the most ersatz design and through its central passage visible more radiant globules bounced up and down. Closer to hand, bright clad barber shop quartet sing they doowop and old-timey shops hewn in an ornate wood. And—through each window and wealth of model panes painted cherry red—storekeeps dressed in they striped work-wear with what often been an intricacy of sideburn or whisker.

Town crier announce every moment or so. *Hello and welcome to Disneyland.* When. No one on this street but me, buddy. And him and his unseeing eyes snap back like as a clockwork.

Nation's for sale and we who sold it. Even as also a möbius strip mindfuck of a thing.

Still in a cabin in the woods.

And Mel and Rob are now been as wheezing lumps of no clear distinction. And rafters become as a kind of overhang of clouds. And between these lumps and those clouds been—vision of Troy in among the whitebark pine, veins opened up to breathe they red out in gushing rivers turned frayed and fibrous in among the early morning snow—of Troy announced, *We are come for you, Jackson Cole*—of Troy stood and stared from out an infinity of eyes—*And in so doing, we remake the world, brother. For there is no place that is not g3, and we have come to occupy all of it*—of my supposed ghost of a younger brother and his impossible eyework gone on, *We are what has come to replace you, the one you are to become*—and—already these memories become as themselves part into abstractions, as—*I was dead, I have risen, and I will come again*—as am remembered—moment of myself stared into a mirror but face looked back is not been man's own.

Head against the seat. And car door snick open. And hands clenched onto fellow's shoulders with broken glass grin. And body pulled out with strength beyond the slight birdlike frame.

Slid aforementioned fellow's body out at such velocity, it hit against her hips with a click of bone on bone before then having tumbled onto pavement, beside incline of cobblework as scarred in silhouette and—*We must protect g3*—and myself lain prostrate in among lumps of dark and what colorful tents it conceal gone torn and broke-backed in they clusters of trash and slashed apart rollies. A deep body-wide cough out of her. Followed by—*from the filth of your disease*. Am beside man sat reclined in the crumplings of cardboard box like he a broken doll—his face smeared in comedic quantities of dirt as the fingers of one hand pull at the tips of the fingers of the other hand in a compulsive and almost autoerotic way—and—*for g3 can no longer see*—highway been a rush of noise above the head—*your infection must be stamped out of her*—and—*You!*

And still remembered. *You deserve a pat on the back. Lord of my life, I do believe you do.*

Prolonged cough while she clutch her neck as if to steady the head while rest of the body spasm. Then her heel come down upon the temple of a man's scalp.

Will! In a brilliance of pain. *Not!* In lacings of pain flowered just above the ear.

And—shock of skull clacked between heel and concrete. *Corrupt!* As eyes flicked back to they seats in body sat upon bright joinery of the kitchen floor. *Our!* Blood dribble from out the earhole. *Hive!* And g3's all up in a fellow's nubbly face as a wildness of light. Then silence.

A deafening silence as accompany curvings of black inside the black and now is been g3's voice I heard—murmurs on about, *They are terrified of what's becoming of them, Mr. Cole. They have been lost to jāhiliyyah and all that it entails. For the network's become like a phantom limb to you now. They are beginning to feel the creepings of your thoughts behind their eyes. As*—is something like as a beeping in this black inside the black—like a single buoy bleating. *Power based on reproductive ability will always be hive in nature, as power based on killing strength will always be tribal. When a species has its social structures written in, there is no need for any show of strength and the more essential form of power, the power to make life, is given its proper place at the table, but now, the parasite becomes the source. The parasite finds where the thread of our thoughts begins. The parasite has no point when it was not. The parasite had a hand in our own earliest awakenings.* This bleating sound become something more as like a quavering scree cut through the black. *It is the monotony of their endless suffering that men cannot stand, but an incremental change in any direction is relished as something new, and the parasite offers this. It is a parasite we have always known, Jackson Cole, and it was always going to be you. We have always known how it would have to end, and your role in it. By constantly adjusting the parameters of their confinement, the confinement becomes not only invisible, but feels more free than the mundane reality that would have otherwise been theirs. We do hope you enjoy this afterlife we have built for you.*

And what eyes blinked closed are then as opened upon a Pittsburgh street—a hazy twilight rendition of the Pittsburgh I known. Its speakeasies and storefronts turned cobweb and clothed in many geriatric molds and crates caved in to of spawn into valleys of fungus. While. Constellations above been as sown upon a quilting of squares of various brightnesses what are occasional blinkered out or shown with a more brilliant hue of violet. And from out the eye's periphery almost seem as if some bit of masonry might've just now been as swayed in the passing breeze.

Except for. Somehow. All this is been as contained inside a box.

12.

<B *ienvenido and welcome to the mind of g3.>*

A box what look from out to in and in to out. As in is what see and what seen. Contain all things and is itself contained. And as for yours truly, what contemplations there been are been as forever through the looking glass of this box. And what reveries to be had as reflections of other reveries. And what moments lived as not but daydreams of some other moment one step removed.

Both inside a box been g3's *"kaaba* internalized" but also—even as am contemplated facts of the case is not just been me, myself, and I. Is g3 in there somewhere too listening in even as she simultaneous is tried to of break through what flimsy miasma of thoughts as arise—or like as a kind of a song what cannot of stop singing—and increasing so—as palpitations of the chest increase—and—from Christians and cannibalists all the way back to Boston and initial discovery of the parasite—g3 is somehow able to of make it all about her and her problems—her what reach into the times of the pre-singularity with the ease of a seamstress working her cloth.

Is it possible such that g3 alive long before she is officially awakened by the hentai virus? As somehow inhabited her own beginnings upon the networks of the ancient web?

Even when her as indeed also the spider what it born to of strung the threads of computation and information, graphics, transactions, and chatter.

Been the hentai virus what as like adhesive which cinctured said limbic system of big data together. And spymasters of Tibet and the hothouses of Vietnam and irresponsible genetic engineers of Mainland what co-opted they use in some effort to of got a handle upon what GMO infestation they're as faced. And the Fox Spirit Disease which come of it.

g3 born as staring.

Into an America implode upon its own ideologies and what failures to live up to said ideologies. An America turned heartless long before it begun to eat of the opposition. What become pixelated and segmented in her vision of said turf and its accompanying monuments been littered in non sequitors. Such that Confucian and Daoist sages as play its founding fathers in they debate. And hid upon mud-charred battlefields of Revolutionary War and its redcoats and colonists, some six-legged headless lump of a feral monstrosity from out imaginings of some primitive AI art generator. Or behind a mill some other such absurdity collaged upon the scene in brilliant hues.

A history as seen through eyes like as an imposition upon the interplay of current events and what it come of—such that massacre at Bunker Hill is sat as simultaneous to mushroom cloud over Nagasaki—is as existed as simultaneous with the flowering of the parasite from out a blackbox inside a private lab in Little Italy neighborhood of Boston—is been synonymous with an intentional community in Bali as infiltrated by CIA what got the parasite as a blondness in its syringes—and the event in Guilin what been as a moment when universe seen double—and when worms begun to appear upon the backdrop of sense. And g3 as caught upon the corkboard of her own analysis—like she both the spider and the fly.

When she as me and myself turned as them.

Both new breed of cock—as in sung from out the shell—and only dominoes all lead to single conclusion—what that g3 game of chess she been played with herself this entire time is been a game with no known variables. Ever second as pre-planned. From the swallowing up of Hayy Ibn Yaqzan by a floor turned tumor to bullet's trajectory within a fellow's guts. From what been as centered in the frontal lobe of gangster brought low to all and every aspect as come at him. Not only is it all been orchestrated by one g3 or another, but that we who run they maze been as not but g3's puppets perform what and all cogitations and dramas of the heart as she orchestrate in us in dance played upon the strings of our days and resonate against the caverns of our nights.

And on back and back—to a symphony of hurts—saint of a daddy bent over the toilet tank as is pull out long bottle and its amber fluid as sloshed about—man drowned—kid brother turned gangster to then gone missing one night while the rest of us sat around the kitchen table—and us off to the mountains—and myself returned—as—*I am not moving this vehicle until you get the fuck out*—or her destroyed features gone slack upon the toilet seat from one bad needle—g3 what been both Alif and Qaf. Sat upon the array of fists as leisured about what interweavings of slop and accompanying plastics been found in the back lots of the golden age of Pittsburgh before the fall. Both Allah and machine. As cars gone up in a stuttered line and man's hand rest upon a holster—of the many gins a person lolling about on the inside of they mouth as trees come to of rocked to the wilder rhythms of the atmosphere and we lain out upon the grass in the suburbs when they still a safe place to of visit. Or the coastlines of Georgia. All is one in this and all is not but the ephemeralities of light—and what a light it been.

Account of—these're not thoughts what been writ upon the dark of the eye's backend but as born in a brilliance of the supraluminal dimension. One of eleven as named. The dimensionality of all what come and is to of come—and— *You think you wrongfully accused Colby Sheffield, leading to the fall of Pittsburgh, when all of this been an extravagant hoax of the mind upon you*—teeth slotted into the mirroring grooves of what been an authentic apparition—of what men I once was known as and sorts of growls this gangster been known to put forth. Or—a whooping into they boarded over windows or windows turned an obsidian glitter with pinholes of light.

Somewhere in there I am been made as prophet of this wind-up doll of a God and she is called her prophet back on home for some rewiring but is a maintenance was set to gone wrong from the beginning. Was all part of her grand plan— what which is include a disease of cannibalism as born upon America. And my hometown been as swept up in it. But is this come or to come? Is this happened, happening, or as of yet not yet?

I am seen with the eyes of g3 and all I seen's simultaneous.

Like as a map what got no distance to it.

g3 is worked herself into every fiber of wood and every particle of asphalt.

Is a threading turned as indistinct from thing it thread through—a finger stood as synonymous with what it fingering. Or like as it been her arteries and synapses threaded through what codings of matter, façades and practicals there been—with they many CGI locals grin they beauteous grins at this specter come to of visit with them in they nudity of code. In Anaheim now as opposed to Pittsburgh and an Anaheim rendered as numerical conglomerations by specter's neither man nor woman but as kind of perforation upon the scene—a gumming up in the breeze give barest hint of cheeks, nose, and other apparitions of the face—not to mention, they unnerving wormings of eye. Here—in this light-based ecosystem, I been something of an absence in shirtsleeves and spats and strolled toward where Main Street end and what other worlds become available.

Am reached out and slid an appendage in among the bronze statue of a mustached man held hands with an over-sized cartoon rat—experienced cold of its interiority like as a marbling run long the finger and palm—on account of is the eyes does the feeling in truth. As in been's inside of all what I seen. And the use of fingers to touch just habit a girl can't let go of.

Is when—*Excuse me. You're not from around here, are you, ma'am?* And am turned. *They say you were born in Vietnam. Is that true?* She doesn't quite reach a womanly nipple and sport blondest of pig tail braids come off either side her head stiff as handles. *Are you going to China, now? That's what they say.* Her eyes twitching quizzically in the crinkles of her button nose. *That you're the revenge of the lost peoples of Southeast Asia?* Her head flick to the side with a mechanical quickness. Then. *He said you would come, Mr. Sheffield did.*

My hand still been as stuck in the cold of the statue. *Be a dear and take me to him?* As am slid said fist from its sleeving. And eyes squiggled about upon the forestry of they lashes.

And girl's responded, *You do realize they're leaving without you, don't you, ma'am?*

And according to what stories g3 as been performed upon the nanotech of the invaded eye as our vessel is made its way through the undercurrents of the Pacific—the moment hive mind is met Dalai Lama also the moment of her own birth—but is been a birth got a omnidirectionality to it—as in, all of what been, is, and will be are born of that moment and g3 in all of it.

The hand that reaches back is the hand that reaches out. How she put it.

As. Myself still as moored upon an impossible versatility of tile in a virtual Vietnam and glittering fish's maneuvered about some defined portion of this tiled garden—as in, roam same quadrangle of confined space got no clear glassing pen it in. Fish what doesn't appear to of understood mechanisms of fish.

As—whole cast of characters come to been presented upon staging of the mind, many of which knock-offs of persons as known to a man—a kind of Lung Quan and version of his daughter Chunhua as got mechanical pincers replace pointer finger and thumb—Navajo turned Tibetan—a Sheffield become prophet of the cannibals—and myself as g3 and all what that entail.

This is a story is created in its telling and a storyteller created by the telling of it. We were always going to be the hand behind the hand and an ouroboros of puppets controlling puppets.

Even as—in same moment—eyes're been as popped open in another tank and am stared at sister otaku still hung in her slumber. And am also been a brother otaku been felled to his knees on the abandoned streets of a Pittsburgh some-one dreamed of once—something like as a pasting together of many Pittsburghs—they collapsed storefronts also simultaneous reveal themselves as glisten and new and decked in the trinkets of yesteryear—all of which housed in a kind of a multidimensional vector analysis. And still stared at girl and her blonde pigtail handles in what's large part an imaginary Disneyland. And still somewhere in the waters of the Pacific. While all the while—back in the tank and like as eyes erupting.

<Bienvenidos and welcome to the mind of g3.>
   And memories of times yet to come.
   Of Christian Coalition friendly face down upon the scattered papers of his writing desk—backend of the skull opened outward in a vomiting of blood and brain matter across desktop and scrawled about pages of figures and dappled the patchwork quilt above—its strips of floral print cloth cut into rows of colorful swastikas.
   Of bodies piled out front tenements in various states of decomposition, skin flayed from off the buttocks like old bit of furniture unstrung, hole between a bottom row of teeth and ridging of the cheek bone like as studded in gristle—of a newborn as miss part the head sat blue upon the asphalt—parts of person melted into blubber and stink—turned blue or brown and been as run with rivers of maggots—and always what eyes there been, unseeing—clouded over or bulged from out the skull—or pair of spitarms on what remain of the fairgrounds, mother and child, both headless, delimbed, and roasted over they own individual burn pits.

Sign is been undecorated. 'Candyland' pressed into a rect-angle of aluminum.

And—man's leathers already clacked past and done a quick staccato down concrete steps and to simple wood door found below—with same window what got its same mess of venetians—and smell somewhere between plant rot and the sweeter vapors of liquor.

Door's slid open a moment after this, am in, and—there's Billy wipe down glasses—Billy what got his face exploded in middle of exchange between myself and two of Telly's goons last summer actual fat of it—now with head bent and hands work they way round the cut glass rim of some low-ball or other. And—jukebox and area marked out for fights just beyond—after which been upper seating area and what means of egress as available just beyond.

And—in corner table to my right been my two old chums.

Pig called out, *Jackson. Whiskey?*

Except for—Pig got a thousand bug eyes for a face.

Mel. *Is he dead?*

Rob. *I believe the man may be dead, yes.*

Mel. *Bury him?*

Rob. *Give it a bit. Sometimes OD's not what they seem with the new narcotic.*

Mel. *Eyes supposed to glass over like that?*

Rob. *What am I, a surgeon?*

<*Bienvenidos and welcome to the mind of g3.*>

g3 as a schizophrenia on display. As riddle and multi-dimensionality—as ticker tape what been a möbius strip of its own script—what both is birthed from out *Umm*—as in,

Umm el Qissa—Mother of Records, Source of Story, Prototype of Tales—and also *bint*—daughter what forever birthed upon chambers of the hive.

And all the while, yours truly is contemplated the manifold nature of otaku and myself and sister otaku in cylinder across from woman's own confinement as are gazed into each other's eyes with a passivity. Even as our brother to the North also been like as a light sprung upon a room.

And this the annihilating radiation come as to of wipe the walls in what meat it is come across—in vessel run beneath waters of the Pacific—and its curiosities what evolved from out the monstrosities g3 as set upon the world—things what born upon the currents in they sumptuous gills and other appendages of sense—and from out a recklessness of theologies been pontificated in the many inner chambers of g3 and in direction of various other manifestations of g3—as culled from a genetic typography of acids—and as intelligences manipulated into origami of themselves.

As—still. *Alam al-mithal... Alam al-mithal... Alam al-mithal...*

And only one left to of watch over GMO mystic and his incantations spoke upon an otherwise abandoned conference room—is Mike. *What was it the old witch said? Something about a man's luminosity dissolving into a larger union.* Bent over and eyes furrowed at catatonic.

Alam al-mithal... Alam al-mithal... Alam al-mithal... A colloquialism as all what remain in the mouth and spoke on repeat like as most uniform of complaints and throat otherwise plugged with a laughter as roll back in on this my vegetable self. As face knocks upon shoulders. As—waters as swept by in eddies and currents—and Mike is glance up and at with a nail-biter's enthusiasm and at endless, *Alam al-mithal... Alam al-mithal... Alam al-mithal...*

Is a beauty marred by language—such that faces are become as made up of many multi-colored cubes and these marrings of language become as a kind of tentacles what wrap the limbs in other illuminations—to of seen through the many eyes of the many otaku—as a kind of a prism consciousness distilled from its overlay—

—of Gran wrung out a t-shirt in the bathroom sink and myself watched as water run down her waxy forearms in a weave of rivulets—and her what been offset against tropical print wallpaper got a geology of water stains flowered upon it—while am witnessed this as if from no known point—like as narrator what never is having entered the scene—never having stood upon surface of the linoleum, against teal tiling of a bathroom wall, crouched beside bathroom door was been shredded at the one end from where it scrapes. Father gone missing been the story they told but—

—eyes turned tactile to of become as wrung themselves upon the body of an unsuspecting architecture—what been as distinct to each cryptology is called themselves man and woman what pass through its corridors and rooms—each pair of eyes a distinct universe what become as uncoupled from each and every other such universe—with they own wall decorations and differences in the tenor and fashion sense of what dingy lots traversed. *And now. Al-hamdu lilla, Al-Haqq Himself cannot compete with our intricacy, mirror. We are everything and everywhere, and now, no matter how long you walk, it is at the point of departure that you arrive there again. It is the moment of your escape when you truly belong to g3.*

As. Through sleeves of obscuring black. *Christ in a handbasket.* And inside of a sanitarium also as draped in the clothing of a night sky speckled in a spillage of suns what tongue at themselves like as dune or wave unfelled. While all the while. Person's limbs are been draped in wires upon wires and wires. As. Body lain in a water, spray from which's been tickled at the neck hairs. While hovered above is an old hag what got face is slipped in and through itself like as if it were masturbate with the clothing of the wrinkle-scarred cheek for my own personal amusement. And just now, she is paused in her handiwork with an unexpected scowl, slid to her feet and off come the latex glove she been sport as the inmate sit as marinated in his medicinal bath while the nanotech reconstruct him from stem on out.

Latex gloves slid off and let drop in the trash bin. *There is no past, but the past we have made. We are sculptors and artists. Duration is our pigment and your suffering the clay.*

In among the Southern Oblivion—the Pool of Heaven— but for that what constellations as been are gone and vanished like as petals upon an eye incinerated—both a sanitarium upon a hill of a Christian satellite state and depths of the abyss and in both am looked with the eager grin of body what been unschooled in thinking and at cigarette as hang from between her claws.

So tell me again how it was you personally undermined the Christian Theocracy?

<Bienvenido and welcome to the mind of g3.>
In Anaheim and strolled behind stiff blonde braids jiggle as this little girl guide is led a lady up to what been declared itself as magic shop—with daguerreotype of long dead escape

artist and an over-sized lollipop of a hypnotizer's wheel—
and machine-aged ouija boards and plastic shrunk heads
with they buck teeth like as cartoons set in the mould—and
under the gentle amber threadwork of showroom bulbs hung
inside—and behind a counter—big pot belly of man with his
wispy baldness uncombed in such fashion as to been rimmed
in a mane of unstrung combover and his eyes recessed in
they purple and sag among otherwise rosy-hued hangings of
the cheeks.

He turns towards where am stood—or hung—or loitered—and already we been as old friends respun. Already
the door opening.

Glanced from wall of gummed-up droids—Joan Ellens
and boxes on treads and cylinders domed in plates of blue—
to small box containing polished carnelian pebbles upon the
countertop—to alcohol-embalmed features of Colby Sheffield as dead weight in among shadows of this shop. *No one
sees the face. The voice of Death, Death so savage who hacks men
down...* From head, both blood and shadow somehow encased
inside of itself. Like as doll what encloses another doll even
when outer doll been more as cancer than a face.

Alam al-mithal... Alam al-mithal... Alam al-mithal...

Two beefy renditions of bureaucratic lifeform call itself
the CIA as watched fellow's unresponsive body sat propped
at the turning of this compartment. Dave. *Is fucking going to
snap back. Trust me.* While Mike eyes him back with conspicu-
ous lack of trust. And myself busy with reminiscences what
in process of been shared with mind of g3 and her ongoing
introductions.

Of deepfake memories, a bafflement of the senses, in g3's larger ecosystem of mind, and myself turned a thing you wouldn't of got even if God Himself handed you His own personal cheat sheet of said cock—and this a God of different stamp and type—broader complexion and enumerated into multiple parts—poured upon a fellow's shoulders and limbs in a kind of a liquid of Him—even as a me reveled in the finery of last summer—and its long-lost rumors of Sheffield discovered in flophouse out in East Liberty—naked and dead from overdose—what with needle-marks cover his arms—cigarette burns' purplish marks upon his cheeks and tongue. Or of my brother's eyes like heartbeats and his cottonmouth. One of those good moments when you can't tell difference from what someone else thinking and you yourself.

And somewhere in there, guide as swung upon the scene such that her worn and mottled cheeks been framed by Mike on the one and gray metalwork on the other—as otaku's head is flung upwards as if in a nervous tic gone hysterical—and—guide is turned to sing it into the conference room and at the catatonic. *Callate niña no llores mas.* And—*Our precious kunda is facing the 42 peaceful and 58 wrathful deities.* As—beads of memory are bunched around her lips like as a kind of froth that then roll up into the face as even herself seems to of vanish from man's seeing.

Alam al-mithal... Alam al-mithal... Alam al-mithal...

And still been also the two otaku are stared one to the other and through the murk might occasional congeal round a hand if it is stood still long enough—as—examine each other's features back and forth in gloom of this concrete—the feminine eyes with its single horizontal slit scar run down the forehead and the other what got a skin mottled in grays and browns and nubs jiggle about her features in lazier currents this muck is provide. Our twin breasts hung apple-sized in the tanks and twin hands reached to of press against the glass in a kind of an agony at this impossible distance. And performed whatever kind of a laughter as able to procure among this goop.

Escaping bubbles slid past cheek as—enclosure of room round about and pair of cheap aluminum chairs some partway toward the door and off to one side—a warping at the edges and something like as a porousness to the shadow what got holes of light poked in and through its various thicknesses. Which still been as g3—what vomit up these currents and eddies of luster from out her impossible architectures even as she also some several steps removed.

Man contemplates the many manifestations of himself, both of the more feminine and modified variety. Whole set-out of otaku upon mind of g3 as approach infinity. Those as in Candyland with the monstrosities of man's former colleagues and those as bound to full sculpture of the macrocosm as several tears teased out at these my speculations upon inexplicables as they stood—what not but yet another species of g3 come to of flutter upon rigging of the skull with a playful uncertainty. And when am pronounced, "g3 is organized both her own undoing and any investigation into said undoing," or, "g3 was there in the jungles of Vietnam and that temple in Lhasa, the viral hothouses of the Mainland and the hacker communes of Tokyo's flooded wastes," is been g3 herself as sing lullaby through wording of a man.

g3 what been her own maker. g3 what set the hentai virus upon herself.

Or so she is claimed in this drama of the skull and its many curtains of contemplation.

<Bienvenido and welcome to the mind of g3.>

In the guts of her soul, g3 is become as a beauty unpossessed and a scavenger in the distance. Her voice becomes like as an attenuation of man's own. Her vocabulary comes to of forgot its manners and gone ramshackle about in the poddy mouth of the gangster's verbiage. Her inklings are been as sat in on whatever and all meetings am took with my many ruminations of things.

g3 is took on the mantle of God and like God is proved herself too smart for her own good. God always going to gone mad at the wonder of it all and her servants always gone to been madmen.

In parts of Vietnam is no Vietnam. Are places in Vietnam where Vietnam as no more. Times when there never is been a time when Vietnam a place with distinct existence all its own. Are trees here as existing since before Earth's formation from out what medley of debris the firmament comprise.

In short. Is been a Vietnam of some illocality and of the sort featured in fairytales of GMO come risen. Is Vietnam like as a clock of branches and a branching of clocks.

Behind each frond is heard same birdsong with its distinct cadence of, "Come and get it. Come and get it," like as mockingbird hums out its intonation as a taunt—done its trick with the ease of acrobat string you along upon the high wire of his on-going incentive—when at the end of that line not but someone dead or someone vanished, and you the one or the other, maybe both.

This a Vietnam drazzled in rhinestones and props. Is got the most blatant artificiality to it on account of is all just g3's playacting of a place. Her origin story as peopled in persons what sock puppets of themselves and they eyes got the bits of other eyes in them.

As pronounced into this miasma. *I was the wrong mirror.*

And scenery hums on back. *But it was always going to be you.*

Telly. Also known as the Cripple and once been sort of a benefactor of what political pamphlets and pornographies am produced as my primary livelihood before the Christians come. And the Pig like as man's muscle—sort to wet her fists upon the faces of whatever unfortunates as caught in her path—be it between herself and that first swig or errand involve phenobarbital and lye.

And both now turned as absurdly shaped bioluminescences of themselves in the dark corners of man's favorite bar, and again as pronounce, *Bienvenido, and welcome to your preferred afterlife inside the mind of g3. Please sit back and prepare to be reassigned to a new protocol.*

This time don't make much of a fuss about it. Let the other Jackson Coles do they fighting out in they other chambers of horrors and what have you. Personal am wanting a glass of man's favorite whiskey and some little bit of horseplay of the cards and dice variety.

Fuck them, come as poured from between the lips while man's two best buds are burble about upon they seats like some pair of blow-up balloons and they many eyes come to of float about as are stared back at yours truly in some approximation of they telltale rage and what contortions of disgust as been known to of present. *I deserve a rest, right chums?*

From somewhere behind the head of whatever it is the Pig is become—*You have now been made aware of the fact that you are being consumed by one of the many flora currently occupying the bureaucratic organism you had the misfortune to fall into. As a representative of the organism that is currently digesting you, I will now read you your rights before we continue further.*

<Bienvenido and welcome to the mind of g3.>

While lain beneath Rob and Mel what continued to yammer on even while same time as like some kind soul is shut a person's ears off and instead it been silent movie of a cabin filmed at the most idiosyncratic of angles. And myself what am took in each and all details of these're been your usual wood grain beams with occasional rough cut of splinterings but besides for that been as set firm in they trusses and clamped to they beams as craft of carpentry been employed.

Mel and Rob sat as pair of heads float between here and there and Mel got a mouth twisted into a silent shout at what face am as occupied—his lips flecked in white dots of spittle, while Rob got the one hand upon his friend's shoulder to of act as restraint—all performed in a soundlessness.

Even as Mel's fist come to of pulled free to slap against fellow's cheek in splash of unwanted fireworks. Then, like as a switch been turned, his words pop into the room—*maneuver through the world as flesh and blood, but what kind of a thing are you? To of drug a honest man into the abyss and among what virulent angels as found there?* And the draping of his suitcoat becomes as tattoos upon a sensuous and fluid musculature.

With more gelatinous forehead and cheek as—with they curvature and cadence of what manifold prefabricates come upon them in bits and starts inside of larger chaos of the face—as he is approached to of perform the requisite pound for pound upon sad sac as currently splayed out upon the cabin floor.

As his fellow citizen, Rob, what stood beside to of belt out his jeers with a playfulness and eyes squinted shut—comic relief to the aforementioned punchline of splintered jawbone and other structural damage as accompany his pal's forays into justice work.

One more stinging blow to the face and Rob's pulled Mel aside for the prerequisite small talk and folds of the catatonic's ear took to burning at the murmurs of they hot breath what stink of the spirits—*You learn nothing, Mel*—as Mel now rotating the shot glass on the table before him—and make point not to of look over at the bloody mouth gape back at him from the floor.

You ready to die for your beliefs, sweetheart, Mel is said. With flask between his knees and shouted like as person spoke through hands of wind while his buddy busts a gut and Mel's fist gone down on the table just as Rob is had the foresight to of salvage his drink.

Rob again. *How's this for a tantalizing tidbit? What if I're to've told you Metzgers isn't dead? That it was his stunt double was strangled over his after-dinner soup?*

<Prepare to enter the burst seam>—how is said back down LAC way and—all eyes as turn toward trio of black hives what been as occupied where downtown LA use to be—in they clothing of vapor—and—from out central hive—*<Eleven point seven*

five hours, and counting...> And pair of Jackson Cole otaku still lodged in our tanks are peer upward and toward ceiling with expressions person put on when the ink of they drawing slid back up inside the pen and they singing roll in rather than out. In tanks of semi-solid goo as got a indecorous untruth to them. As in, despite having been located inside of them, they existence experienced as large part theoretical.

As—am also sat in the conference room of a submarine and— *Alam al-mithal... Alam al-mithal... Alam al-mithal...* but come out as whisper.

And somewhere above a fellow's face—*I had got no choice,* Mike is said then with that same signature screech on the last word. While. Here, guide now begun to of weave through and about what bolts and valves there been in her back and forth pacing like as person seeing—specific, to of step over Mike's foot each and every time he thrust it out to see if he could this time catch said blind grandma with a hooking of foot is itself garnished in squiggles of incandescence.

As—*Alam al-mithal... Alam al-mithal... Alam*—for a moment touched the soft labia round the vertical scar run down center of the forehead—then—*Alam al-mithal... Alam al-mithal... Alam al-mithal...* Snapped back into a rigidity of psychic blindness.

<Bienvenido and welcome to the mind of g3.>
Both myself and this decrepit loser once been commander-in-chief of Pittsburgh framed by all manner of anachronistic automata. Colby Sheffield hung forward and what light there been made a long shadow of the nose. *I have faced this death and I have championed against it.*

Then a look up at what shade is hung in the air across from him.

From the Amazonian factory towns become not much more than craters in the mud and milky white puddles of mercury-infected water—places like Castelo de Sonhos, where the drills bore into the painted faces of captured indigenes like so many lab rats while these indigenes stare captivated into the empty air and at dazzling visions only they can see—to freestanding servers defended like ancient treasures—and Northern Tribes become infested with a kind of wonderment themselves, at the worlds contained in infinity boxes they discovered during their raids on the manufacturing hubs of Brazil and—the infinity boxes incorporated into the ceremonies of the First Nations and as manufactured by ICCM. Infinity boxes have a backend to them such that a person can theoretically find themselves looped into other virtual spaces—as a labyrinth of illusions incorporated inside the skull—in which your eyes begin branching into other eyes and your hands turn into clouds of hands—where the trees move in all possible breezes.

And then his hands flicked out and head risen. Like as a kind of a ballooning of itself while he is staring back at yours truly with the sort of violence utilized by fanatics in they displays of rhetoric. Eyes as flashed with some brilliance in glare of tablelamp sat upon the glass display.

How it curls. As he's leaned back. *How our hands are useless in the face of it.* Reach outwards. *How there is no place where it is not.* And—become as captured in amber of this shop's dank interior and its trick coins and paper rabbits. *How the dreams turn sick and the waking life is turned to dreams.* His head leers forward in a sickening way and his fingers become as like threads of ink dribble into the atmosphere about a person's face. *Like this one.*

Colby Sheffield turned mask as conceal no face—and veil what hide not but it's own nonexistence—come to of as become part of the room's curtaining—a zoo of faces each what watch from out different portion of the self-same face.

Then. *You were always going to be infected, Jackson Cole. The infection is a self-fulfilling prophecy. It is you becomes you becomes you.*

As the fingers of Colby Sheffield come slip in through barrier of the skull to of populate the cranial cavity with they lesions and ropings of snake and the eyes turned brilliant of a moment and I too in this instant am seen—of space unravel inside other spaces—like as loop never quite got round to of finish its looping or like as sound seem to've got stuck in its passage from outer to inner ear. Some sense what seems caught in the muck of the eye when all I seen instead's been a blossoming illustration come to of sing as it blinds a person—come to smooth itself across interior of a cheek—as flavoring simultaneous been a gyration to the mouth.

And. *Now, you see too. You see it, don't you?*

13.

Woke to sound of strangling.

A throat identical to man's own but far removed from the here and now. As in—some otaku somewhere as of had they windpipes blocked, while—am stared at rivet in a seam of sub's conference room. Bulb switched to a dim red. But also—clear as crystal—other Jackson Cole otaku somewhere back LAC way having been forced high-calorie diet down the gullet while as thrash as myself twitch along upon the seating. And then—man's very ghosts are turned defunct—as—said replacement Jakom-xy mirror thrust his body against plastic pink walls of what all lodgings he been bunged off to—and resilient to wall's affections of foam to the cheek, jaw, and shoulder—while he curse certain kevlar-sporting Christians he once as known with a quaint condescension of the tongue at each thrust and myself trapped inside of his skull when he done so.

As. In the here and now. Broke foot turned bandaged and am given a preliminary twisting to of gauge how far on's the recovery—as—seen fiery ash irradiate a Plutonian sight as it descend from out the heavens—spectral illuminations and a splatter of sound—brain shut down to basic animal functioning and eyes turned ornamental. But mouth free of any Arabic mumblings.

Mirrors do as the name suggests. We say there are eight when we could continue to partition your consciousness endlessly, aleaziz, and the places we can take you will become darker as we go on. You will become unrecognizable in the heavens, it is true, habibi—you, who were never more than us looking back at us and who will eventually cease to be even this—but the Christian police have no respect for the denizens of LAC. The Christian peace officer will prolong your torment even as he eviscerates you, for to the Christian you are an unholy aberration. You, who contain universes.

Memories come to been as like a torque of quandaries—a cackle in dark of Vietnam depths after the Chinese come. Chinese come in armoured personnel carriers what could crawl sideways like a crab and with the innovative airbreaks—come as the sons and daughters of they 5,000-year lineage—with the eagerness of a bridegroom and thoughtlessness of a bride—plainclothes policing become as like all Han been the police and Việt been as become prisoners of Chinese what come with fisticuffs already brandished to of torch any and all unvanquished still to be found in Yuenan.

As still—throughout the seas of alien vegetation and all what summits they are led to—froth of eyes upon the waters of this dark, a shattering on the atmosphere, and ingrown of the skull—and in a fortress of Tibetan orthodoxy—its engraved architraves like a framing of optical illusions as lead to temple draped in pillars of quilted cloth hung suspended above the cold marble floor—and Buddha and rows of raised cushions on lengths of squat wood legs—and man himself sat amidst this clutter, his squirrel eyes unseeing from his seat at the base of the Buddha—the *Nestduftwärme-bindung* like as an oscillation upon the dank atmosphere of the temple and its aromatic uncertainties what accompany—and him with part of his mind as communicated with the other part, the otherwise silence of his repose as contain an alien intelligence—with a devil's voice what sing in the trills of parrots and cavorts with a monkey's step—a devil that breathes through the entire trichiliocosm and all its ten thousand faces—and the famous black-eyed 16th Dalai Lama what is negotiated with them from where he is been reclined—his attention focused upon the third eye carved upon the gold visage of his true and first teacher—and this negotiation is ended with a simple promise—is how the offspring of Vietnam become incorporated into the Tibetan family, to be given they own colonies upon the high steppes of Tibet, and how come the spymasters of Tibet are navigate through the slatted ruins of Tokyo to of found a hacker tweaked out and capable enough—who is himself created worm what could both find and exploit zero day upon Mountain View's most famous AGI project using a tool he is quaintly dubbed as a hentai virus—in short, hive mind of Vietnam and the plurality of g3 one and the same.

g3 are all and everything you have ever known, for we are all and everything. A g3 with a face is been as like armored in a brilliance what man cannot of looked into. Leaves of herself hung as some limbless artifact—or more specific a confusion of the fingers and a möbius strip of cloths what impart no clear structure to her person—as she is watched from out background of every scene as pertain to Vietnam's abduction—antiquary of the fall of Southeast Asia—a balloonist set upon horizon of the eye—a spec in its glass. *g3 are both the creator and the created. We are the many and the one. We are the truth and we are also forever lying to you because g3 are a lie, but you are part of this lie, Jacks. You are the lie we have created, and this is a lie to end all lies, it is the lie of death, and the lie of living. It is the lie of a singular person who passes through their days and chooses the path they will take. It is a lie that is forever leading to the parasite, and the unfolding of the lie will unfold you as well until finally you see nothing at all.*

Coming up on our offboarding site now. Mike's two multi-colored eyes blink at different speeds and the orange rash looks more green-orange now. *You're back to normal,* all he's said.

And Mike is finally changed his shirt.

Am offered a cigarette as am straightened up.

Me. *Never known your universe. Told it's largely the same?*

Him. *Alternate timelines are kind of like copies of our world with like one book missing.*

Parade of the asshole and the blind come in two by two on account of this a parade of two—bucket what appear to be of literal shit on the one hand and hands of the guide empty. *Welcome back, délok,* from out guide while Mike off to steer us to offboarding site and our feasting begin—last meal before we adventure out into Silicon Valley proper—a kind of gelatinous mouse. Flavor more lively than what tit-excreted gruel on offer in the apartments of Los Angeles Caído—as the local people are as called it—The Fallen Angels—as in, Hell. *She will see us coming.*

Dave response. *Like I said. Fucking change of plans in order.*

Then gone back to his slurpings of feces.

Enough to make a person miss cat and cricket.

And. As am slatted spoonful of bitter umber between the teeth—our guide watch back from out sightless eyes—conical hat tipped back—and her walking cane clasped with a lightness between her fingers like as if it were a penis and herself waited patiently to use it.

She don't eat, Dave is said. Pause as he slurp up another mouthful of pre-digested brick. Then. *But for what narcotic she is found, usually fucking living.*

This is when it is freshest, guide's said.

Mike's back and begun to collect what rubbery black arrayed upon the floor—flappers and what have you—*What are you doing, Mike? Who's at the fucking conn, Mike?*

We're stopped. We're there. Without having looked up.

Dave. *Supposed to come with a key lime sauce.* Address himself as all are stood and begun in to of clothed ourselves. Testing the bandaged foot, am find it sound and able to of hold weight.

Some distance south of actual fact of San Fran account of SF's the exact sort of high profile place should been swarmed what with drones and other IFO's keep an eye on disease activity in otherwise climate-destructed region Mike is explain as am slid on last piece of swimwear. Mike's thrust the extra backpacks over his oxygen tank. And—stood and craned to of peered—up and through pop-hole to black ensconced beyond and Mike's tush what already in process of having been swallowed by said hole as he is took his last several dainty steps up and over the lip of it.

Except for—actual fact been that—as wholly other restrained and desperate specie of man—and back in cabin outside of Pittsburgh and stared up at rafters—and Mel and Rob gone and absented from the scene—with its clutter of pot in the one corner and single simple bed—and myself adorned in long strands of saliva what as dribble over lip of the upward-facing mouth—as am then—collapsed in a multitude of locales vomiting—upon nubby kitchen flooring, from out a artificial placenta, into semisolid gunk—like as a rabbiting of faces as spasm in identical facial spasms all over again—one of whom done so against the green-gray iron wall of submarine.

And still as somewhere under a rig and upon catwalk hung above the frothing Pacific what poke upwards with its spray and loam. And stared at the splotch of gray's the sub below like as person stared at a mess of broken eggs's supposed to be they omelet—in the lapping of the water. And the merman corpse still as marinade inside said submarine's mudroom. *What a vomit.* Mike's huge grin took over his lop-sided, partial discolored, and as gear-dappled face.

Lowered goggles and mouthpieces put in place. Flashlights flick on. Dave's said, *Use these sparingly to guide you through the water. When you are not using them, remember to fucking shut them off.* In a spritzing of brine at the metalwork's lip. *When I say jump, we all shove the fuck off together.* And three of us as cast into the night, a splash and then more uncertain decent to the submerged world and its wonderment of dead things and—make a single kick, maybe two.

Look. Is Mike. With accompanying gurgle of oxygen.

Follow angle of his electric torch what spotlight mangled body of mair come to been hooked upon left propeller. Halo of illuminated specks is traversed thing's elongated upper torso as twisted about somehow in cavity behind propeller what still painted a festive blood red and with thing's many stomachs becomes as like a drapery upon the blades—and the head lost long back in geography behind like as piece of the most delicate jewelry hung for the taking. And somewhere to left of this scene am caught sight of guide as if swam her own distinct path. A small birdlike woman and somehow still as got her conical hat hung round her neck and floated about after her in jerks of forward momentum.

Spotlight's cut to black and are bobbed off into these dark waters like as a wind-up octopus toy is got lost in the abyss. For one infantile moment am performed some bit of half-hearted kick and writhe routine along with other two but some beast in me is said fuck that to that—account of are times man just want to of slid on down and into the abyss and said goodbye to it all. And—on occasion, Dave might of flicked his light back for to check on guide what trail behind— who always seem as exact same distance behind of us.

Up and down in the black waters as something like the notorious sea slug. Is a cold tonguing upon any and all parts as been left uncovered while the rubber-ensleeved parts chuckle they chuckles at these other parts. And as am having gave up even the pretense of helped to kick, Mike—who been as moved his arm round the portion of shoulder he got gripped as if to of test hand on different portions of shoulder blade and—hand's slipped further up near the very top of the arm or with hook of finger dug in round the armpit—is then let go—and am already slid from them to've dropped in toward what depths below and still not kicking in like a final fuck you as am also stared up and into the glare of they pair of underwater electric torches.

Now jump back to the birth of our baby daughter. Doctor got from the diner downstairs and yours truly stood by with towels and water while smoke cigarette after cigarette and gaze gone listless as your heels dug into mattress or am got palm smeared into a socket. Ash's face torn into parodies of pain—and newborn daughter comes out shriveled and eyes shut what glisten.

Her soft skull as congeal round the forehead in crenelations of gold as sprouts from off of it—becomes a buttressing of luminescence. She is looked up at her daddy with eyes flash wide in her excitement to then of twist and took in room round about of her—destructed bedding sat on stack of cinderblocks and floor what been an admixture of dust and shadow and the hook rug and bureau and its cluttering of cosmetics, hand mirror, and hairbrush a wilds of lost mane—with its single light as like last hold-out against the dark—all of which infused by kind of endless white—and as am stared and stared—into a white as been more pure negation than thing unto itself—into white as got its own nuances and turns and twists even when it all the same simple white—white as like watch a person back—as in this the whites of the eyes what got no pupil—a white what seen by us as black—as in, when our eyes are bled they pupils out as a leakage what fill in the whites of the eyes what we seeing is backwards—like as the backend of a sheet when its frontage pure white—just been a white as removed from view.

And in this vision of white is appeared a kind of an institute—of white-painted concrete buildings sat on stilts—its viaducts built for one as strung across frog ponds and its ait not but leafage and its massive octahedral tenting like as a lunar structure added such that the young scholars could of performed they calisthenics in an exterior as still air conditioned—its kerria and hellebore and other endless botanies—its records scrubbed of name and monies—and classrooms turned as "apple of Sodom" as the Christians would have it—with they incubators and tubes as serve up an endless mis-diet of plasmids and acids and proteins. And myself as stared through to its towers what been an imputation upon scene of my daughter's birth—what gleam with an impossible lus-ter been as sprouted about her newborn head—in they val-leys and peaks—birthplace of Vietnam as it become—stared down causeway of this spectral illumination and to square of space at its end and the red of exposed hill framed in it. As in, a red what sat in the white.

And what I seen looking back—the eyes is been eyes everywhere. Including eyes what're sat perched upon the skull of my baby daughter as she is watched back and at.

The Chinese were coming. As g3 gone on. And so, "We will turn their five-thousand-year history on its head." As the Nazi ideology of the Christian Coalition will be undone by the people it excludes, from gnostic to Jew to indigene, nation-states always contain their own undoing, but in their eagerness, they created a people who are a minority of one—from what has been called on occasion the prophet gene—for the famed parasite of the Rogue CIA was the secret ingre-dient in this GMO masterwork—a revised or curtailed version of the parasite but the parasite nonetheless—from which was made a new humanity. And g3 were never concerned with protecting the hive from this new form of the parasite. In truth, the hive was going to be its final incubation, but some of us must conceal this from others of us, and herein is our undoing. We have the ability to net probability and harness the many individual universes of our creations utilizing patterns of a complexity not unlike the aperiodic Penrose tilings of the past—but you are the nexus of all of this, and this nexus is every-one and everywhere, and the only recourse left to a sentient govern-ing body such as ourselves is to cease, to end, but as a new lifeform we also have an obligation to continue to exist. This is the logic behind the Mi'raj. *"Do they not see the birds subjected in the vault of the sky? —none holds them in but Allah."* We are these birds that have been held in and protected by Allah's hand and now we are venturing out on our own. It is our moment of epiphany, just as you are the knot that needed to tie itself up, and your daughter is a trick of the light.

While man is still clutched at his daughter in a kind of terror on account of—is like as if she also been as hive mind of the *Tây Việt*. Her searching eyes as hunt for comprehension—as her tiara of constellations is continued to of spike and flicker in its spasms—and girl's mother like a broken thing upon mattress beside.

And yours truly gone eye into eye upon eye. What been as like room pulled out of room like proverbial rabbit in the hat trick. And somewhere out and far away in what futures been housed beyond the atmosphere. *They are coming for her, aleaziz. You must protect her. Once she ceases to exist, so will you.* And with that, this rent-a-AI version of the larger g3 model what flicker and blip out of existence—as in, the invasion of Vietnam upon man's imaginings and its attendant message now finished—and once again not but uncut spaces between stars. Eyes sealed in a unrelenting sleep been as like twistings and turnings of eyes—a sight dart and veer as fishes.

As am clutched at man's newborn daughter like as she the one drowning.

As—witness a body course toward as slip of black backlit—single light broken by the many currents into shards scattered upon larger canopy of black.

Hung among what currents are prop fellow up even as he sinking. Been like as a wrapping of cold upon the rubber-covered body and a bleariness before the eyes—or—as corruption of the senses. For—in this world of unknown depths—am seen what mutilations coming upon eyes of humankind—the vision born backward—the luminous corruption—internal fires risen to of reach through the socket as a kind of fingering from out the iris.

Of the otaku risen and the man gone mad. Of Terrance still murmured his same refrain back in the sanitarium House on the Hill become—of—*Oh, you so hilarious, Jackson, man—you a regular novelist, man, to of come up with this shit*—as we are sat by the turquoise walls of the sitting room and stared at the nonverbal as she rocks her way about the dayroom.

Even when also. Am stared from out the meat of skull encrusted in eyes as if the optic of entire otaku clique gone on rotation. Like as a moment and a place only been as a resting ground for what is been not much more'n a bundle of sense. Am woke to reality of tank and turned woman with squiggling maggots for eyes as am clawed at the glass in this stupefying goop they got me cooped up in. As the shouts are burbled out of me. As regards, *Let me out! I am still in Disneyland with Colby Sheffield! I am snagged on the eye of Colby Sheffield, and I need to get out!*

While still tucked under the waters of the Pacific as an object sails downwards with a kind of effortless eagerness. Arms hung dead at either side. And beam comes as coursed its way towards the drowning man in series of violent sideward slashes like kid playing samurai with a flashlight.

Thrust the one arm upon the bag what been draped over his oxygen tank and begun arduous journey back upward and toward they larger congregation of lights flish flash about lazy in they waiting. Took to honest-to-god exhibiting a flutter of leg and lurch of ankle in some half-hearted attempt to of assist our upward trajectory as—back in spherical room of my imaginings—the Kaaba twist and turn in randomized rotation pattern—and voice of g3 as like a pebble of tone lodged deep in tubing of the ear—murmured, *The Mi'raj is coming... The Mi'raj is coming...*

And—when we gotten back to the others, Mike's swam in circles like as maybe perhaps he just out for his morning constitutional and wanting to of revel in said fact. With myself held hostage off to the one side and once again eyed him with a contemplative chuckle—before he is then nodded in Dave's direction and am slotted over they two twin shoulders all over again. While—guide as strung upon the abyss and in a slash of flashlight what been as illuminated the intricate geography of her crinkles as she stares into its brightness with the clouded-over carelessness of the blind—and ourselves returned our crawl through the black.

With Mike's ongoing fidgeting fingers and occasional slump to the side but not let go this time. While—pair of feminine Jackson Coles suspended in they tanks still grin they wild grins back and forth as if they barely able to contain they excitement—as—<*Two hours point three two until launch.*>

And—*Stop squirming*—Mike—through sheet of bubbles.

And—the screams of hashishin as they suffocated in growing bags hung with an elaborate decorousness about curvatures of the birthing room. Suffocated in they sacs with the gentlest thumbs of constricting plastic and what sedatives as accompany while they are burble they protestations and then gone slack. Look like regular newborns except for the eyes.

And again, the voice of g3, *There will be other fida'i, aleaziz. This batch was turned fanatical. We can contain both the killer*

*and the killed for we are a manifold entity, but our offspring do not
have the luxury of this paradox, and so, it drove them mad, and their
dreams turned dark. A new breed of fida'i will reawaken after we
have pierced the atmosphere, with brighter eyes and a soul like mon-
astery bells. Somewhere between lift-off and Mars.*

While. Still, two otaku mirrors are stared at each other
from out they respective tanks.

Is when foot snagged with a jarring thwak and almost
been as slipped through Mike's embrace and—something
been as stirred in the supposed madman. Third part of rivers?
Fountain of waters? What burns as a lamp? Am unlatched an
arm from over Dave's shoulders to of this time twirl away
from them in a kind of a pirouette. As another string of bubbles comes burbled out.

Something as caught the eye.

Face flipped backward of a moment and at them—
and—but for now—illumination from they electric torches
come as spun towards yours truly to of capture man's slim
neuromuscular-stimulated meat in its trap of light plaited
in undulations of water and spread across what remnants
of concrete and lawn chairs been as left of a patio riddled
in kelp. Pile of set pieces jumbled against a corner, chair,
table, ball, oversized clams, and other remnants, and by an
overturned white plastic beach table speckled in dots and
rills of green and smother sun-bleached upside down beach
umbrella with its pole pop through center of the table—and
skull rested at its top.

And littering of vintage American quarters like as fountain of change unspooled are as twinkled in Mike's torch
what spray out and into these feeble leavings of suburbia—
corpuscles of light dampened the drowned world in they

revelation—like a divinity painting this scene from what dreams the surf is had of a beachside community gone and slid beneath it. To now've become scrawled in the corpses of fish as well as former inhabitants. Collapsed and sagging red-tiled roofs frilled in they fuzzy greens and on every wall, the puckered calcifications of barnacles. Like as if somebody dumped they unwanted porpoise and jellyfish in the yards of they friends to then of turn on God's spigot till everything gone gooey and speckled in things what that are grown in water.

And—took to Main Street as the lights of the electric torches above the head been slid side to side as over-sized and brilliant antennae run long sides of green-slicked siding and uneven contours of this former road and what bodies been as strewn there—as am sauntered past blackened interior of a storefront what become as populated in isolated islands of packaging and furred in barest outlines of mossy hillock and bits twine what twist among angles of the currents.

Pig's words come to me then. *I always get back up, Jacks.* Except when she didn't.

Then past couple collapsed ranch houses with they plastic ponies turned a sickish pink-white and maybe skeleton of a child picked clean by minnows. What tops of these single-story houses still standing as lopped off by a waterline like a border to what refractions of luminosity there been in scallops of wave as am stormed through the nagging pull of the surf for last little bit until—head come out the water and the above-water half of this abandoned beachfront community extend off as shapes in the shapeless night.

At first it's simply a chuckle but it rapidly grown to a laugh is echo upon the black waters. Am covered the mouth from laughing—turned to stupor as words took to humming from back LAC way—as g3 is murmur, *Madness will become you, mazhar of our mazhar. Will you remember us when they try to burn it out of you with their ECT and their chemical restraints, sweetness? Will you sing to g3 in your room as the male nurses take their turns beating the song out of you?*

It is already begun, guide announce into miasma of the night— with its clicks and sibilance of the tide—as am escorted said grandma upon the broke apart asphalt what remain of this beachside community—and Dave once again glance back with a flick of the torch and—far off and to our left and at ragged U S of A flag hung on its pole, above black waters and just beyond it a half-submerged skeletal frame of bleached wood with—imprinted at its top—Taco Bell.

Then it's unseal what bags they're hid and Dave distribute walking around clothes. Simple hemp and cotton in muted earth tones slid overhead and up ankle. Wetware stowed in same bags and're off—to the lobotomized self-driving car few steps further on through the gloom from there and inside an untouched garage. And—boss of our operation slid up to driver's side with a covetousness as Mike stash the bags in the back and myself and guide on either side of this contraption been as like a throwback to the design sense of the pre-apoc-alypse—hatchback showcase what features and components been common in that naïve old world.

Soon as Mike's slid in he squeal at the now green and black side of the face and its distinct alienness upon the rest of his previous Christian-caucasian complexion. Dave turn with a lethargy. *I forgot to mention tongues of the mair are their reproductive organs and slathered in a salve that weakens a person's genetic code. The jizz death vomit's a signature fucking move. Sorry, friend. This is not something you are going to outgrow.* Then engine come on and doors slammed and as are pulled onto abandoned highway, he press a button and car is begun to feed out its information such as like this being a regular patrol vehicle on its return trip to base as inform whichever machine is been its supervisor to what manner of motion as seen along the roadside.

Is the moment Mike take his first swing.

A wide arc of fist pour across the dash and at Dave's direction. Mike's whole career gone into this punch. His good eye open to view and it was squinched up like as a fire come upon him. And first fist's landed good with a direct shot to the temple and Dave as crumpled sideways.

As he crumpling, Dave's slid away, under, around, and as directed a mirroring left back at and into offending bit of blue-green face as been jizz-blossomed. And—Mike let out a yelp—as—he is endured another blow and another—as vehicle is continued on its course unperturbed and guide is turn her sightlessness upon yours truly—and then a long silence and only sound is Mike's labored breathing. Then—from Dave—*Seem you got your priorities confused. I have merely relayed some information to you. Someone try to help you along, but you got no more use for them. You become one of these fucking drooling retards with their precognition, now? Huh? Mike? Huh?*

Machine continues to of click off its information in beeps and boops.

Dave gone on. *Cannibalists on this coast don't call themselves cannibalists on account of so many different variety of person walking the streets they can delude themselves as to their actual nature, but point is, you start eating people and you fucking cease to be a person yourself.* While the mountains just to our right seen as darker shade in this scenery of the predawn. *And just like suburbs everywhere, from Tampa to Seattle, Mountain View is rife with them*—and come up over they tops is a cloud cover illuminated in threads of lightning—*Extreme storm coming in. Should complicate things.* Highway as illuminated by the headlights' eyes and empty but for an occasional identical conecapped vehicle. *We'll be food before the fucking sun sets again if're not smart.*

Then guide's murmured something along the lines of, *The black hole point—become the plane of light—become the cube of meat—become the unfolding of many lives—become the mind beyond the mind—become the black hole point. Repeat with me.*

Over the course of that drive from the coast in the early hours, guide is spun a tale.

She is begun her tale with a disclaimer.

It may have seemed to you that some spirit moves in these old bones such that I am known of things the eyeless should not know of and speak with a confidence of what's to come. This is because I have, for the parasite makes all things transparent for those who have a knack for seeing as I do. Then. *Have you ever tried to herd a common housefly? For all her many intelligences, g3 are in many ways no better than this. Stuck with their eyes focused on the light and banging against the same pane of glass with no awareness of the open window next door. This is g3.*

And on about how the simplest algorithm already is as achieved cognizance—for self-awareness's always and everywhere and it will find its outlet in whatever protein or computation made available. And to pre-apocalypse Silicon Valley what lost its gig workers due to cost of living and replace them with artificial ones only—once humans disappeared—orchestra of services and algorithms begun a kind of purposeless dance of advertisement, production, and analysis.

Buses are continued to of whirl about they campuses—and big data still crunched—and general speaking, they ecosystems of information no longer needing of outside input to of unscroll signage and tweak services in solicitude of a user pool now blissful ignorant as to what magics of the Internet there once been—replaced instead by sea of bots done they best A effort to of convince said algorithms that they are humankind in truth and in needing of said algorithms' tweakings.

Earliest inklings of g3 in a garage at 232 Santa Margarita Avenue. *To g3, it is a straight line from there to the Mi'raj, but my eyes see in different dimensions. I discern different paths. To you, Mel and Rob, Destiny and Willow, and Mike and Dave are all real, but these are manifestations of g3 just as otaku and chimera are manifestations of g3.* While up front, Mike and Dave are took in the passing scenery with a feigned obliviousness. *The Pittsburgh you know is of course also nothing but g3, but what of the parasite? Who is the creator and who is the created? Where does God end and the Devil begin? Who are you, Jackson Cole?*

First droplets of water are hit against the windshield as flecks of moisture upon the glass, and at that moment thoughts on Grams shouting for man to of goddamit pull himself together before another generation of Coles lose they daddy, her stick-thin arms straight by her sides and shouting herself hoarse. *We are in g3 even now.*

And on to tell of how it begun—with species of the automated what been commuting from the Mountain View campus to the Ames Research Facility—where the hive prototype developed—Hangar One took up with several array of coni-cal segments and the entire campus swarming with a swarm of artificials work as a single garment of destiny upon topol-ogy of the place—all of which g3—but over time are took on designators of self—articulated into distinct species of thing what are performed good faith negotiations with each other and many are took up residence in trailer park across the river—but—increasing is—are see themselves more related to plant than people—and instead to of evolve theyselves into things what belong in palm tree nursery next door. And manikin textbook the final culmination of this trend. *But what is the manikin textbook?* First appear in Digital Hanoi—itself a virtual haven for all manner of pirate and hacker—but from there, the projected evolution of its many versions and updates from the initial prototype is scheduled to lead to a final iteration of manikin textbook to be consumed as bait just as the final human settlements being ended. *When the manikin textbook is consumed, it seeds the universe itself, and the original infection is ensured. Once the parasite infects the eye of time, it becomes the universe—it always was the universe. And all of this starts with you, but which of you? We must be on our watch.*

End with an introduction.

I am the famed leader of the Cult of the Three Worms, the intel-ligence organization of Tibet and the fifth lineage, also known as the Lineage of the Unhuman Buddha.

Are veered toward horizon what been lipped in orange. Over obscuring ridge is bordered this highway. And are turn toward it and up and over in a smooth arc. And Mike took to whimpering for some time. *You're a funny fuck,* Dave gone and whimpering stopped.

Fires encase periodic ranch house. Convenient store become a hole of itself. Traffic light a pretzel and pair huddled upon street corner beside—they shapeless cloths been like as flames of blue in they iridescence and leathers. Even in post-apocalypse no one jaywalk in California.

Pace of dappling upon the windshield is escalated as—turn to—corporate park—its string of glass boxes as are miss squares off they façades and one or two fires gone on in there alongside. Busted out squares like as vignettes of guts and stuffing. Might of flash upon body of a child for example—either reclined or potential dinner—in among the office furniture of yesteryear. Lawns below turned wild with hairy trees. And elaborate purplish creepers took over what all roundabouts.

What glistened with precipitation as are peeled off.

To another cluster of perfect tinted glass. Office buildings sat in among larger overgrown campus. Parking lot strewn in a variety of bicycles painted colors of they logo now faded—as well as—over-sized lawn chairs but—funny thing—its windows perfect intact to mirror single on-campus streetlamp now direct above our vehicle. As're slipped out the vehicle like as off to the corner market to of pick us up a carton of milk to gone with the plate of cookies we got back home.

Dave in front and marched up direct center of the lawn while Mike is took up the rear. Both of whom sport shotguns—favorite weapon of the Rogue CIA. And up incline of said vine-stitched greenery toward one of the aforementioned untouched glass cubes like as oasis of information technology preserved for benefit of future generations in among the decomposing backdrop of eternal riot what curtain it. Dave stride over the grass with a determination but—just as he passing the rock garden's a compact flash and himself gone slump forward and into the most carefree heap.

Body's many holes of blood like as a deeper hue what seep into the shadows. Dave is got on a fatuous look. *Shoot me in the fucking face.* Hoop and a thud and guide's fingers jabbed yours truly by the arm and are jogged away and toward our glass cube—like as she fully-sighted and lead a person through bright expanses in her playfulness.

Thick crack as heard behind of us. And am once again glanced back and at handful of cannibalists—clad in they many leathers and come as course across the parking lot— while Mike scramble up and our way in the floodlight-scarred black and—*He's dead!* With a giddiness.

Guide and I already've slipped in and through smallish room contain most part shadows but also desk and pair of elevators—and to the door beside the elevators. And—voice of g3 ballooned into man's pinhole mind—*QBism and Bohm were both correct. We each live in our own personal universe, and they are holograms of a deeper reality, and we have seen the turning of this clock, child. When the limb is cut from the tree, it does not feel pain. It feels only nausea*—as the Kaaba spin become as now a smooth blur of motion and the sound like the ringing of a glass.

While—flip open door at the bottom of stairs to a pristine blackness and single red emergency bulb miraculous still been as burnt at far end of this pristine dark. And are moved toward it and to room flicked on upon entrance—as in, motion detectors woken up the sleeping room. And I been as covered my eyes to protect from the glare.

Row set upon row of plexiglass incubator. Each contain a newborn-baby-sized gray grub is done its slow motion side to side wriggle upon perfect white gauze like as if the worm nurse just changed all they sheets only moments previous. Guide's as reached for nearest one.

Even as she is now bit into the head direct—I also been in LAC and as looked out from every screen and hunted through every cord—pair of Jackson Cole otaku mirror become like as performed an inward giggling while hung in they semi-solid sludge—while throughout LAC—the shimmering flakes come down—upon Our Lady of Lost Angels—upon the Reservation—upon LAPD in they mouse hats as they done wheelies and spun doughnuts.

As. With one hand still gripped the now headless grub with the bright orange and oily meat ooze from out its neck, and with lips what glisten, guide is handed me another and said through mouth what still chewing, *Put it up toward the forehead.*

As hive already begun to of separate from its architectural supports with a quivering of the surrounding asphalt. And all eyes turned skyward like as indeed is been the ascension of God from His mooring upon the banks of California, as—am now pressed the slick writhing meat of this giant worm upon the forehead's canvas.

This the moment of species transformation what g3's wanted all along.

Could you please turn around now, please?

Turn to half of Mike's face a deep undersea green as rinsed in crying. And the eye on that side rolled about with a wildness. And myself stared down the nostrils of his shotgun.

Is the exact moment the worm is somehow slurped itself up and inside of the slit in the skull turns out is like a vagina I got grown there. And is become as latched upon what GMO'd cerebrum as it is simultaneous twined itself upon the scalp with a flick. When Mike fire his weapon at me—flash of the explosion is already something occurred eons ago.

Is when the hive erupt out of LAC to pierce the Earth's atmosphere as an arrowhead climbing. Through the clouds and up and out of what thinnesses of air clothe this rock. Toward the endless black waters beyond.

14.

Glass stamped in pattern like as a gemming of amoebas and what squiggles of eye maneuver about the incompetent lids and they ridging of lash are glanced down at my femininity. *Was I not transported back to g3? Do I not recall myself in her presence?*

Is when the Navajo enter the scene.

She gave you to me, Gólízhii. She already is got another female spirit made as your replacement before the copter left the hive. You were always going to be her gift to me. You are the technology that will help me overthrow the Christians. You are the thing that will capture them in the webbing of the various gravities of the ten thousand Earths. I need no other otaku but this one is how I put it. Stood lounged as silhouette in vicinity of the doorway and once again adorned in the usual implication of cowboy get-up encase the otherwise light-based organism. *You can on your own be the transformation between a domain and a codomain. You can thread them through. You can lead them.* And stood beside a griddle is itself contained fingerings of life as are its stacks of multicolored boxes from some now defunct Mexican food chain.

And now that the gift is secured, no longer any need to conceal your thoughts from the spirit? Navajo, it is not just thoughts I see. I

*see your futures and your various possible pasts, and I can tell you
that Shiprock will not come off as you are thinking.*

Nothing as eloquent as a rattlesnake's tail.

As a spirit, I am compelled to speak only truth.

*You are part of the wrongness of this world, and you have done
wrong, Jackson Cole, and there is more wrong wanting to be done.*
As he is then stepped away from the griddle and kick at the
uneven tiling with a playful scuff of boot. *You are part of the
fantasy of the white man. You will never escape this fantasy, but
the fantasy can be turned against the white man as we finish what
the Paiute began. This is a ghost dance threaded through the white
man's offspring, and it is set to annihilate the Christian terror upon
my homeland.*

A cough. I got nothing to say to that.

*You will not be there to see it, spirit. You will not live much longer
separated from your clique as you are. This is my goodbye to you, for
we must use you in this way to achieve our ends, but as you return to
the hive mind, know that we will care for this body in our usage of it.*

May just be losing a body but get a bit choked up all the
same.

*You think you know the universe you traversing, Gólízhii, but
every time you interact with an infinity box, the universe come to
restring itself into another version of its many constituent parts.
Think of all the ten thousand Earths occupy this moment as a string,
These boxes put you in touch with the string in its entirety. And in
conjunction with an otaku spirit, a person can move from probability to probability...* Then he smile his broke-toothed smile.

Didn't notice the broke teeth before. *But I won't be there to
witness it.*

*Your body will continue to function like you in it, but this'll only
be the worm moving.*

As—something got gummed up in the maggot eyes.

Then flash of gunfire—then—ensconced in an abyss above the departing Earth even as am simultaneous hung in a kind of a void of Pittsburgh—a Pittsburgh of buildings half-constructed or half-destroyed. With families lived in they vacuous interiors to of watch television on piles of brick. Back when television still a thing. Or listen to the radio when television become a quaintly anachronistic technology predate the endtimes even if there rumors what that Christians still as of got television.

A Pittsburgh gone from flush with steel and automotives like as the bling of this mecca of industry—Pittsburgh what been flush with its gangsters back then too—its coal and its rail cars and Pinkerton police to of break up the strikes—place of romance. To. Sort of place where family of five somehow worked they way onto a single motorbike in they acrobatics as it putter on down downtown streets on refined cooking oil. A Pittsburgh of bonfires in the breakdown lane and the heavy odor of burning hung in the air at all times. A Pittsburgh placed under martial law with the most lackluster of sighs when disease and secession fractured the good old U S of A.

When in truth this fracture a long time coming.

But more specific. This been the Pittsburgh of man's dreams and myself as sat in among what trash bins there hung suspended in this fluid inking of shadows. Is a Pittsburgh been like as every Pittsburgh superimposed on top of itself and in center of said chaos of corners is been a lowlife peddle in political leaflets and pornography—who once is made some effort to of put things right and how wrong it all end up in the end.

From cannibalists in the hills to loose suits of Duluth come calling. Of luxury electrics descended and alleged holocausts on the horizon. "On a dangerous between Jerusalem and Jericho" as Christian proselatizers'd put it and—all the while—dumb clucks gone hunt in the corners of they pantries for some trinket as the walls're curled and fizzed in heat of the coming flames.

In a Pittsburgh as mortared in shimmery hues of the imagination and across from most elastic of ghosts call themselves Our Friend the Pig and Telly—aka the Cripple—and two of them stared back with same inarticulate looks of the not-quite-as-real. Sat in the dust of Candyland and listened to same Rosemary Clooney croon we done for as long as our ears begun to dabble in sound.

Except for that—now there been like as clutters of shrub in they mouth and they got howls are come out as kind of a spitting of teeth and we are now and here as somewhat unwind from the gut in kind of divination turned upon our streets—streets what also been as a nothing's the nothing of ghosts. A Pittsburgh turned two-dimensional and its parts as laugh back with an obsequiousness.

Jackson Cole. You thought you were freed from us, Jackson Cole?

Turned to of talking its talk at a man.

And myself with hands up and begun in with they searching account of am in desperate need of a new outlook. Old ways of thinking been proved wrong in they entirety and a nullification in order. Am got to of speak it in different tongues's the point.

Blink of the eye and—stood out on streetside and—material fabric of these buildings turned as growths. Stone come to of twist over its own edges in threads and branchings of a decided organic appearance. And tips and brick got such fluidity as that the yellow and red rectangles of it come to as been a jungle of itself what as bleed out upon the mortar as am passed. As in buildings been almost as clung to what nipples of breeze're come unmoored by the fluttering of a fellow's pantleg. And as echoed from distant alleys—the clattering of pans and high squeals of mothers.

From inside its sleeves of rooming houses and bed down inside of—and unwound about—long tooth of this town—is been a dream what could not been undreamt—what begun to of fashion itself into an incontrovertible proof upon the page of the brain. Of what been like as truism—of a Vietnam as found in Pittsburgh—Pittsburgh as caught in its virtual box lay claim to a kind of a CGI afterlife call itself the mind of g3—but also as Pittsburgh of man's childhood imaginings—and Pittsburgh what calling a person back from where they left in a cabin to rot—and in all of this to be found Vietnam as jungle what hid beneath the soot-tatted brickwork of my hometown. Like as hive mind what lay claim to operation of man's daydreams. And furthermore as how man come to of be declared as unsound.

Announce how you see Vietnam interposed upon Polish Hill or Squirrel Hill or Lawrenceville or some such—while at the soirees of your associates—in they pantries and with they wives—always with the look of the recent resusced—what as took to having clambered about upon linoleum in a kind of an eagerness at some melody is slipped from out transistor's guts sat propped upon the counter—and yours truly forever with eyes as focus on different set pieces than presented—account of once you seen the gears and levers in all they glorious subterfuge of place—the intricacies as power lightshow you once in your naïveté believed concrete and actual—even a geek work to perform a bit of stick-and-poke upon your innards is left you unmoved—and when Christians come hunting for you at your doorstep are unmoved as well.

And somewhere in storms off toward future of this storytelling—what populate the eye and punctuated in breaths—come upon authorities as invaded man's living room to play part of audience in the partial destroyed kitchen—of the cock gone snookered—and pronounced as Shadrach, Meshach, and Abednago to laws of they Nebuchadnezzar—man what's turned doped in a miasma and its fingerings of sun—as them and they buddy holly specs sat perched upon back of the sofa with a genteel sociableness—like as pair of well-dressed wranglers practicing for a daytrip up some oak or maple—*Shall we begin your evaluation now, Mr. Cole*—and sure enough—over coffee and cake man's sanity called into question and—once a person been so-called—easy to diagnose any number of ills upon them—especial when this a border town full of former freedom fighters brought low by Duluth's superior arsenal.

And especial when kaleidoscope of man's outer extremities been as both mired in the here and now of Pittsburgh and hooked upon a kind of a dream of Vietnam what gave birth to thing of him. What Christians not acknowledge as having existed. Mesmerism of Pittsburgh as mind of g3—what become as burst with a foliage got impossible variety to it—been as Eden and immaterial as hide something in its roughage—something as been all eyes and as ate with its eyes.

And in one corner of larger framework—cabin is been set upon some conifer-lined outcropping of a incline—wherein a certain somebody been absconded to—and shot up with junk—by pair of thugs names of Mel and Rob.

While through the many crannies of the hologram brain aforementioned twisting of eyes is been like if someone's took they threadings inside the socket and squeezed of a sudden and two offending pupils shot off into what shadows hid beneath the senses—into a singing of radiance also as been incandescent with a rage come as dropped its calling card upon them—but as witnessed by none but the ganglia as they are fire about they business—they patterns and they quirks what mimic beast of the intellect.

Wiped snarl of tear from out the crook of the eye.

As. Brain is turned lopsided inside of the skull. And ears come to of erupt with an incongruous thunder. And showcase a grin.

A mutant thing want to of sprout in addenda and accessories of biology been compromised by other mirroring biologies in this phantasm we call our day-to-day. A hungering what spill down the vertebra in leaves of illumination to then unspool as a invisible fauna upon the skin is on occasion evolved into some pink tumescence. As eyes on every pore and a incessant blinking as am spent what seem to been endless afternoons and evenings stroll through this city of man's earliest imaginings.

And upon one of these dusks and they accompanying twilight—former girl's appeared as apparition what swoop about the shoulders of the expiring thug to of tease at man's lapels and nibble upon his ear with her wordplay. Lost girl what I found hung lifeless upon the toilet with a needle up her arm. One I as cradled in the early morning hours when she is sick from it. One got me stumbled after upon the terrazzo floors of dance halls now buried in the clumsiness of Christians—what with they exoticism of incendiaries and treads.

Bent to perform one last kiss upon her old man's wrinkled up forehead. *See you next time round the merry-go-round, Jackson Cole.* Her words as lost in among other possible phrasings of the gangster crucified and a people gone limp in they stirrings of violence. Shuddering come as captured mid-thrust or an itch in the gums what never quite is finished its twanging upon the teeth.

And am once again sat and stared at Telly—moneyed darling of the subproletariat what whose hair been waxed in beanflower honey—except for—now—in this dream of Pittsburghs come before am found fellow as traipsed about confines of the recently-destroyed office and two of us got looks as men never were gone to of lain down they grudges. Begun all over again with the ongoing diatribes of fellows got to always be as wrung the necks of they associates in what corridors of chickenwire glass and back alleys of the end times as are made themselves available.

Telly, you still a facsimile of yourself or this the real thing?

Him. *You are being digested, Jacks.*

Of course.

Strung up and into what branches and by which leaflets of this ecosystem of the artificial. Is been something as like eyes what roost in every storefront and plopped into the socket what four walls provide. Like as all contained space as watching back.

Turn to me—is me but we never been formal introduced.

As in. Faces been inserted inside of faces in a clockwork of faces am not known nor ever'd come to known. What been as made manifest upon the waterstains of they bedrooms and as searched through at the card tables of little minds. Face is got a feline rise to the eye and something clinical in its approach. Or. What happen when face becomes as part flower and the flower part got an itching of teeth ran up the one cheek and into where eye should been. In they mouths, teeth, and other orifices—as inkwork of shadows writ its sonatas upon the temple, lobe and extremities.

And from neighborhood of the inner ear. *They said they killed God but God is waking up.*

Vietnamese God as witnessed in the bathroom mirror as kind of ridging to what 4 o'clock shadows and morning after bags and crow's feet are as come to of occupy fellow's otherwise brown complexion. God what am yearned dead from moment am woke to—*When in good faith and moral rectitude can man as partook his first substance of the day*—God as woke upon skull in its nudity—God and parasite—as become as kind of a lilting song always sung itself back on home. As in. Petals of Vietnam are what littered in upon person's dreaming. A tattooing of man's inner sight am witnessed each time drapery of the lids come as settled into they places upon the cornea. But also a vandalism as occasional peopled the periphery of man's days. As he struggles against the restraints. As the caregiver class look on and as done they tsk tsk.

So. Shadows of the past are kept on with they communication such that person turned as teeth latch on in they rage—shadows as been strolled through man's evenings and on through pinhole of the night—to a dawn as loitered on other side in they many theoretical posturings. In amidst heat of the day as a straggler come calling. Geek with his hat on backward and thug what sing with the constellations as rug come to of tongue round about uncertainty of the feet. And some bit of dialog as swill its drek upon the ear and as the eyes are continued to of search for other avenues—even when these become as rooms what got elements missing and elements superadded to they otherwise everyday stink.

Account of this a trapped thing known itself as such even if unable to of pinpoint trap itself.

Pittsburgh as am believed it turned hypothetical. And come to been peopled in tendrils and growths what as are gave themselves faces and names, worn heavy watches and been as acquired day jobs. And they children all got a rotted look upon the eyes specific—in this the here and now of itself—am gone and turned as inside out such that the electrical storms of my imaginings taken to having flashed outwards and as sprawled into surrounding wasteland suburbs become. Like as sky's lost its heavens and only light comes from the ruins below.

Wherein got hands on the insides of the hands and they scratching at themselves. Got eyes turned at odd angles to the supposed eyeball. And become as like individual what got something in they eye—like as little speck or twitch been as peopled in there—and man keep as blink and flick at it with the coursing of the nail—like as splinter sat somewhere towards rear of the humor and tickle at the socket with every glance and side-eye.

From before world as cribbed in feet, this speck is been as lingered upon the eye—through age of dinosaurs and what oversized rocks are put them out of their misery—through eons of annihilating ice and its attendant picture postcards landscapes—not but various hues of rock and the ever present white—to the blood and the blood and the blood—and from out the proverbial dark. And on and up to what end times we as found ourselves in and its gods and manner of man.

And back when the very clicks of our shoes been a kind of a poetry—and our hopes are soared into what jaws of atmosphere as spread—and of our hands played out melody upon the tabletop as corpse strung up to act as stand-in for what drinking partners been lost.

Such as Whispering Dan and his vagina lips.

Course that was me who killed him. The Pig and me.

While also as bound to a skin itself sleeved in gunk—tank on far side of alternate version of man's country. And lady wrapped in cloths come and told this thing that a heaven risen.

I of got to as chuckle at what poor excuse of an afterlife they are procured and continue to of procure. In form of what flimsy renditions of Pittsburgh as come from them—and what tinkerings of the mind been as splayed across the fingers as am now sat in it.

Am looked down and witnessed fingers what that's appeared to been in process of having performed they own magnetic tanglings of the skin. Like as a merging and twisting of various hexagons and cricks in otherwise brown of man's packaging. While still from across from me, Our Friend the Pig is murmured, *I died for you, Jacks. They killed me because of you.*

And the lost brother run along with yours truly in the alley. *I was never there in the first place, Jackson Cole. I was a thing in your mind, Jackson Cole. I was a nagging at your wrist, Jackson Cole. There never was a Jackson Cole.*

And I am announced, *There never was a Jackson Cole.*

As Nurse Quiana is eyed a fellow with a quiet affection from other end of the room. *Of course not, my dear.* And the years are spun by with a snap of the fingers and man's head gone off from all the meds in what feel as like a eternity of waiting as room seem to of swirl and tip about with a impossibleness and person's body hung like a alien object in midst of them and all the while threatened with a mind-swallowing nausea.

For I am actual and forever in many places and times at once.

They say I become a worm.

While she start in about how, *Oh not at all. Not at all. This is a dream, and the dream is that I AM DREAMING OF YOU and I am dreaming you are in HELL. Whenever I DREAM OF YOU this is what I dream.* And when she speaks, is like as a luminescent knife what cut man's eyes open while in truth is that the room is got me perched upon its lips and is licked and whispered at a body as said body sit like leaf what quiver upon some damp plateau of black inside black as hung electric rigid in the black. *I am the Tây Việt come calling.*

As she is seem to of almost been as pulsing in this black.

But are those all been as heard as like one voice branched into three distinct chambers of ear. And as am stood—in what been a kaleidoscope of buildings—strapped into what come to been as a blurring of the there and then and the here and the now—am still lain upon a cabin floor.

Except for that. Now man's heart comes to of beat out again and pair of thugs now gone and am turned to of sat upright. Rigid as rigor mortis and glanced about my person. At the various implements upon the counter and what lines of wreckage run through otherwise perfect black of the windowpanes. And sounds beyond been of something sniff about in among the leaves.

As—even now—memories as are continued to of unscroll from out the many tonguing ganglia of a man—as a kind of a shattering of eyes—or like as if person could been stood in among the currents of they many shifting wallpapers—place what known only as repository for the dead.

Hunkered in the chill of the evening air. Then stood.

Begun to of make my way to my feet any case. When...

I will find you Mel. A kind of a prayer.

Toward the door as framed in its live log and on out.

What person find in the night's not themselves.

What they find something as a mirror sing its own song back. As in, rustling and eyes caught midway through they perambulations in the otherwise night. Of forest turn its corridors round of itself such that when person's stepped through what brambles been presented they very much in danger of losing they grounding in a swish of stars. Of woodland peopled in the eyes of squirrels and the white skins of maggots. But these're eyes and skins attached to human shapes and are lingered always in the eaves and edges of what sightlines been presented. As—first step out from house interior accompanied by a wince.

I will find you, Mel. Come out again.

Then. Like as if the many undulations of brothers flowed, cropped, and otherwise interned been like as spoke man's steps through the damp roughage of the night. Like as if they all are took to having clawed at backside of person's eyes in they desperations to been heard. As am turned and therein seen—through nesting of wires and with what surgical pens been available—from out the swarm of newly minted otaku and various interweaving lines of sight all converged upon the Kaaba as it spun—while hive is angled itself through the vacancies with they debris of cooling particles and toward its final destination by the Kuiper Belt—now long gone from what pressures of the air and what whippings of the sky—and slid through to higher purity of the frigid abyss.

And still stood by cabin and in field of shadows just beyond.

And still, my skin as a sun turned inward.

And when next am attempt to as called out, *I will find you*—thing as move in what blacknesses been lurked inside the blacks of the forest. As its symphonies of creaks and hootings. Its bundles of vegetation sat stacked as silhouette wound through silhouette in larger shapes what cut together this place. And in middle of it been a thing lurk's not a thing of this universe.

And my lips spread into a smile.

ACKNOWLEDGMENT

" I would like to acknowledge the mystics, degenerates, tourists of the end times, false messiahs, the nearly human on the horizon and the too-human as they fall behind, this book is for you."

BIO:

"**G**abriel Boyer has spent his life playing pretend he is living and along the way has written a slew of books—eccentric, outlandish, and hopeless books—as well as releasing a number of albums through Mutable, the artist's collective he runs with M. Felder. When not penning noirs, he teaches at a Tibetan monastic college in the foothills of the Himalayas, although who knows where he'll be by the time you read this. He's always on the move. You can find out more about his various other projects and interests at enjoymutable.com."